METHOD OF MURDER

"I had Timothy take another look at Ruby's exhaust system and he didn't find anything unusual." Bill looked agitated.

"That makes sense two ways," I said. "First of all, it sounds like it's easy enough for carbon monoxide to leak into the car; and second, I like Timothy a lot, but mechanically speaking he's never been the brightest bulb in the chandelier. Now if—"

"Dodie!" Bill rasped.

"What?"

"I wasn't completely satisfied, so I had the state police give the engine a second look…go over it with a fine-tooth comb."

"And?"

Bill peeked over his shoulder, taking in the near-empty dining room. "This is why I need your discretion. The state guys found a hairline crack between the manifold and the tail pipe connection—except it wasn't caused by a bad repair job or rusting."

My stomach churned. "What are you saying?"

"Someone with a detailed knowledge of car mechanics cut a thin gap in the pipe so that fumes could leak out."

"Ruby was…?" The words stuck in my throat.

"Murdered…"

Books by Suzanne Trauth

SHOW TIME

TIME OUT

RUNNING OUT OF TIME

JUST IN TIME

Published by Kensington Publishing Corporation

Just in Time

Suzanne Trauth

LYRICAL UNDERGROUND
Kensington Publishing Corp.
www.kensingtonbooks.com

LYRICAL UNDERGROUND BOOKS are published by

Kensington Publishing Corp.
119 West 40th Street
New York, NY 10018

All Kensington titles, imprints, and distributed lines are available at special quantity discounts for bulk purchases for sales promotion, premiums, fund-raising, educational, or institutional use.

Special book excerpts or customized printings can also be created to fit specific needs. For details, write or phone the office of the Kensington Sales Manager: Kensington Publishing Corp., 119 West 40th Street, New York, NY 10018. Attn. Sales Department. Phone: 1-800-221-2647.

Lyrical Underground and Lyrical Underground logo Reg. US Pat. & TM Off.

First Electronic Edition: September 2018
eISBN-13: 978-1-5161-0721-6
eISBN-10: 1-5161-0721-7

First Print Edition: September 2018
ISBN-13: 978-1-5161-0722-3
ISBN-10: 1-5161-0722-5

Printed in the United States of America

Thanks to everyone who entered the *Just in Time* recipe contest, especially the winners: Debbie Proud, Ian Hughes, and Katherine Wortman. You'll find your favorite dishes inside the pages of this book! I am grateful to everyone who offered advice for this latest Dodie O'Dell mystery—Kate Trauth and Ginny Gahl Trauth on *Bye, Bye, Birdie* rehearsal techniques, Christopher Cannizzo, Chief of Police, East Hanover, New Jersey on department procedures, and Grace McCormack on Dodie's love life…

...as always, thanks to Elaine for reading, guiding, and laughing.

1

"If the Etonville Little Theatre was doing *Carousel* instead of *Bye, Bye, Birdie*, I could sing 'June Is Bustin' Out All Over!'" Lola Tripper said, humming and sipping a cup of coffee in a back booth of the Windjammer restaurant, which also functioned as my office. "I love June. Such a gorgeous time of year."

"You're in a pretty chipper mood. Guess it might have something to do with the Creston Players?" I signed off on the inventory sheets for the week's menus. Windjammer's chef/owner Henry was experimenting with some new specials, and I had to order an unusual amount of avocadoes, cilantro, acorn squash, and curry paste.

"Should I speak to Walter?" Lola asked, a mesh of worry lines creasing her forehead.

"Why? What's he done now?" Walter Zeitzman, the on-again-off-again ELT director and Lola's former love interest was in a snit most days now. Professional and personal jealousy if you asked me, Dodie O'Dell, manager of the Windjammer restaurant in Etonville, New Jersey, a stone's throw from New York City.

"You know how he feels about Dale."

I knew. Lola scored a trifecta last month: She met Dale Undershot via an online dating website; Dale turned out to be a member of a theater company in Creston, the town next door to Etonville; they concocted a co-production between the Etonville Little Theatre and the Creston Players. Lola and Dale were the romantic leads in *Bye, Bye, Birdie*. Walter was chewing nails these days, as the designated director of the production.

"Last night when he was setting light cues, Walter made a snide comment about Dale that, according to Penny, had everyone screaming their heads off. Very unprofessional behavior." She frowned.

Lola, actor, director, and ELT diva, had been my BFF since my arrival in Etonville from the Jersey Shore following the destruction of my home and place of employment during Hurricane Sandy. Henry's cousin owned the restaurant I had managed down the shore before the hurricane and had recommended me for my current job. I thought about moving to New York as I'd headed north across the Driscoll Bridge from the shore. I got as far as Etonville and settled in—managing the Windjammer, Henry's moods, and the staff. I'd also become an honorary member of the Etonville Little Theatre, celebrating its successes, commiserating with Lola when productions went off the rails.

I was sensitive to the fact that Lola had been actively boyfriend hunting for the past year. Dale was a good fit: charming, handsome, and unattached—definitely a keeper. "What did Walter say?" I asked gingerly.

"Something about Dale's hair piece."

"That's dangerous territory." Everybody knew about Dale's explosive temper and great head of hair, but no one mentioned it—until now. "I guess Walter's feeling neglected."

Lola wiped her mouth on a napkin. "I can't keep playing his nursemaid. He has to get over me and grow up."

"Easier said than done." I paused. "What exactly did Walter say?"

"Oh…something about if they didn't get the cues straight for Dale's 'Put on a Happy Face' number there'd be hell 'toupee.'"

I tucked an inventory sheet onto a clipboard. "Actually, that's kind of clever—for Walter."

"I guess so," Lola conceded.

We both giggled.

"Hey you two," Benny, bartender and Windjammer assistant manager, sidled up to the booth. "You gotta cheer up."

"Wise guy," I said.

Things definitely felt more relaxed at the restaurant these days. Henry's specials were attracting more traffic than at any time in the last year. He was almost on a par with his crosstown nemesis La Famiglia—since he'd gotten an extra half star from the *Etonville Standard*'s restaurant reviewer this spring. The Windjammer came in with three and a half stars to La Famiglia's four. We were gaining on them.

"Henry wants to know if you're going to announce the contest winners tomorrow night?" Benny asked.

I'd been promoting the Windjammer/Etonville Little Theatre connection for several years now by producing some pretty hot theme-food ideas: a seafood buffet for *Dames At Sea*, Italian night for *Romeo and Juliet*, a 1940s food festival for *Arsenic and Old Lace*, and early American concession treats for *Eton Town*. Each event had its own hiccups, but those are other stories…

Bye, Bye, Birdie had me stumped. What to do with a 1960s musical about a hip-thrusting rock star drafted by Uncle Sam? Inspired by Elvis Presley's actual army induction, *Bye, Bye, Birdie* had a good run on Broadway and in the movies, but my usually peppy creativity was snoozing and I was ready to say bye-bye to the entire theme food project.

Then it hit me! In the musical, there's a fan club competition to choose a young woman on whom Conrad Birdie would bestow one last kiss before he's inducted into the service. Why not an Etonville contest to choose dishes to serve during the run of the show? When Etonville got wind of the contest, there was a deluge of entries. Who knew the town was so competitive? Appetizers, salads, entrees—the whole enchilada. Henry chose the winners, since he'd be responsible for actually creating the meals. As usual, he grumbled his way through the process, but, secretly, he was pleased to have so many people interested in his menus. We ended up with three entrees and an appetizer.

"Announcing the winners is a good idea."

A loud crash from the kitchen yanked our attention toward the swinging doors that led into Henry's inner sanctum.

Benny and I locked eyeballs. "Wilson!" we both said in tandem.

"How's Henry's new assistant coming along?" Lola asked tentatively.

"I miss Enrico," Benny answered and headed back to the bar.

"Me too, but he has bigger fish to fry now." Enrico, Henry's second-in-kitchen-command, returned to cooking school to up his future prospects. He now worked part-time, mostly on weekends. In his place, Henry had taken the suggestion of his restauranteur cousin and hired newly minted sous chef Wilson. I was the last person Henry's cousin recommended for hire. That worked out. Wilson was a young Haitian—a new culinary institute grad. Cheerful, full of laughter, always smiling—

Another clatter. "Wilson!" Henry bellowed, his voice audible in the dining room.

—and sort of gravity challenged. He dropped things.

Lola winced. "It was good of Henry to hire Wilson. Being a mentor—giving him a chance to kick off his career."

Henry poked his head into the dining room. "Dodie," he hissed, and motioned for me to join him in the kitchen.

Customers were trickling in for lunch. I jumped up. "Gotta soothe some ruffled feathers."

Lola finished her coffee. "I have to run too. Don't forget you're coming by rehearsal tonight. Last run-through in the theater before we move to the park. I'd like you to see Act One—some new choreography for Dale and me."

"Benny's closing so I can sneak over after seven."

* * * *

Dinner was well under way. Regulars stopped in to eat before rehearsal next door. Henry, though cautious, let Wilson try his hand with some items this week and the result was definitely multi-cultural. Sole meunière—complemented by rice and beans and fried plantains—were served on Saturday. Tonight's feature was moules frites. I tried explaining to customers that it was simply mussels and fries. I'd eaten variations on the dish down the Jersey Shore many times.

"We know Wilson is very continental," said one of the elderly Banger sisters—Etonville's gossip mavens who kept their arthritic fingers on the pulse of the town's affairs.

"Very French, don't you know," said the other. They bobbed their curly gray perms in unison.

"But we'd be happy with the other type of French food," said the first one. I refilled their coffee cups. "What other type?"

"French fries, French toast—"

"French onion soup—"

Geez. "Nice to see you ladies. Have a good rehearsal," I said and scooted away. Walter was no particular friend of mine, but I had to sympathize with him on this one. Directing the Banger sisters in *Bye, Bye, Birdie* had to be an act of self-flagellation. Of course they were only in the chorus, like a number of other Etonville citizens, but—

"I hear we're going French tonight?"

I looked up from the cash register. My heart did a flip-flop whenever I heard Bill's husky voice, the corner of his mouth inching upward in that quirky smile, and glimpsed his former NFL running back-physique. "Hey handsome. Leaving work early?" I leaned over the counter exposing a bit of cleavage.

Bill's ruddy face turned a shade deeper. "Shh! You want the whole town to know our business?"

"What parallel universe are you living in? We're already the topic of steady conversation." The occupants of most tables in the dining room had swiveled their attention in our direction. "See what I mean?" I murmured.

Bill ducked his head and walked to my back booth. I followed with a menu and a table set-up. "Must be a slow gossip day."

"What happened to privacy?" Bill grumbled.

"That ship has sailed in Etonville."

Bill settled on the moules frites and a glass of cabernet, digging into the mussels with relish. "Wilson is a good addition to the staff."

A racket in the kitchen made us both flinch. "Agreed. Are you going to rehearsal tonight? I'm dropping in later and maybe I can catch a ride home…" I let the image dangle before his imagination. Bill and I cemented our growing relationship two months ago when we'd begun sharing living accommodations: most weekends at his place because it's larger, tidier, and he loves to cook, and occasional weeknights at my bungalow, which I scramble to make presentable.

"Your Metro out of commission?" he asked innocently.

There was nothing wrong with my red Chevy and its one-hundred-thousand-plus miles. "No, but after you tread the boards tonight you might need a little rest and recreation," I said provocatively.

Bill shook his head vigorously. "I told Walter I can't rehearse tonight. I have a stack of paperwork. I don't know why I let you talk me into acting in this musical anyway."

I straightened up. "First of all, you're not really acting. You play a cop. Second, all you do in the scene is blow a whistle and interrupt the onstage chaos—like you do in Etonville. Third, it's your civic duty to support the town and its citizens. The mayor is certain this will bring positive PR to the municipal building."

"My civic duty is preventing crime and keeping the town safe," he argued and drank his wine.

"Chrystal told me today she needs you to try on your costume," I said.

"Why can't I wear my Etonville PD uniform?"

"Because it's a show and you're an actor."

"You said I wasn't acting." He wiped his hands on the napkin and pushed his plate away.

Bill was being ornery. "This will be fun. You'll see," I said with more enthusiasm than I felt. Maybe it wasn't such a hot idea to have Bill play a police officer in *Bye, Bye, Birdie*. Even if his onstage presence lasted seconds. It seemed like a nice gimmick at the time. Lola bought into it. Walter was skeptical.

"Any more opinions on vacation?" Bill asked.

We'd been discussing summer plans for weeks now. I wanted to spend some time down the shore in August and he was itching to travel to the great outdoors in upstate New York. Camping, fishing, rafting, and generally, according to Bill, communing with nature. I would be communing with bug spray and a bottle of wine. We had yet to come to an agreement.

"I have to make reservations at the campground," he said.

I hated to throw shade on his plans but…"Maybe we should think about this some more." I moved out of the booth. "Gotta get to the rehearsal. Talk later."

"But Dodie—"

"I'll have your costume delivered to the municipal building tomorrow."

* * * *

"O'Dell, this is going to put us on the map—doing a show all frisky," Penny said and slapped her clipboard against her stocky body. Penny Ossining, stage manager, was Walter's most loyal minion, a trusted sidekick for many years, a longtime veteran of the Etonville Little Theatre, and part-time worker at the Etonville post office. She saw herself as the cornerstone of the community theater, and loved to dole out theatrical wisdom. Her whistle was legend among theater folks.

"You mean…al fresco? It's Italian for outside."

Penny squinted at me. "Whatever. It's in the park. First time for the ELT."

"Lola said it's the first time for the Creston Players too."

"Yeah." Penny jerked her head over her shoulder and watched Walter in the center of Etonville and Creston high school students who were playing Conrad Birdie's fan club. They were rehearsing their fainting spell for the moment when Birdie propelled his pelvis at them. They practiced standing, then falling, then standing again, then falling again—until they were laughing hysterically and Walter threw up his hands in frustration. "You are squealing when you should be swooning!"

The kids gawked at their director, shrugged, and remained on the floor.

"Squealing is an exhale." Walter let loose a high-pitched whine that brought the entire theater to a standstill. "Swooning is an inhale! It's a moment of awe! Of astonishment! You are overcome by the presence of Birdie!" He took a deep breath in, fluttered his arms, and plunged to the floor. The kids guffawed. "On your feet," Walter ordered.

He wasn't too keen on this co-production enterprise.

"You're right. Walter hates this co-pro stuff."

Penny was still in my head. How did she do that? "Maybe next year you'll do Shakespeare in the park. You know, like Central Park in New York," I said.

"O'Dell, you crack me up." She checked her watch. "Time to round up the troops."

"10-4."

She blasted her whistle, and the sound waves reverberated off the walls of the Etonville Little Theatre. The cast and crew were holding their ears. Lola and Dale, sitting in the back of the theatre, their heads together, were oblivious. *Yowza.* She had it bad. Penny prodded and threatened and, gradually, the cast gathered in the first rows of seats. Walter lectured them on the challenges of performing outside—gnawing mosquitos and humidity doing a number on their make-up. The ELT crowd was used to Walter's eccentric tutorials, but the Creston actors displayed a collective "Huh?"

"Lola? Lola, could you come up here?" Walter called out plaintively, eyeing the two leads in the midst of their cozy tête-à-tête. "I need your opinion."

Lola and Dale moved down a side aisle of the theater. Lola was smashing in a snug, black, knit top, her blond hair flowing gently around her face. You'd never know she had a daughter in college. Dale was dressed in a blue knit shirt that accentuated his muscular physique. Lola squeezed her leading man's hand as he joined some actors in the first row, and she made her way to Walter's side. I couldn't help but notice Dale's straight jet-black hair—a toupee all right. Looking at Dale's hair reminded me that my own auburn waves were due for a trim. I needed to call Snippets in the morning.

A hacking cough interrupted my train of thought. It was Ruby, the rehearsal accompanist. She was one of Creston's contributions to the co-production. Word was she'd been working with the Players for a number of years. Mid-seventies, wizened, with close-cropped gray hair, Ruby was an inveterate smoker who had to decamp to the loading dock for a cigarette during breaks. Always in the same uniform—sneakers, rumpled trousers, and an over-sized button down shirt— she was also something of a musical savant. She could scan a score and then play it by heart. "Hi Ruby. How did it go in the park last night?" Lola mentioned that Ruby, Walter, and some crew set musical cues in preparation for the "all frisky" tech tomorrow.

She coughed. "That Walter's a horse's patoot."

She'd hit the nail decisively on the head. "Hard to take sometimes?"

She hacked again, letting out puffs of breath smelling of alcohol. Ruby carried a hip flask in her bag and usually had a few nips during her smoke breaks. "I've worked with the best of 'em and the worst of 'em," she said, her voice raspy. "Him? They broke the mold."

"Well...as long as the show gets up." I was channeling Penny.

"Hah. I told the Players this two-theater thing would be a disaster. Bunch of amateurs and no-talents."

Was she referring to Etonville or Creston actors—or both? Might as well shift to more pleasant territory. "Lola said you're a terrific accompanist."

Ruby studied me. "What's your name?"

"Dodie. I manage the Windjammer next door," I said, nudging her memory.

Ruby's watery eyes glimmered. Then narrowed. "Oh. That crummy restaurant. Tried to eat the food. Made me sick."

"Sorry to hear that," I said politely.

"Well. At my age lotta stuff makes you sick," Ruby said. "Getting older's not for sissies."

Out of nowhere, I felt for her. Maybe her life wasn't so easy. "I guess not."

"You're young but some day you'll see it."

See what? Walter motioned to Ruby to join the musical combo sitting in the pit below the stage. "It was nice to talk—"

"You married?" Ruby asked.

"Me? No! Not yet." I said awkwardly.

"Good. Lemme give you some advice."

Over her shoulder, Walter was anxious to get the rehearsal underway. Penny signaled the actors, and Lola gazed into Dale's rugged face.

"Stay single. You can't trust anyone. They only get you in the end. I know from experience," she said emphatically, easing the flask out of her bag to take a sip.

"I guess that's true sometimes. You think you know a person..."

Ruby brought her face close to mine. "It's not what you know about 'em. It's what you don't know."

Yikes. Some history there. Ruby toddled off.

* * * *

The first act of *Bye, Bye, Birdie* was in progress. Lola and Dale were the starry-eyed couple Rosie and Albert, all cooing and cuddly, with Rosie lamenting Albert's songwriting career and Albert promising to give up the music business. The ELT hotshot, we all called him "Romeo," swaggered around the stage as the rock-and-roll superstar Conrad Birdie. He pretty much played himself. Janice, a lovely young girl from Creston High played the ingénue Kim, a member of Conrad's fan club in Sweet Apple, Ohio. Vernon, the narrator from *Eton Town*, and Edna, the Etonville police department dispatcher, were Kim's parents. Abby, manager of the Valley View Shooting Range, was Albert's overbearing, aggravating mother—typecasting according to some. The actor playing Hugo was a tall athlete from Creston, cute but gawky...I figured basketball. He flirted with Janice, which annoyed Pauli, my teenage tech guru, who hung around the theater as the ELT photographer and had designs on Janice himself. He was crushing on her badly. Finally, there were the Etonville citizens in the chorus—Vernon's wife Mildred, a church choir director; the stars-in-their-aging-eyes Banger sisters; and Imogen, the shampoo girl from Snippets, making her first appearance on the stage. Bill, who didn't have an entrance until the end of Act Two, would be missing the run-through.

Things moved smoothly through the first half, the high school kids having fun with "The Telephone Hour," sashaying in and around old-fashioned telephones on pedestals while Romeo strutted across the stage in way-too-tight gold lamé pants and greasy hair.

"I thought there were no costumes until later this week," I whispered to Carol, who sat next to me. She was the owner of Snippets salon, the moderator of rumor central, and Pauli's mother. Carol was my other BFF. She did hair and make-up for the theater.

Carol sighed. "We tried to keep those pants off Romeo, but he stuck out his crotch and said 'Hand 'em over.' Said he needed to do some method acting tonight. Chrystal gave in."

He wiggled and jiggled the lower half of his body, his arms around the teenagers from Sweet Apple. Romeo was in his element...method acting, all right. "Hey, can you have Edna take Bill's costume to the municipal building tomorrow? He doesn't understand why he can't wear his own uniform."

Carol chuckled, her salt-and-pepper curly hair springing around her face. "That's cute. I'll tell Chrystal. Hey, have you made arrangements for your birthday?" She raised an expectant eyebrow. "It'll be here before you know it."

"Nothing definite yet."

Conrad Birdie sang "One Last Kiss," at the end of Act One. Carol dragged herself out of the theater seat. "I've got to get backstage to give notes on hair and make-up."

"Can I pop into the shop in the morning? I need a trim," I said. Carol was good about accommodating my last-minute appointments.

"Sure." She scurried off.

The curtain fell on the last notes of the Act One finale, with the company reprising "A Normal, American Boy." The theater lights rose along with the noise of the usual backstage hubbub. The crew set the scene for Act Two. Actors dashed around. Some of them wandered into the house, and Walter admonished Penny about taking charge of the production. She blew her whistle to get everyone's attention. "Take fifteen for intermission. Performance conditions!"

Alex Milken, the musical director, and other members of the Creston Players, winced at the detonation of Penny's whistle from their seats. I'd met Alex when he stopped by the Windjammer for a meal. He was a recent addition to the Players staff. Ruby stole out of the orchestra pit, bag in hand, and made a beeline backstage—no doubt for a rendezvous with the loading dock.

Dale intercepted Ruby. He drew her into an alcove on the left side of the stage. With the usual intermission turmoil in the house, no one paid attention to the two of them. He snatched Ruby's arm and bent down, talking rapidly. She flung her head back, yanking herself away from him. Dale glanced around the theater, smoothed his hair, and said one final thing to her before she traipsed away. Some squabble. More than likely, Dale was giving Ruby a tongue-lashing about a musical cue. He certainly was a stickler when it came to his performance.

"Hey."

"Hi Pauli. Getting some good rehearsal shots?" His digital camera hung on a cord around his neck. Since enrolling in a photography class at Etonville High, Pauli had served as the ELT production photographer—a role he accepted with great pride.

"I dunno." He fiddled with the camera.

This was not the eager, upbeat kid who'd cheerfully assisted me on a couple of murder investigations—email hacking, digital forensics, and deep Internet searches. "Something wrong?" I asked gently.

"Like, Janice," he mumbled, brushing a hank of brown hair off his forehead.

Aha. Girl trouble. It was a year ago that Carol was fretting he'd never get a date for the junior prom, and here he was, twelve months later, mooning over a female. "The actress playing Kim. Pretty awesome. What's the problem?"

"It's that guy who plays her boyfriend," he said.

"The tall kid from Creston High."

"That's the dude."

He was feeling the competition. "Pauli, they're acting. You know, it's the...method." I flashed on Romeo parading around in his gold pants. "They have to be convincing."

"That dude is too convincing."

"Why don't you ask Janice out after rehearsal?" Pauli was now officially driving the family car. "Maybe you could take her home?"

His eyes lit up for a moment, then went dull. "That means, like, I'd have to talk to her."

I proceeded carefully. "You haven't spoken to her yet?"

"Nah. Like she doesn't know I exist. This love thing...it's bogus," Pauli said solemnly.

I got it.

* * * *

I told Lola the show was in great shape, begged off Act Two because I was exhausted and had an early day tomorrow, and moved to the lobby. The door whooshed open behind me. It was Ruby. She stared, blinked, and scanned the expanse of space—empty except for a banquet table and folding chairs stacked in a corner.

"You seen my bag?" she rasped.

"Your bag? No," I said. "Did you leave it somewhere?"

"Duh. That's why I'm out here," Ruby said sarcastically.

The trill of Penny's whistle leaked into the lobby. "Guess it's time for Act Two."

Ruby coughed. "They can't do it without me." She stomped back into the house.

What was that about? She left with her bag—which contained the flask—at the end of Act One. How did she have time to misplace it?

It was nine-fifteen, but felt like midnight. I'd gotten only six hours of sleep last night thanks to a chaotic camping nightmare featuring me being chased by a black bear into dense woods while Bill climbed a tree and hung out with his fishing rod. I *had* to win the summer vacation argument. I hadn't been camping since my Girl Scout troop spent a weekend by the Delaware River when I was ten years old. It rained so hard the tents filled with water, all of our clothes got soaked, mold blossomed on our hot dog buns, and no one could get the campfire lit. Wet, cold, and hungry. Some outdoor fun!

I stepped into the June night air, inhaling deeply. The temperature had risen to eighty today. The summer humidity was like a wet blanket. Walter was right: The outdoor production might dictate that the actors deal with drippy make-up. A light breeze kicked up and it felt good on my face and neck.

I climbed into my sturdy Metro, flicked the ignition switch, and backed out of my space in front of the Windjammer. Through the window I could see Benny at the bar and Gillian, our twenty-something waitress, serving the last of the dinner customers. I was over the moon to have an early night. A glass of chardonnay, the latest thriller by my favorite mystery author, a speedy check of my Facebook page, and a date with my bed.

Then I recalled Carol's reminder. My birthday was creeping up, and though I'd casually mentioned the date and a possible celebration, Bill had not picked up on my hint. Without warning, the hairs on the nape of my neck quivered and I shuddered—my radar whenever something was bothering me. Was it the wind blowing in the driver's side window? My birthday? Or something else?

2

A ping from my cell phone coaxed me awake—and away from a beach where I was luxuriating on warm sand, the sun hot on my back, sea gulls wheeling overhead. Now *that* should be my summer vacation. My cell pinged again, demanding attention. I reached for the phone and scanned the messages: the first was from Bill, asking if I was up and wanted to meet for breakfast at eight thirty at Coffee Heaven. *Of course*, I texted back. The second was from Carol asking if nine thirty was too late for my Snippets appointment. *Not at all*.

In the shower, the water was warm on my shoulders as I lathered my hair and rinsed my thick mop. I pulled on lightweight khakis and a pink cotton blouse, which complemented my Irish hair and complexion, and grabbed the car keys. I had settled into the Metro's front seat when my cell rang. It was Bill. *He was eager this morning.*

"Hi there. I'm on my way." I lowered my voice into my sexy register. "Little impatient today, aren't we? I mean I know that—"

"Sorry to cancel. There's an incident down by the highway. An abandoned car," he said.

"Isn't that something Ralph could take care of?" Ralph Ostrowski was a patrol officer on the Etonville police force—genial, mildly capable, and a regular at the Donut Hole coffee shop. Talk about a walking cliché.

"He's directing traffic on Belvidere. A streetlight blew out." Bill grunted. "I haven't had my first hit of caffeine yet."

"I'll swing by Coffee Heaven and deliver it to you on the job."

"Don't bother. I'm not sure how long—"

"No bother. See you soon," I ended the call. After all, this is what couples did—tended to each other's needs—right?

I analyzed our relationship as I cruised down Ames and over Fairfield. Bill and I had had a great couple of months sharing our homes and getting to know each other. Sometimes we binge-watched Netflix while exploring Bill's latest gastronomic marvel; or sipped wine in front of his fireplace while a sexy Norah Jones serenaded us. Or I modeled new lingerie from Betty's Boutique, Etonville's version of Victoria's Secret. Occasionally, we wandered the streets of Greenwich Village in New York, experimenting with new restaurants. I was getting into the girlfriend routine.

I pulled into a space in front of Etonville's old-fashioned diner: a handful of booths and tables, a traditional breakfast menu, and two or three coffee specials in an affirmation of the twenty-first century. My obsession was caramel macchiato.

The welcome bells above the door jingled as I entered and made my way to the counter.

"Hiya Dodie? The regular?" asked Jocelyn, the Coffee Heaven waitress.

"Sure. Make it to go, and add a black coffee."

Jocelyn put her hands on her hips. "The chief's car zipped away a bit ago. Wondered if he'd had his coffee yet."

Our relationship had become the go-to topic of conversation around Etonville. Folks asked "how we were" with a wink—as if we were the town mascots. I'd become accustomed to Etonville's prying eyes, but Bill was still skittish.

Jocelyn placed lids on the take-out cups and then leaned over the counter. "Speaking of relationships…"

I groaned inwardly.

"Have you seen Walter lately? He's looking really fine," Jocelyn murmured.

Walter? The ELT Walter? The temperamental guy with the crazy warm-up exercises who still had it bad for Lola? "Well…uh…I was at the theater last night to see a rehearsal and Walter was…" How to explain Walter's demonstration of the difference between a squeal and a swoon? "He was working with the actors. I saw Act One. The show is coming together and—"

"But what about Walter?" Jocelyn asked optimistically. "I'm inviting him to dinner one night next week."

Uh-oh. "Jocelyn, are you and Walter…" Talking? Interested in each other? Did Walter know Jocelyn existed outside of waiting tables at Coffee Heaven?

"A couple yet? Nah. But I figure with Dale Undershot moving in on Lola, I'd better get ready to claim some territory before Walter decides to play the field again."

"Right." I paid and left in a hurry before I had to listen to more of Jocelyn's strategies for organizing Walter's love life. I tried to imagine the two of them. I pointed my red Metro in the direction of State Route 53.

Within minutes, I had veered onto the access road that ran parallel to the highway. Up ahead, I could see Bill's black and white cruiser, lights flashing, parked in front of a blue automobile. I eased off the roadway and came to a stop several car lengths behind the blue car, a Toyota Corolla. It was familiar. Where had I seen it before? An ambulance swooped in and ground to a halt in front of me. *This was more than an abandoned vehicle.*

Bill's hand punctuated the air, as he appeared to be speaking rapidly on his two-way radio. I carried the container of coffee to the rear of the Corolla, but an emergency medical technician halted my progress. "Sorry. Can't let you by."

Bill waved me over, the technician nodding as I passed him.

"What's going on?" I asked. "I thought it was an abandoned automobile."

"So did I. Turns out the vehicle wasn't abandoned."

Ralph drove up in another police cruiser, his siren blaring.

"Cut the sound," Bill shouted.

"Copy that, Chief." Ralph alighted from the car. "Heard over the scanner that you had an 11-83."

Bill shot a look at Ralph. "Don't you have an 11-66 over on Belvidere?"

Ralph jammed his hands in his pockets. "They're about done repairing the street light. Need help here?"

"Make yourself useful and get on the horn to Timothy's. We'll need a tow truck to get this thing off the shoulder."

"10-4."

Ralph was a cop in search of an incident, though he was usually assigned crowd control whenever there *was* an incident. "Is he or she...?" I asked carefully.

"Yes. Had to jimmy the lock to open the door."

The emergency technicians were in the process of moving the body from the car to a gurney.

"Oh no," I murmured. Something wasn't right. The blue car, the size and shape of the deceased...

Bill's walkie-talkie squawked. "Yeah Suki?" He had a brief conversation with his second-in- command, and then pivoted to me. "The car's registered to a Passonata, first name—"

"—Ruby!" I cried. My heart pounded. Dead. Wait until the theaters found out—

"You know the vic?" Bill asked.

"It's Ruby. Don't you recognize her?"

"No. Why should I?"

"The rehearsal accompanist for *Bye, Bye, Birdie*?" Then I remembered that Bill had come to only a couple of rehearsals, begging off with the excuse that he had to work most other nights.

Suddenly, I could identify the Toyota—dented rear bumper and all. Ruby often parked in front of the Etonville Little Theatre, sometimes illegally, and complained bitterly when she got a ticket from the town meter maid. What was Ruby's car doing out here on the access road? Had she been on her way home to Creston? The last time I saw her was in the lobby of the theater, before the start of Act Two. I peered into the front seat of Ruby's car. Her bag was open, some of its contents strewn around the seat and the floor: her wallet, empty cigarette packages, a comb, vitamin bottles, Kleenex, assorted pens, a small notepad, antacid tablets, a Styrofoam take-out container with the remains of a hamburger and French fries, etc. The rest of the car was empty.

"Where's her flask?"

"What?" Bill glanced up from a pad where he'd been making notes.

"The silver flask?"

"Was she known to…?"

"Yeah. She was never without that little guy."

Bill poked carefully around Ruby's purse. "No flask. No apparent signs of trauma. Locked doors, windows shut tight, ignition on—like the engine ran out of gas. She might have had a heart attack or a stroke. Or maybe she was too intoxicated to drive so she pulled over and fell asleep."

"What she was doing out here, anyway," I mumbled. My good mood evaporated as the EMTs covered her body. The medical examiner arrived.

"Who knows? We'll have to wait for the ME to determine cause of death. And don't go getting any wild ideas," he cautioned me, running a hand through his blond hair, which was glinting in the summer sun. "I'll take that coffee now."

I handed him the paper cup. My investigative instincts often had been on target in helping to solve recent murders in Etonville, but this was a tragic accident and I did not intend to investigate Ruby's death. My imagination was on hiatus. "I have more than enough to keep me busy these days," I said pointedly.

Bill gazed at me over the rim of his coffee container. "Dodie, I'm on duty," he whispered.

"Yes, sir, chief." I saluted. "See you tonight?"

"If I get all of the paperwork done on this."

It was difficult to banter back and forth when Ruby lay dead on a gurney, twenty feet away from us.

Ralph marched over from his cruiser. "Chief, Timothy's tow truck'll be here in a minute. Where do you want it to go?" He jerked his thumb in the direction of Ruby's car.

"Timothy's for now," Bill said patiently.

"Copy that."

"Guess I'll head out. Got a date with Snippets," I said.

Bill arched an eyebrow. "Can't envision what the gossip crowd will make of Ruby's death."

I could.

* * * *

The hair salon was buzzing with activity by the time I walked in the door. Imogen was shampooing the two Banger sisters at the back sinks, and assistant manager Rita snipped and styled Mildred's shoulder-length locks. Two customers sat in the waiting area. Meanwhile, Carol juggled the appointment calendar and the phone. Snippets was the beating heart of Etonville.

"Things are hopping in here," I said.

"It's always like this near an ELT opening. Everyone insists on getting their hair done, even when they're wearing wigs in the show," Carol said sotto voce.

"Thanks for squeezing me in." I followed her to a cutting station and she flapped a cape around my neck.

"Why don't you get Bill to take you away for your birthday weekend?" Carol asked as she waggled a pair of scissors and studied my wavy mane. "Maybe an inch off. The ends are splitting."

"Fine," I said. Carol went to work.

"Dodie, it's your birthday?" The Banger sisters had settled themselves into chairs on my left.

"In a couple of weeks—"

"You're a Gemini?" Mildred said from my right.

"Yeah." I laughed. "That's me. The twins."

"My first boyfriend was a Gemini. Very moody, unreliable, and dishonest," she said.

"Really?" I asked. "I was under the impression that Geminis are open-minded, fun-loving, and great multi-taskers with good instincts." I scanned the group. Both the Bangers and Mildred eyed me skeptically.

Imogen waltzed over to join the conversation, newspaper in hand. "Have you read your horoscope for today?"

"Not yet," I said through gritted teeth.

"Says here you're 'going to meet the love of your life—a quiet, intellectual, book worm.'"

They stared at me expectantly. That certainly didn't describe Bill.

"And 'that if you come upon a puzzle today, don't be afraid to solve it,'" Imogen added.

"Not sure what that means," I said, aiming for light and noncommittal.

"Good thing nobody has died this morning," one of the Banger sisters said solemnly.

Uh-oh. Wait until the news about Ruby arrived.

As if on cue, the front door opened and Edna rushed in. "Have you heard?" she screeched and flapped her arms frenetically.

All eyes swiveled to face her. "What?" Mildred asked.

"It's Ruby. She's gone!" Edna exclaimed, strands of gray-brown hair popping willy-nilly out of the bun on the top of her head.

"Gone? Where?" asked Carol. "I hope she's back in time for the tech rehearsal tonight. I know she can be difficult but she's a whiz on the piano and nobody knows the score as well as—"

"The chief was called out for an 11-24—and maybe an 11-54—on the highway, but when he got there it was an 11-41 and..." She gulped. "And then an 11-44. Of course, we all know Ruby liked to take a sip now and then..." She mimed a bottle to her lips and her audience nodded in unison. "So it might be a 23152."

Drunk driving?

Edna wrung her hands. "What are we going to do?"

"Edna! For Pete's sake, stop!" Mildred put up a hand like a traffic cop. "What do all of those numbers mean?"

I tiptoed into the discussion. "There was an incident this morning. Ruby—"

"She's dead!" Edna hollered.

Stunned silence. We were off to the races...

* * * *

By the time I reached the Windjammer, word must have ricocheted around Etonville like a billiard ball off the rail of a pool table. I had barely entered the restaurant when Lola texted: *Have you heard?* I texted back with words of support, and suggested she stop by so that we could talk. Though

Ruby's loss of life was of utmost importance, I hoped that her death didn't delay the opening and Henry's creation of the contest winning recipes.

"Some news about that piano player." Benny cleaned the soda taps and prepped the bar. "They're saying she was probably drunk…"

Possibly.

"…and that the chief had to smash her window to get in."

"He didn't actually *smash* the window—"

"And that a witness saw a man running away from the scene."

What? "Who said that?" I asked.

Benny gestured. "You know Etonville."

I certainly did, and it took very little to trigger the rumor mill grinding. Ruby would be this week's grist. "Walter will need to replace her if *Bye, Bye, Birdie* is going to open on time."

"Henry's already working himself into a lather over the food contest. Hope this doesn't throw a monkey wrench into the process."

I needed to calm Henry's frazzled nerves. I pushed on the swinging doors into the kitchen.

"*Do-dee*," Wilson sang out, accent on the second syllable, and, grabbing me in a bear hug, swung me around, "I am so *hap-py!*"

I bounced against his mid-section. "Wilson, you can put me down." My feet touched the ground, my knees flexing, my legs wobbling. "What's up?"

A grin creased his brown face. "Henry *iz* beautiful! You are beautiful! And me? I am making my blanquette de veau!" He kissed his fingers and released the smooches to the air.

Tonight was the rollout of the winning appetizer—stuffed potato skins with avocado and cilantro—backed up by a simple dinner special of roast chicken and rosemary potatoes. Why in the world was Henry relinquishing the kitchen to Wilson and his white veal stew? "Where is Henry?" I asked.

Wilson smiled broadly and enveloped himself in a chef's apron. "In *ze* back."

I walked outside. Behind the restaurant, Henry cultivated a garden that produced an abundance of basil, rosemary, thyme, oregano, parsley, and dill—and kept the kitchen stocked with fresh herbs. They were his secret bullets. He tended his plants like an over-protective parent.

"Things are awfully green out here," I said, as he pinched leaves and cut bits of stems here and there.

Henry grunted.

"Wilson tells me he's doing the veal dish tonight. Thought that was next week. You know, introduce the palates of Etonville to his French-Haitian recipes gradually."

Henry sighed.

"What's going on?" I asked gently.

"I miss Enrico."

"I do too, but give Wilson time and he'll be—"

"And my daughter got engaged to a nincompoop," he finished darkly.

"Oh." Henry rarely talked about his home life. His wife worked in the city at a Wall Street investment firm, and his daughter graduated from college two years ago. This was the first I'd heard about a match gone wrong. I flashed on a picture of my father's reaction to one of my high school boyfriends. Also a nincompoop. "When's the wedding?" I asked carefully.

"When hell freezes over if I have anything to say about it. Which I don't." He tossed a spray of rosemary into a basket. "I said 'yes' to Wilson in a moment of frustration."

"Right. Is it too late to walk it back?"

Henry ducked his head forlornly.

* * * *

Ruby's passing was all anyone talked about during the mid-day rush. Henry's potato leek soup garnered limited attention—which was too bad because it was one of his best recipes. As Benny poured drinks and Gillian hurried from table to booth, I topped off coffee cups, rang up bills, and eavesdropped on conversations.

"Here we go again. Another ELT production, another death." Unfortunately, true.

"At least she wasn't murdered." Also true.

"Good thing she's not from Etonville." A member of the Etonville Little Theatre.

"What will happen with the show?" The question on everyone's lips.

At two o'clock, just as the steady stream of hungry townsfolk dwindled, Lola swept into the Windjammer. She didn't bother looking right or left, but headed straight to my back booth by the kitchen door. She slumped onto the bench and I signaled Benny to bring us coffee.

"Are we never going to get a show up without a crisis?" she cried.

Crisis was Lola's euphemism for sudden death. "Sorry Lola. I know this is the last thing any of you need."

"I feel terrible about Ruby, of course. She wasn't the most agreeable accompanist I've ever worked with, but Dale said the Creston Players couldn't have gotten along without her." Lola twisted a length of blond hair around her index finger. It was a nervous tic I'd seen before.

"She certainly knew music. I mean, scanning a score and then putting it away? That's a rare talent," I said.

"Dale said they were lucky she showed up some years ago. He actually brought her into the Players. She was an accompanist for his voice teacher," she said.

"Where did she come from? Does she have family in the area?"

"According to Dale, she lived alone," Lola said.

"So now what?"

"Penny is contacting the cast. We're going to have rehearsal at the theater tonight and cancel the tech for one day. Our new accompanist needs to get up to speed with the piano," she said.

"You have a replacement already?"

"The only possible person at this late date," Lola said. "Alex. The musical director. He knows the show. He's not as talented on the keyboard as Ruby, but..."

Beggars can't be choosers, she left unsaid. I didn't have much contact with Alex, but he seemed like a decent guy—polite, soft-spoken, and patient with Walter. That in itself made him an asset to the production. "So he'll direct the combo and play the piano?"

"It's done a lot. He's done it before, he says." She bit her lip. "I had such high hopes for *Bye, Bye, Birdie*."

"It's too soon to get depressed. There's time to pull it all together," I said.

I left Lola with a bowl of Henry's potato soup and replaced Gillian at the cash register so that she could take a break.

Other than seeing Ruby at rehearsal and when she ate at the Windjammer, I didn't know her well. I felt down about her dying and wondered who would miss the older woman? Who knew her well enough to miss her? What was it she'd said to me last night? "*You can't trust anyone...they only get you in the end...I know...from experience.*" Sounded like a bitter memory, if you asked me. Of course, no one was asking my opinion of Ruby's life or death—and it was just as well. I wanted no part of this latest catastrophe. I had enough on my culinary plate.

Gillian waltzed through the swinging doors and into the dining room. A crash and a loud exclamation followed her.

Wilson again.

3

I flicked off the lights and locked the front door of the Windjammer. It was almost midnight; I'd sent everyone else home over an hour ago. Sometimes, being the last person standing felt like a good way to wind down from the day. The afternoon had been hectic, preventing my normal three o'clock break. Instead, I prepped the inventory sheets for the winning entrees, assuring Henry that, though he was iffy on the contest dishes, patrons would love them as much as they did tonight's winner. The potato skins earned raves—this kind of an appetizer was definitely in Etonville's wheelhouse. I was not sure about upcoming specials.

Wilson's *blanquette de veau* was another matter. I'd say it was a fifty-fifty response. Some patrons thought the veal stew was fine, though a trifle too *chichi*. The other half of the crowd speculated on why it had to be so white. Where was the color? Wilson insisted on the classic version prepared by his Haitian grandmother, and was adamant about no carrots or peas. He and Henry sparred for three rounds until Henry yielded, still dejected by his daughter's impending marriage. Wilson gave him a bear hug as a consolation prize.

I stopped on the sidewalk outside the restaurant and gazed upward. The sky was inky black and clear, promising a sunny day tomorrow and hinting that the weather might cooperate throughout the week. The last thing the theater needed was to be rained out on opening night. I sank into the driver's seat of my Metro and cranked the engine. My mind skipped to this morning and witnessing the EMTs placing Ruby's lifeless body on the gurney. I took the leisurely way home. All was serene, quiet. I drove through the empty streets of Etonville to the north end of town, though I lived in the south end. I was in Lola's neighborhood which made me speculate about rehearsal, the musical director's handling of the accompaniment, Walter's pre-show exercises, and Penny's antics...

As if on autopilot, my Metro headed to the access road leading to State Route 53. Timothy's Timely Service station was up ahead, and I slowed down. As I drove by, I located Ruby's Toyota parked prominently among the cluster of cars awaiting service. I had personal experience with Timothy's earlier in the year, and "timely" might have been a slight exaggeration. I gazed in my rearview mirror. A pinpoint of light flicked on inside Ruby's car. The service station was closed. I tapped my breaks and when I looked up into the mirror again, the light had disappeared. Was it my imagination?

I brushed off a spooky sensation and pressed the gas pedal, beating it back to Ames and my home in minutes. I climbed out of the car, scooting to my front porch. Inside the house, I yawned, looking forward to hunkering down in bed, maybe reading a chapter or two—

"Hey."

"Argghh!" I jumped and released my bag.

Bill leapt off the sofa. "What's the matter?" he screeched groggily.

"What are you doing here?" I gasped, my heart doing a trampoline act.

"Thought you'd like some company. I came over a couple of hours ago and laid down on the sofa for a minute. Guess I fell asleep," he said.

"I guess." I collapsed into my recliner and exhaled my fright. "You scared me. I didn't see your cruiser outside anywhere."

Bill rubbed his beard. "I like to keep things between us on the down low. I drove my BMW and parked it down the block."

"It doesn't matter where you park your car. Etonville has eyes and ears on us."

"Sorry to frighten you. I meant to text earlier but got sidetracked by the ME's office," he said.

"Ruby?"

"Yeah. Her blood alcohol level was .06," he said.

"Not at the illegal level." I'd become aware of the legal blood alcohol level during an earlier investigation.

"No, but high enough to make driving slightly dicey. Especially given her petite build and body weight."

"Does he know what she died from? Was it a heart attack or something?"

Bill nodded. "It's preliminary, but the ME says it looks like carbon monoxide poisoning."

"She was asphyxiated? Don't you die of carbon monoxide poisoning in closed spaces like garages? Ruby died on the open roadway."

"I'm having Timothy go over her car in the morning. Maybe there was a malfunction in the exhaust system. A crack in the manifold or something," Bill said and rubbed his eyes.

I shivered.

Bill put a protective arm around my shoulder. "You cold?"

"Tired," I said. No sense in sharing what I thought I witnessed at Timothy's tonight, especially since I couldn't be one hundred percent positive that I actually saw something worth sharing.

Bill smiled slyly. "I guess we'd better get you into bed."

OMG. No mystery chapters tonight.

* * * *

The alarm buzzed a staccato rhythm and I woke up. Buttery sunlight streamed in the bedroom window and I winced. Time to get up already? I pulled the sheet over my shoulder and promised myself ten more minutes to snooze. I was in the middle of a delicious dream…lounging poolside at a luxury resort, soaking up rays and cool breezes, while a handsome man served me a pink drink with an umbrella poking out of it. Was it Bill? Speaking of which…I peeked at the left side of my bed. Somehow, the shrieking of the alarm hadn't awakened him, though he'd been the one to set it. I studied his blondish beard, spikes of his sandy brush cut sticking up in all directions on his head, and frown lines in the space between his eyes, firmly closed. He must have been exhausted. I kissed the tip of his nose. His eyes fluttered open.

"Yep. It's six thirty. You wanted to be gone before the neighborhood woke up."

"Price I pay for a private life," he griped and threw back the cover.

As if that was remotely possible. "I'll put on some coffee."

"Don't bother. I'll get some on my way to Timothy's garage." He rolled out of bed and dressed in a flash.

I whipped on a bathrobe and followed him to the front door, barely keeping up. "So, talk later?" I asked as he strapped on his belt and holster.

"Sure." He hugged me, yawning in my ear.

Truly romantic. "Did Edna bring your costume to the municipal building? Until you hear different, the show goes up the end of the week."

He opened the door.

"And let Penny know if you can't make the tech tonight. It's in the park."

"Got it."

I grabbed the back of his uniform shirt. "You're a man of few words this morning."

He laid a whopper of a kiss on me. "Actions speak louder than words." *Yahoo*!

Bill had no sooner stepped onto my front porch when two of my neighbors, each attempting to control a frolicking dog, immediately stopped their conversation. They waved merrily.

"Hi, Chief," one said. "Gonna be a beautiful day."

The other agreed.

Bill ducked his head, practically ran to his car down the block, and I gamely waved back. "Morning!" I was standing in my robe for all the world to see. I scampered back inside and shut the door. Oh well, life in a small town...

I toyed with the idea of hopping back under the covers, but I was too wide-awake now to surrender to my dreams again. I luxuriated in an extra cup of coffee, a slice of toast, and the *New York Times*. By eight, I was ready to face the day. I stayed in the shower longer than usual, letting the warm water ping off my face and run over my shoulders. Funny that Bill hadn't mentioned our vacation last night, as he had nearly every day since we first agreed to plan one together. He was so gung-ho about sleeping in a tent, fishing for dinner, preparing a gourmet meal on a camping cook stove. Had he been that preoccupied by Ruby's death? I pushed thoughts of her passing out of my mind, as I slipped on my black skinny jeans and a stretchy, red, knit top. Red was my power color, and I needed to dive into the day with some energy. Wilson, Henry, the contest-winning entrees—

My cell binged. It was Lola: *Are you up? Coffee? Need a favor. I'll explain.* I texted back that I was up and would meet her in twenty minutes. I picked up my keys from the coffee table in the living room and spied a manila envelope. Bill's name was on the outside, official looking papers on the inside. *I'll bet he needs these today.* I'd swing by Timothy's on my way to Coffee Heaven.

By the time I left my bungalow, the neighborhood was a beehive of activity. The beautiful weather coaxed people outdoors to mow grass, water flower beds, and powerwalk down the street. I whipped out my cell phone and pretended to have a call—never mind that no one was on the other end. If I appeared to be busy, I wouldn't have to acknowledge my neighbors with anything more than a perfunctory wave. I settled into my Metro and, phone to my ear, my simulated conversation rattling on, I backed out of my driveway. I ditched the phone as I hit the street—no sense tempting fate by pretending to chat illegally.

The roads were already crawling with Etonville residents as I swerved my car down Main Street, avoiding the manhole covers where the Department of Public Works was paving the road. Ralph directed traffic in the opposite direction—standing in the street, gesturing with his arms, blowing his whistle from time to time. I wasn't sure his actions weren't clogging the roadway. Glad I was heading north instead of south. I inched along until I could turn left to cut over several streets and swing by Timothy's service station.

Up ahead I saw Bill's squad car. Good. I was hoping he was still here. I pulled over on the side of the road and clicked off the engine. I snatched the manila envelope off the seat and strode to Ruby's car where Bill and Timothy had their heads tucked under the hood.

"Hi," I said.

Timothy jerked his head out. He shoved his ball cap up his forehead and ran a hand over his grizzled beard. "Hey there, Dodie."

Bill followed suit. "What are you doing here?"

Was that a suspicious glimmer in his laser baby blues? "You forgot this." I held out the envelope.

"I did?" Bill asked sheepishly. "Guess I was distracted this morning."

Timothy considered the exchange between Bill and me, stifling a chuckle.

"You could have delivered it to the department," Bill said. "No need to track me down. But thanks."

"I wasn't sure how important the papers were." Bill was right; I could have stopped by the municipal building on my way to Lola's. Then I realized what was bothering me. The light in Ruby's car last night was an itch that required scratching. "Have you found anything? About Ruby's car?" When Bill and I had officially "gotten together" back in March, I had assured him that I would stay out of future investigations—at least in public. It would be easier on both of us—but I had my little hairs to keep track of, and right now they were giving me a hard time.

Before Bill could stop him, Timothy said, "Well, you know, carbon monoxide is deadly stuff."

"Even outside a garage?"

"Dodie…" Bill gave me a warning glance.

Timothy was oblivious. "Uh-huh. CO_2 can get into the engine compartment and then the body of the car. A cracked exhaust manifold. A leak between the manifold and the heat shroud. The tail pipe not securely connected to the—"

"Can you take a closer look at the engine and exhaust system and let me know if you find anything?" Bill asked.

"Uh-huh." Timothy removed his cap. "Course she was due for an inspection. Maybe they woulda' caught something with the exhaust system." He pointed to the state decal on the front windshield. Ruby's car was overdue for its date with the Department of Motor Vehicles.

New Jersey was a stickler when it came to car inspections. The DMV didn't mess around. I should know. I'd missed the inspection deadline by two days years ago and had to pay a fat fine for my mistake. "What a shame. If she'd had the inspection, she might be alive?" I asked. I had always found the state inspection to be relatively inconsequential. Until now.

Timothy shrugged. Bill was silent. Was now the time to mention the light?

"Give me a call later?" Bill said, tipping his hat at Timothy, and leading me by the elbow back to my Metro. "Dodie, we had an agreement."

"We do. But this isn't a murder and I thought I saw something last night."

"What?"

"On my way home, I was driving past Timothy's and—"

"This place isn't on your way home from the Windjammer," Bill said.

"Not exactly, but I like to drive around Etonville late at night when the streets are empty and everything is quiet, so I came down to this end and—"

"Dodie!"

"Right. I was cruising past and when I looked up into my rearview mirror..." What did I really see? "A light went on in Ruby's car."

"A light? Like the dome light?"

"Not that bright. Maybe a flashlight? Could have been a cell phone flashlight," I added.

"So you stopped and investigated?" he asked.

"Me? No! I drove on. When I looked up again, the light was gone."

Bill exhaled slowly. "So you can't confirm that what you really saw *was* a light. You only think you *might* have seen a light?"

"I guess so." My cell pinged. "Lola. I should go." I backed away.

"Stay out of trouble," Bill called out.

* * * *

"You gals all set?" Jocelyn asked as she rang up our coffees to go.

Lola took a sip of hers and snapped the lid on the container. "Thanks, Jocelyn."

"By the way..." Jocelyn tugged on the front of her uniform and leaned over the counter. "If you see Walter, tell him I said 'Hey.'"

Lola gazed at me. "Oh. Sure."

I held it together until we were safely in Lola's Lexus—a cleaner, more comfortable ride than my Metro—which I parked in front of the Windjammer. "Guess who has the hots for your director?" I hooted.

"Jocelyn?"

"Yes."

"No!"

"Yes! And she's serious about it."

"Does Walter know?" Lola asked.

"I doubt it. You know how oblivious he can be. Besides, he still has eyes for you." I sipped my caramel macchiato.

Lola steered the Lexus out of town and onto the highway. "You'd never know it from last night's rehearsal."

"Bad time?"

"After we suffered through one of Walter's warm-ups—we had to be trees in the Etonville Park...you know, swaying, falling, branches bending in the wind—he gave notes for an hour. They included an especially detailed critique of Dale and me. Everything we did was wrong. The timing on the choreography was off, the blocking was incorrect. He gave me line readings. Me!" Lola concentrated on the road. "I tried to be calm and supportive of Walter, but Dale was so fed up he nearly burst a blood vessel."

I'd seen Dale explode a couple of times at rehearsal over blocking notes. "Guess he doesn't like to be corrected?"

"I could have throttled Walter. Penny was getting frustrated too."

"And that takes some doing." Penny was protective of Walter. "How did Alex handle the accompaniment?" I asked.

"Fine. There were missed cues but by opening night he'll be good to go."

"At least he knows the show."

"True. Even Walter had to compliment him on taking on the extra load."

"Maybe if Walter knew about Jocelyn, it would improve his mood?" I suggested.

Lola cut her eyes in my direction. "Can you picture the two of them?" She approached the Creston turnoff and switched on her GPS. "I don't really know what part of town we're going to."

"You never did explain why we had to go to Ruby's apartment," I said.

The GPS directed us to continue down the main drag for a mile and a half, and then turn right on Barrow Street.

"I didn't want to go alone. Thought it might be creepy. But both Walter and JC said Ruby had taken notes and created music cue sheets from the rehearsal in the park Monday night."

The night before Ruby died. "Wouldn't Penny have that?" Penny carried her prompt script and clipboard around as if they were the Holy Grail.

"You'd think so, but Walter said Penny was busy doing I-don't-know-what while he and JC and Ruby were timing music to light cues. Ruby insisted on keeping her own record of the cues, and said she was taking the sheets to work on them. Since we didn't need them until we moved to the park for the technical rehearsal, I thought Ruby might have left them home. They weren't with her score. Of course she barely looked at the score."

"I suppose you could create another set of cues?" I asked.

"We might have to, but finding the cue sheets will save us a ton of time rewriting all of Ruby's notes."

"So you called her super?"

Lola checked her GPS. "I explained it all to him. Not sure he understood but he agreed to meet us at her apartment to unlock the door."

We traveled over Barrow and onto Hamilton Avenue. Lola eased her Lexus to the curb and we stared at 119, the address she had for Ruby's apartment building. The neighborhood was old and worn, like Ruby herself. The faded red brick structure housed four floors of apartments. The courtyard had remnants of a dried-up fountain. In its heyday, the courtyard must have been an attractive setting. Now, however, debris littered the empty fountain. Single-family homes bordered either side of the apartment building, and parked cars lined the curb. On the opposite side of the street were a deli, a post office, a tavern, and a church. The streets were uninhabited.

"This is it," said Lola.

We got out of the Lexus and followed a cracked cement walkway, through patches of dry brown grass, to the back of the courtyard and the entrance into the building. Lola called a number and in a minute, the super opened the door. "I am Nikolas. Come, come. I am sorry to hear about Ruby. She was nice woman."

I judged his thick accent to be Eastern European. About forty, with thinning dark hair, he wore a plaid work shirt and a tool belt that jingled. He led us to the elevator and explained that he had not entered Ruby's place in the seven years she'd lived there. Ever? Ruby was on the verge of elderly, and she'd never needed help with the plumbing or heating or electrical? She'd been self-sufficient.

We rode to the third floor in silence, and then moved down a hallway to an end unit. Nikolas fiddled with the keys and pushed open Ruby's door.

"We'll only need a few minutes to find the papers," Lola explained.

"I will come back in fifteen minutes." Nikolas left us alone—as though we needed discretion to search among Ruby's things.

Lola and I walked to the center of the two-room apartment. There was an efficiency kitchen, with a refrigerator, stove, and sink on one wall, and a table, chairs, and bookshelves on the opposite wall. A laptop sat on the table. A door led into a miniscule bedroom that allowed for a single bed and a chest of drawers. A sofa facing a flat screen television and an upright piano occupied the remainder of space in the apartment. Everything was neat as a pin.

"Wow. Doesn't seem like Ruby," I said.

"I know what you mean. The flask, cigarettes, her scruffy look like she'd spent days in the same clothes. Where are the ashtrays and empty liquor bottles?" She sniffed. "Even the air smells clean."

I poked my head into the bedroom. Nothing strewn about, some clothes in a closet neatly arranged on hangers. Two pairs of dark slacks, several blouses, and knit tops. "I've never seen her in nicer clothes—like these. Are we sure it's her place?"

"Yes." Lola found a piece of junk mail addressed to Ruby on the bookshelf.

"It's pretty sterile," I said.

"Well, it shouldn't take me long to find the cue sheets—if they're here." Lola took a glimpse of the room, gazed at the bookshelf, and moved into the bedroom.

Out of sheer curiosity, I ducked into Ruby's bathroom. It was a bad habit of mine…checking out medicine cabinets. Ruby's held the basics—toothpaste, dental floss, face cream, hand lotion, an outdated prescription for an antibiotic, and an open bottle of Ambien. It was half full; without thinking, I snapped the lid back on.

I re-entered the living room and walked closer to Ruby's books. I was always curious about the things that people read, or at least pretended to read. Ruby had a handful of romance novels, biographies of presidents from Eisenhower to Obama, and a series of books on Indiana—its history, a text on its native plants, and a phone book for Indianapolis dated 1970.

"I can't find the cue sheets. Ruby must have left them somewhere else," Lola said, frustrated.

A light bulb went on. "I didn't see anything that looked like a bunch of papers in her car—but maybe Bill has them."

"That makes sense. Could you ask him?"

"I'll text him now." My fingers went to work on my cell phone. "You know, it's strange. Not a single picture in here. I'm thinking of my great aunt Maureen. By the time she was Ruby's age, family photos decorated every surface of her home. Where are Ruby's?"

Lola ran her finger over the edge of a bookshelf. "Who knows? I heard she was from the Midwest."

"Indiana, I'm betting." I pulled out a history of the state and showed Lola.

"I suppose the police will try to contact her family. If she has any."

I replaced the book and, shoved to the back of the shelf, I noticed a worn binding that covered a fat sheaf of pages. A thick rubber band held everything together. "What's this?"

Lola crossed to my side and watched as I withdrew a scrapbook, eight by ten, apparently jammed full of newspaper clippings and memorabilia. "Ruby's?" Lola asked.

I lifted off the rubber band and opened the cover. In block print were the words Ruby Passonata. "I'd love to see what's in here."

"Nikolas will be back any minute," Lola said apprehensively.

"Maybe I could borrow it. I don't think Nikolas would mind, and it doesn't look as if any immediate family members are racing to Creston to collect her things."

Lola bit her lip. "I suppose we could say we're using the scrapbook to write a dedication to Ruby in the program."

"That's a lovely idea!" I jammed the book into my bag as Nikolas knocked softly on the door.

"Missus? I must lock up now."

We joined him in the hallway. "Is someone coming to remove Ruby's things?" I asked.

Nikolas motioned his uncertainty. "The police…they say they are looking. I don't know."

He seemed dejected. Maybe one of only a few who would miss Ruby.

4

Lola wound her way out of Creston while I texted Benny to alert him that I might be running late. He texted back: *Be prepared...Cheney Bros. missing asparagus. Henry second thoughts on tonight's contest winner.*

I'd been going toe-to-toe with Cheney Brothers food delivery service for two years over orders missing items. I wanted to replace them with another company, but Henry had a long history with them. Anyway, he hated change: new staff, new specials, a new son-in-law...

"I think, for the moment, we should keep the scrapbook to ourselves," I said.

"I agree. Although it's not like anyone would care," Lola said and scooted onto State Route 53.

"Timothy thinks Ruby's exhaust system was defective. That the carbon monoxide leaked into the engine and then into the interior of her car."

Lola's eyes widened. "What? Didn't she die from a stroke or something?"

Ooops... "Lola, you have to keep that to yourself until the official word is out. I don't want Bill to think I'm speaking out of turn."

"Mum's the word. Carbon monoxide? Don't you have to be in a closed garage or something to die that way?" she asked.

"Not if there's a problem with the exhaust."

"Speaking of Bill..."

Lola's eyes twinkled and I might have blushed a bit. I wasn't used to having everyone check in on my love life. Sometimes I yearned for the anonymity of my Jersey Shore days. "All good."

"And your summer vacation?"

"Negotiating. That camping thing is a big deal for him," I said.

"We went camping once. Tom and I."

Tom was Lola's husband who had died years ago. Long before I came to Etonville. "You did? You never mentioned that."

"He claimed he had a thing for the outdoors, but the weekend was a fiasco. I fell out of a canoe, Tom burned dinner on the camp stove, and we both ended up with poison ivy." She winced at the memory. "My advice? Keep negotiating."

Lola and I chitchatted during the rest of the trip to Etonville, but in the back of my mind Ruby's life competed for my attention. My powers of invention went to work. What did Ruby do, besides work with the Creston Players? Did she have a circle of friends outside the theater? Not that the Players were very friendly with her. What about her background? Family? How long had she lived alone? The questions piled up, and I gently pushed them aside as Lola approached the Windjammer.

"So you'll be at the park tonight for the tech rehearsal?" she asked.

"Right. Benny's closing the restaurant and I want to check out the picnic area where we're setting up the food stand." A previous attempt to supply homemade concessions for an ELT production backfired when a murder investigation waylaid the opening. Not to worry, I told myself. This time we were only selling drinks and snack boxes—also provided by Cheney Brothers. I hopped out of the Lexus. "See you later."

Lola waved and drove off. I swung my bag over my shoulder. It was heavier now that it contained Ruby's scrapbook. I was dying to dig into it—maybe during my break this afternoon.

"Good thing you're back," Benny said, greeting me at the Windjammer door.

"That bad?" I asked quietly. Customers had begun to wander in and tables were filling up.

Benny jerked his thumb over his shoulder. "You better check it out ASAP."

I hurried to the kitchen. "Mmmm. What smells so good in here?"

Wilson flashed his wide, wide smile, abandoned his knife on the cutting board—where he was preparing vegetables for tonight's special: curried squash and eggs with raita salad—and put his arms out to grab me. "*Do-dee!*"

At the stove, Henry brandished his soup ladle.

I put up my hands in a defensive gesture and sidestepped Wilson's embrace. Henry stared darkly into his soup pot. "I guess we're not serving the cream of asparagus. I'll call Cheney Brothers and get the order here for tomorrow. Escarole and white bean soup is a good replacement," I said optimistically.

Henry grunted. I could understand his second-guessing his decision for tonight's winner. I felt the curried squash might be a trifle experimental for Etonville's taste. Unfortunately, he'd chosen the winner last week—when he'd been in a euphoric mood because business was brisk, customers were complimentary, and Wilson hadn't dropped anything for several hours. Now he was living with his decision. I patted Henry's arm. "It will all work out." Huh? "I'm sure people will love the squash and eggs."

Wilson beamed. Didn't anything get that guy down?

*   *   *   *

Henry's grilled three-cheese sandwiches—a staple at the Windjammer— sold like hotcakes and his soup special was holding its own, except for three or four peevish customers.

"Today's soup special was supposed to be cream of asparagus," said one of the Banger sisters.

"We had a slight problem with the vegetable delivery," I said apologetically.

"We like cream of asparagus soup," said the other sister. They waited expectantly for me to respond.

"That's nice." I moved on.

"Dodie, what's with all of the white food?" asked Vernon, Mildred's husband.

White food?

"Vernon, let Dodie alone. Can't you see she's busy?"

He ignored Mildred. "Last night it was white veal stew, today it's white bean soup—"

Mildred tsked. "Next time I'm leaving you home."

"What?" Vernon asked and cranked up his hearing aids.

I moved around the dining room, gauging the gastronomic satisfaction level of Etonville's citizens. I'd say about a three on a five-point scale today. Wait until they taste tested the contest winner tonight...*Yikes*!

I rang up Edna's take-out order for the Etonville Police Department— tuna salad, grilled cheese, and Henry's special burger for Bill. He was crazy about them. "Busy over there today?"

Edna tucked stray hairs into her bun and leaned in. "Well, something's up," she said knowingly.

"Yeah?" I handed her change for the two twenties. "The chief's been in and out three times, had Suki on the line to the Creston police, and didn't bother ordering anything when I made my run to Coffee Heaven."

"Sounds like something *is* up. Any idea what?" Edna was usually good for police chatter.

"It could be something simple like an 11-25 or 11-54…but I'm thinking it's more a 10-29."

Edna loved her codes, no doubt about it, and I'd become so accustomed to speaking to her in police shorthand that I recognized some of them. "10-29? That's a 'subject wanted.'"

She tucked the change into her purse. "Yep. 10-29F."

A felony. What was going on? I'd have to wait to hear from Bill.

"Gotta scoot." Edna dashed off.

* * * *

I went behind the counter to take a breather and drew myself a seltzer. I kept one eye on the dining room and the other on my cell. Lola texted asking if I'd heard from Bill about Ruby's cue sheets.

A polite voice interrupted my messaging. "Could I have a menu, please?"

I glanced up and saw the friendly face of Alex, the musical director. He sat down on a barstool. "Of course." I handed him the laminated card and a glass of ice water. "The soup special is escarole and white bean, but we're also featuring our grilled three cheese sandwich. People love it."

He pondered available choices, then, brushing light brown hair off his forehead. "I'll take the special. I hear the chef is a master at creating soups and chowders."

"Good choice." I wrote up his order and handed it to Gillian, who headed to the kitchen. "We haven't formally met. I'm—"

"Dodie. Yes, I know. I've seen you at rehearsals, and here of course. I'm—"

"Alex. Ditto on seeing you." He put out his hand and I took it. His courtesy was old world, but nice. "I hear you're taking over Ruby's place at the piano," I said gently.

His affable features clouded over, his dark eyes dimmed. "It's awful. I'll miss her."

"I'm so sorry for your loss. Were you…close?"

"We weren't what you'd call close. We'd run into each other at the Players theater, maybe coaching an actor, or doing incidental music for a show, but this was the first musical we worked on together. Ruby'd been with the Creston Players for ten years. I'm new this year. I've been doing musical direction for them since last September." He hesitated. "Ruby was a memorable person."

"I'd say."

"She had her own way of doing things, that's for sure." Alex took a sip of water.

"She could read a score and then do it from memory," I said. "That's amazing."

"Exactly. I've only met one other person in my life who could do that," he said.

"Good thing you know the score so well. Now that you're playing the show and conducting."

"It's fine. I've done it before. I wish Lola had found Ruby's cue sheets from Monday night's rehearsal. Tonight's tech would be so much easier," Alex said.

"We looked all over Ruby's apartment. Not that there was much to search. She lived simply," I said.

"You searched her place? I imagine lots of stuff there. Magazines, dusty books, and old picture albums."

"Not this apartment. Tidy and clean."

Alex looked surprised. "Well, knowing Ruby, she stuck the sheets somewhere and forgot about them."

Gillian set his soup in front of him. "Enjoy," she said.

He leaned over the bowl and inhaled. "Mmm. This *is* special."

"Thanks. I'll see you tonight," I said.

"You'll be at the tech rehearsal?"

"I need to scope out the picnic area. We're doing pre-show concessions," I said and handed Alex salt and pepper shakers.

"Let's cross our fingers it doesn't rain," Alex said and dipped his spoon into the white beans.

"Right." I smiled and moved off to ring up an order.

* * * *

I collapsed into my back booth with a tuna salad. I hadn't been off my feet for four hours. Good for the Windjammer bank balance, bad for my arches. I kicked off my sandals, massaged my instep, and rested my head against the seat back. What I wouldn't give for an hour to myself. I was eager to peek at Ruby's scrapbook. What had she saved over the years? My mother kept mementoes of me and my brother Andy: baby shoes, locks of hair, pictures, report cards, newspaper clippings from my seventh grade spelling bee and Andy's soccer tournaments. On rainy days, Mom and I would pull the box off the shelf in her bedroom closet, and pore over its contents. I loved reliving my young past.

"We need to talk."

My head jerked upward. Bill's mesmerizing eyes fixed on me intently. "What did I do?" I asked, like a kid caught with one hand in the cookie jar.

He slid onto the bench next to me, placing his cap on the table and leaving the spikes of his brush cut poking up in different directions.

Wow! Bill was getting a little intimate for the Windjammer and Etonville. Did he have something on his mind?

"Sorry to crowd you."

Guess not.

"I need to keep this quiet," he said.

My heart thumped. Did whatever "this" was have anything to do with Edna's referring to a 10-29F earlier?

"I had Timothy take another look at Ruby's exhaust system and he didn't find anything unusual." Bill looked agitated.

"That makes sense two ways," I said. "First of all, it sounds like it's easy enough for carbon monoxide to leak into the car and second, I like Timothy a lot, but mechanically speaking he's never been the brightest bulb in the chandelier. Now if—"

"Dodie!" Bill rasped.

"What?"

"I wasn't completely satisfied so I had the state police give the engine a second look...go over it with a fine-tooth comb."

"And?"

Bill peeked over his shoulder, taking in the near-empty dining room. "This is why I need your discretion. The state guys found a hairline crack between the manifold and the tail pipe connection. It wasn't caused by a bad repair job or rusting."

My stomach churned. "What are you saying?"

"Someone with a detailed knowledge of car mechanics cut a thin gap in the pipe so that fumes could leak out."

"Ruby was...?" The words stuck in my throat.

"Murdered," he said grimly.

Who? Why?

Bill watched the questions march across my face. "I know."

"Who would want to kill a senior citizen who didn't even live in Etonville? Her apartment was downright Spartan—hardly a trace of her personal life," I said.

"How do you know what her apartment looks like?" he asked. His eyebrows knitted together in a quizzical frown.

I related Lola's and my trip to Creston this morning.

"Her place is part of the criminal investigation now," Bill said. "You need to stay clear of it."

"We never found what we were looking for but I did—"

Bill's cell rang, and he held up a hand. "Yes?" He listened, his head dipping. "Okay. Keep me posted." He clicked off. "I have to go."

"Would you like some takeout?"

He shook his head. "What I would like, the reason I came here…" He hesitated. "I'd like your help with something. Strictly on the QT," he advised.

Yes! Bill was finally appreciating my investigative instincts.

"Because there's really no one else I can ask."

Right.

"Ruby was new to Etonville. She was in town because of the show. It wasn't a random act of violence. Someone planned this and knew what they were doing," he said.

"What do you want me to do?"

"People connected to *Bye, Bye, Birdie* are now persons of interest. I'd like someone to keep track of them while the show is in production. Let me know if you see anyone acting squirrelly."

I was growing accustomed to the community theater life. Many folks from both Etonville and Creston acted squirrelly.

"After the news about her murder breaks, in the next twenty-four hours, someone might give something away, make a mistake," Bill said.

"Okay. I'll be around most nights with the pre-show concessions. But when *Bye, Bye, Birdie* closes and the Creston gang goes home, the opportunity for group surveillance will be over," I said.

"I know. More reason to stay on top of them now." Bill squeezed out of the booth, grabbed his cap. "I'll check in with you later. Keep Ruby's murder quiet for now—even from Lola. By the way, there were no papers with musical notes on them in Ruby's car. Sorry." He left.

My tuna salad had wilted along with my fervor for the food contest. Poor Ruby. She was a tad grouchy and could throw an insult around with the best of them, but murder? Who would want to do away with the crusty old gal who sneaked out for a smoke and a slug between wisecracks? My mind whirled, bouncing from one thought to another. I felt flattered that Bill had asked me to keep an eye on the cast and crew, but at this point in the production process there was usually so much chaos that it would be impossible to keep track of everyone. Besides, it was hard to believe that someone working on *Bye, Bye, Birdie* had it in for Ruby. For once it had appeared that the opening of an ELT show would run smoothly. That horse was out of the barn. Etonville would be beside itself when news of the murder broke…

I lugged myself out of my seat to face Henry's paranoia about curried squash and eggs with raita salad.

* * * *

I held my breath during the dinner rush, as patrons sampled the contest winner supplied by the minister from the Episcopal Church. How adventurous were the town's appetites this evening? Henry and I had already sampled the entrée and it was scrumptious. It was also pretty. Curry paste topped the crispy rings of squash that outlined the baked eggs. The tomato/cucumber/shallot salad was a perfect compliment. I circulated around the dining room, calculating when I'd need to leave the restaurant to get to the park.

"Dodie, this is unusual," said a customer, spearing a chunk of squash. Uh-oh.

"But absolutely yummy."

"Thanks," I said, my spirits lifting.

From a table off to my left, someone gave me the ok sign, and I could see a handful of customers at a booth smiling affirmatively. This contest had been another of my "big ideas" according to Henry, and if it bombed, I wouldn't hear the end of it. So far, we were batting a thousand with the potato skins and squash; two down and two entrées to go.

"This isn't bad," said Abby, who was catching dinner before the tech rehearsal. "I'm used to having my eggs for breakfast, but what the hay. When in Rome…"

What put Abby in such a good mood? "Nice to hear. All set for this evening?" I asked.

"Yep." She tilted her upper body toward me, confidentially. "No one's supposed to know, but I'll probably win the best featured actress award," she whispered.

"Lola mentioned that the ELT was having a year-end banquet and giving out acting honors."

"Think I've got this one sewed up." She scowled. "Closest competition is Edna, but she's pretty green and the ELT likes to reward veterans."

Abby and Edna had been in competition for over a year now.

"Good luck with the opening."

"Normally I'd say 'we need it' but I'm feeling confident about this one."
She swiped at her mouth and pulled out her wallet.

Wait until the news about Ruby's killing erupted.

I manned the cash register—graciously accepting kudos for the curried
squash—and made a brief stop in the kitchen before heading to the park.

"Looks like we have a winner again tonight," I said to Henry. He grunted
his pleasure, never one to wallow in his own success. "This contest might
get us to four stars in the *Etonville Standard.*" The town's local newspaper
prided itself on its gastronomic sophistication.

"*Do-dee*, I am so happy about *ze* squash I make Haitian voodoo sticks
tomorrow," Wilson said.

I squinted at Henry. "Voodoo sticks?"

Wilson let out a cackle. "I fooled you! It's beef on a skewer."

Henry grunted again. Time to take off.

I grabbed my bag from the back booth and waved good-bye to Benny.
"Thanks for holding down the fort tonight."

"It was either this or paint the bathroom."

"Definitely the better choice," I said.

"Hey, tell them all I said to break their legs with the show," Benny said.
"I hear they're killing it."

Right.

5

The night was going to be warm. The Etonville Public Works Department, as well as the Etonville Little Theatre and the Creston Players, had done a terrific job of transforming the park into an outdoor performance venue. The town crew set up ten rows of folding chairs that ran from the base of the stage to the beginning of a grassy slope, where the audience could picnic and then remain to watch the show. Or they could settle into one of the folding chairs. Behind the seating area, a table served as a temporary box office. Tickets were twenty dollars for adults and fifteen dollars for senior citizens, students, and folks who were willing to subscribe to the entire ELT season.

A portable refreshment stand was off to the side—the town trotted it out for other events in the park: movie night, softball games, and Sunday soccer tournaments. Meanwhile, JC erected portable dressing rooms offstage, and—with the addition of curtains and black flats—the crew created wing space for actors' entrances and exits.

"Yep, looks like a real theater," Penny said, knocking her clipboard against her leg.

In my head again. "I can't believe this co-production is really happening without too many glitches." I walked to the inside of the compact concession booth to check out the shelves and bar space.

Penny shrugged. "If you don't count Ruby. You gotta know what you're doing when it comes to carbon dioxide, O'Dell," Penny said importantly.

"You mean carbon monoxide?"

"Whatever. You can't fool around when it comes to maintaining a car. I should know. I change my own oil and spark plugs," she said.

"I'm impressed but I can't imagine Ruby working on *her* car, can you?"

Penny smirked. "Didn't need to. She had a garage she went to in Creston."

My cardio drumbeat picked up its pace. "She did? How do you know?"

Penny pushed her glasses a notch up her nose. "She told me. I was about the only person from Etonville she talked to. We had stuff in common."

I hated to go there. "Like what?"

"We never slept."

"Ruby was an insomniac?" I asked.

"Yep."

"Did she talk about recent work on her car?"

"O'Dell, what are you getting at?" Penny squinched up her face. "Some mechanic screwed up and…" The thought astounded Penny and her eyes grew round. "That's why I do my own tune-ups," she muttered.

Walter waved to her from the stage. He was demonstrating a dance step to Vernon and Abby, who good-naturedly listened and then repeated his instructions. Penny tooted two sharp blasts on her whistle. The sound echoed around this end of the park before it drifted off into the summer night air.

"About time to start the tech?" I asked, checking my watch. It was scheduled to begin thirty minutes ago.

"O'Dell, I thought you had it straight. Tech time in the theater is—"

"Always later than life time. So in real time it's eight but in tech time it's seven thirty," I said. "Got it."

Penny pulled herself up to her full five foot two inches. "O'Dell, are you putting me on?"

"Who me? Never!"

Penny strode authoritatively to the platform stage where actors were gathering while Walter gesticulated wildly at JC, pointing at the light poles. In front of the stage, Lola and Dale stood by the makeshift orchestra pit, conferring. When she spotted me behind the portable refreshment stand, she hurried over.

"Hey girlfriend. All set?" I asked more casually than I felt. Keeping Ruby's murder a secret, especially from Lola, felt like having my mouth muzzled.

"Alex has been so great about stepping in for Ruby—and having her gone has forced everyone else to step up a bit too. Any word on the cue sheet?" Lola asked.

"It wasn't in the car or in her purse."

Walter and Penny lined up the high school kids to rehearse the telephone number.

"At least Walter's in a better mood. He seems to be accepting the fact that Dale and I are a couple on *and* off the stage." Lola dashed off.

I was happy for her. Lola deserved a healthy relationship, but I wasn't so sure Walter felt the same way. I'd observed him during rehearsals sneaking peeks at Lola when Dale occupied her attention. Too bad we couldn't get Jocelyn out here to divert his attention—

"Hey, Dodie."

"Hi, Pauli," I said. "No camera tonight?"

"Like, it's too crazy to get good shots during tech." Pauli was also getting down with theater lingo. "They don't have costumes tonight."

In the makeshift pit where the band was warming up, Janice and Alex apparently conferred about one of her numbers.

Pauli watched the young woman. "So any word on the Janice front?" I asked carefully. I figured Pauli's teenage ego was rather fragile.

"Nah," he said and jammed his fists into his jeans pockets. "She doesn't know I exist."

"You know, you could make a point of taking photos of her tomorrow night. Say they're for the *Etonville Standard*. Some solo pictures? She'd have to notice you then."

"Like, that's a good idea." Pauli perked up, but only for a moment. The athlete actor from Creston bounded off the stage and sidled up to Janice, draping a friendly arm around her shoulders. Oops…

Pauli slouched into a folding chair, arms dangling by his sides, until his spine was nearly parallel to the ground, his mop of brown hair flopping over his forehead. "Major fail."

Time to change the subject. I found the Windjammer website on my cell phone. "Henry would like some website updates: a photo of Wilson and a blurb about him, announcement of the food contest winners, possibly some shots of our summer menu." Pauli had been efficient about keeping the restaurant's Internet presence up-to-date. He'd done a nice job with interior shots of the dining room that featured the nautical-themed décor, based on a nineteenth-century whaling vessel complete with central beams, floor planking, and figurehead of a woman's bust above the entrance.

Pauli mumbled something. I think it was "ok." It was going to be tough getting him to snap out of it.

I settled into a folding chair too. As Penny called the first cues, the lights dimmed and actors moved into place. Penny called "Hold" every couple of minutes as Walter, JC, and the lighting designer conferred, made changes, and then soldiered on. Alex played musical cues over and over. I guessed the process would have been easier with Ruby's cue sheet on hand, but I had to say Alex was very efficient. He knew the show well. I sat through ELT tech rehearsals before. It was a slog, a herky-jerky stop-

and-go, as the technical staff adjusted light levels and coverage. At least this time, the crew did not have to contend with a stubborn turntable—but that was another story...

I swatted away a pesky mosquito, berating myself for having left the bug spray at home. Though the Etonville Public Works Department had sprayed the stage and seating areas, the nighttime critters were persistent. I hoped the audience would come prepared. Maybe we should sell some at the concession stand? JC, thoughtfully, hung a bug zapper near the stage to keep the mosquitoes out of the mouths of the singing actors. As I mulled over stocking refreshments, my mind hopscotched from one idea to another: Ruby was murdered; the *Bye, Bye, Birdie* cast and crew might be persons of interest; she had her car serviced at a station in Creston; her apartment was a puzzle. I wanted to look at her scrapbook before I handed it over to Bill.

Penny yelled "Hold." The actors were getting antsy—talking, checking cell phones, dancing around. The crew relaxed on the stage floor. I scanned the group of actors. I recognized the ELT bunch: Lola, Abby, Romeo, the Banger sisters, Vernon, Mildred, Edna, Imogen, Bill of course, who might not appear until the end of Act Two, if he came at all, and a few others in the chorus. I was getting to know the Creston folks as well: Dale, Janice, the athlete actor, some of the kids from Creston High. What about the crew? Walter? JC? Alex? Who among them would have a reason for killing off the musical's piano accompanist? Opportunity was one thing, but motive? I was enough of a mystery novel aficionado to understand that the perp didn't commit a crime out of thin air. There had to be cause. This particular murder wasn't a crime of passion, executed spur of the moment: This one required planning. Forethought. True to my promise to Bill, I would keep my eyes open, ear to the ground, for any scuttlebutt about Ruby's life, conflicts with Creston Players—

"Penny!" Walter shouted. "I need the ensemble for 'We Love You Conrad.' Where are they?"

Everything stopped on the stage as Walter ran from Alex to JC and back to Alex, waving his arms in a frenzy.

"I'm on it!" Penny roared, "Ensemble on stage for 'We Love You Conrad'."

"*I* can do that, Penny!" Walter bellowed. "I need you to round them up. Some of those kids were hanging around the trees." He pointed offstage—right to a stand of red oak trees where the teenage cast of *Bye, Bye, Birdie* had gathered between scenes.

Penny hauled herself out of the makeshift lighting booth and trucked backstage, clipboard in hand, her whistle preceding her. Soon, a trickle of kids emerged from the wings, laughing, mugging, and improvising dance steps. I noticed Janice and her partner arm-in-arm. Pauli must have noticed too. He pulled himself erect, grabbed his backpack, and marched off without a word.

Romeo strutted up the stairs to the stage, decked out in his gold lamé pants. Was he never going to take them off?

"Alex, JC, let's take it from the top," Walter said, outwardly calm. Inside, he was probably a hot mess.

"Hold!" Penny shouted as she scrambled to her stage manager's desk. "Take it from the top of the scene."

"Lola, dear, could I speak with you?"

Walter and I had our differences over the last months, mostly because I found myself entangled with more than one ELT murder mystery, which didn't always put him in the best light. While I had to acknowledge his talent, his ego needed trimming from time to time. He put a possessive hand on Lola's arm to ask her opinion on some matter or other. I could tell she had her "Oh brother" expression ready.

* * * *

The cast and crew persisted for another hour, stopping, starting, goofing around, Walter reprimanding them, Penny yelling directions, Lola frazzled, Dale solicitous. Through it all, Alex and JC were patient, even-tempered, and focused. I intended to stay until the end of Act One; by then, I'd be bored to tears. I had the information I needed on the refreshment stand, and my butt was weary. I contemplated a glass of chardonnay and Ruby's scrapbook. Never mind that Bill might or might not show up for the end of Act Two…his mind would be elsewhere—definitely not on me tonight. The tech rehearsal had been in process for two hours and they were only two thirds of the way through Act One. I eased my way to the front of the folding chairs where Lola sat with Dale.

I knelt by her side. "Lola," I murmured. She was biting a lip and picking nervously at a fingernail. Every ELT production that I'd witnessed had been a source of angst for Lola; why should the musical be any different? Even if it was a co-pro?

"Hi Dodie. We're moving along…slowly." She grimaced.

"Not too bad," I said. They had hours to go. I motioned that I was cutting out, gave her a good luck sign, and stole away.

* * * *

As I drove away from the Etonville Park, past the municipal building where lights burned and Bill worked, I wondered about Ruby's route from the theater to the road where they found her car. She'd parked it on the eastbound access road, facing the opposite direction from Creston. Why was she heading east instead of west? Of course, her killer might have moved the car. Was it possible the murder occurred elsewhere, and then the killer drove her car to the location? I wound down the window to get a full blast of the evening air. It was ten thirty when I pulled into my driveway. I hated to think how much longer the cast and crew of *Bye, Bye, Birdie* would be held captive at the technical rehearsal. As Penny has said often enough…that's show biz.

At home, I exchanged jeans for sweats, fortified myself with a glass of wine and some leftover couscous I liberated from the Windjammer freezer, and hunkered down on the sofa with Ruby's scrapbook. I lifted the book and inhaled the musty scent of old paper. On the flyleaf, besides Ruby's name centered prominently, was an address in the lower right-hand corner—written in tiny, cramped letters and numbers. Greenburg, Indiana—that explained the outdated phone book in her apartment. I flipped open to the first page, and immediately realized this was no typical scrapbook. There were clippings, but it was a photo album as well. The first pages were full of black and white snapshots of a young couple, probably from the nineteen forties, holding hands on a porch swing, sitting on the steps of a modest brick house, playing croquet in a backyard. There was a wedding photo dated 1941. The young man in the photo was wearing a uniform: World War II. I judged Ruby to be mid-seventies, so a picture of the twosome with an infant that had 1942 written beneath it made sense.

I turned pages until I reached the first clippings. HOME FROM THE WAR was the headline of a yellowed newspaper article. A group of uniformed men stood casually in front of a military vehicle, smoking, and shading their eyes as if squinting into the sun. Under the picture, the article listed one of the men as Edward Passonata—*Ruby's father.* Next to that clipping was another featuring the contestants of the 1948 Marion County fair bake-off. One contestant was April Passonata—*Ruby's mother.* I skimmed a handful of other clippings that focused on town news and then I saw what I was looking for—information on Ruby's life. The last clipping on the page showed Ruby Passonata, aged six, seated at a piano. The headline was CHILD PRODIGY PLAYS WINNING CONCERTO.

Little Ruby had won a contest at a music school in Indianapolis. She *was* a musical genius.

A ping from my cell phone interrupted my reverie. It was Bill: *Are you home?* I texted back that I was and, seconds later, my phone rang.

"Hi," I said. "Working late?"

"Trying to get caught up with paperwork. And coordinating with the Creston PD."

Of course they would be involved in Ruby's murder investigation; she was a citizen of their city.

"Any news?" I asked casually.

"Not yet. How did the rehearsal go this evening?"

"Still in progress when I left," I said.

"I hate to throw a curve ball into the production, but we're going to need to question the cast and crew. They were probably the last ones to see her alive."

"Except for the killer," I said.

"True. I'll contact Walter and have Penny organize it," Bill said.

Penny helped coordinate previous interviews for murder investigations. She fancied herself the ELT production maven and loved strutting around acting important. "I suppose that will include me."

"You? Why?" He asked.

"I spoke with Ruby during rehearsal the night she died."

"You didn't tell me that," Bill said, his voice suddenly abrupt.

"Well, it wasn't important until you discovered she was murdered," I said, possibly a trifle defensive.

"Sorry. I'd like to know what you talked about," Bill said softly.

"Like now? Or later tonight—"

"Tomorrow morning will be fine."

Oh. "You obviously didn't make it to the tech rehearsal." More a statement than a question.

Bill sighed. "Dodie, I have more important things—"

"I got it," I said in a rush. Then paused. "Ruby's death was bad enough for the *Bye, Bye, Birdie* company. When word gets out that it was murder…"

"The *Etonville Standard* has been sniffing around ever since her corpse was loaded into the ambulance."

"You know you can't keep secrets in this town," I said.

"I know, but I've been thinking. Having the details of her death announced publicly might be a bonus."

"Really? I thought it drove you crazy when the *Standard* jumped the gun and published leaks," I said.

"It does, normally. Having the facts out in the open might jog someone's memory—something someone saw or heard. At a time like this, it's good to have a town full of nosey people. In fact, we're going to plaster both Etonville and Creston with flyers about Ruby's death. We're asking anyone who has information to come forward," Bill said.

"I hope you get a response."

"Me too. I'm wiped out. Let's talk in the morning?" he asked.

"Sure. I'll stop by the department before work. Oh, just remembered something. Penny said Ruby had her car serviced in Creston."

"Penny said that? How did she know?" Bill asked.

"She said they talked. They had things in common."

"Thanks. I'll check it out." Bill told me to have a good night and clicked off.

I debated. I needed to get to sleep, but curiosity was gnawing at me. I decided to page through the rest of Ruby's clippings. I picked up where I'd left off, and skimmed articles that summarized her grade school and high school years: contests, competitions, festivals…all won by Ruby. Prizes and awards had accumulated prodigiously by the time she was seventeen. The clippings hailed Ruby as a wunderkind, phenom, and a sensation!

There were blank pages in the scrapbook, and then the clipping that blew me away. Ruby received a full scholarship to the Maynard Institute in Manhattan. The article described the prestigious institute and the stingy acceptance rate, the town of Greenburg's pride in her accomplishment, and the various pieces she'd played during her audition. Finally, there was a quote from the young Ruby. "I am so excited to be studying at the Maynard Institute. It's a dream come true."

The Maynard Institute. Even I—who had little knowledge of the music world—knew about Maynard in New York City. If Ruby were a product of that school, she would have had a career waiting for her. Concerts, tours, and big paydays. I shifted my attention back to the scrapbook and, sure enough, there were clippings, articles, and programs from 1963 to 1969. Ruby had toured the world, giving performances in every major capital. There were photos of her with prime ministers, royalty, and celebrities. She was toasted internationally. I studied the pictures in the newspapers. Ruby, in her twenties, was a beautiful young woman, glowing with success, with the rewards of her efforts, and the adulation of important fans. The scrapbook was probably the product of proud parents living in Indiana— while their daughter Ruby crisscrossed continents.

I sat back against the sofa pillows and sipped my wine, perplexed. The image conjured up by the clippings didn't fit the picture of the woman I'd met during the rehearsal process. The two women didn't appear to be cut from the same cloth. Except for the musical talent. What had happened to that young artist from Indiana who'd blown every competitor out of the water and then created a short-lived career that would be the envy of any musician? Because the career *was* short-lived. In 1969, the clippings ended. Ruby was about twenty-eight when she stopped playing the piano publicly and dropped out of sight. I found no further mention of touring, concerts, or international recognition of her amazing talent. There was one last clipping. A story dated 1986 about a man, also from Greenburg, Indiana, who had died by his own hand. It didn't seem to have any connection to Ruby's stellar career.

I closed the scrapbook. Something was off. The nape of my neck tingled.

6

A loud ringing yanked me out of a weird dream. I'd been wearing a tiara and holding a dozen roses, parading up and down a runway. Was I Miss America? I sat down at a piano to play the talent portion of a competition... it had to be Ruby's scrapbook invading my unconscious. I grabbed for my alarm, slamming my hand on the snooze button—but the insistent clanging didn't stop. It was seven thirty. Who needed to speak with me at this hour? I threw back the sheet and crossed to my bureau where I'd plugged my cell into the charger.

"Hello?" I barked, my voice coming to life.

"Dodie? You sound funny. Have you seen the *Standard*?" Lola cried.

"I'm not awake yet, and no I haven't." I already knew what was in it.

"How did this happen?" she wailed. "Are we ever going to get a production up without there being a murder involved? I am *so* over all of these deaths."

Me too.

"I got off the phone with Walter a second ago. You know how he gets this close to an opening. The pressure is greater with the Creston Players involved. I hope he manages to hold it together."

"Walter needs one of his chill pills," I said.

"That's what I told him. Take a Xanax."

"Let's have coffee. I need to stop by the police department to give them a statement, but we could meet at Coffee Heaven first," I said.

"By the way, Chief Thompson left me a voicemail. He needs Penny to set up interviews with the cast and crew," Lola said.

"Right. Someone might have spoken with Ruby or heard or seen something. Bill wants to cover all bases," I said.

"And everything was going so smoothly," Lola lamented.

"Lola, there's no need to panic. Bill will speak to everyone over the next few days but *Bye, Bye, Birdie* will go on as scheduled," I said soothingly, mental fingers crossed.

Lola said good-bye and agreed to meet in an hour at Coffee Heaven.

* * * *

Forty-five minutes later, I sat in a booth at the rear of the diner, hiding behind a copy of the *Etonville Standard*. The town was, understandably, abuzz. Customers stared at me as if I had something to do with Ruby's death, either that or they were simply gauging my reaction to her murder, and assuming I would be a part of the investigation. I had to admit I was garnering a local reputation as an amateur sleuth and—

"Dodie, why're you buried in the paper?" Jocelyn asked, extending her coffee pot. She refilled my cup.

"I'm reading about Ruby," I said.

"Such a shame." She squinted at me. "Carbon monoxide. It's good for plants though."

"Uh…no…that's carbon *di*oxide," I corrected her.

"Are you sure? Because my mother used to keep a pot of English ivy in the front seat of her car. In the event…"

Huh? Lola slipped into the booth across from me. "I'll have coffee, too. Thanks."

Jocelyn filled an empty cup at Lola's place setting. "I guess the show will go on?"

"Of course, it's what Ruby would have wanted," Lola said serenely, her inner diva surfacing.

"Tell Walter I'm gunning for him!" Jocelyn moved off.

Geez.

Lola moaned. "I don't know who I feel worse for: Ruby…but since she's passed and we don't have any family to console that feels a little empty; then there's the Creston Players, losing one of their company. Alex has to do double duty, but he's competent and seems to have it all under control; and then there's our theater and you know how sidetracked they can get. Walter is always on edge lately, or at least ever since *Eton Town*. Thankfully, Dale is there to support me but—"

"Lola, pump the brakes! Ease up on yourself. It's really sad about Ruby. Bill's probably up to his eyeballs trying to sort out potential suspects and motives. There's nothing you can do except give Etonville and Creston the show to beat all shows."

I fervently hoped that was true.

Lola smiled slowly. "Thanks, Dodie. I needed some TLC today." She took a swallow of her coffee. "Did you see what the medical examiner said?"

"You mean about Ruby's alcohol level? Yeah. She liked her flask, all right, but it wasn't over the legal limit. I don't think she would have passed out from drinking."

"Death by asphyxiation." Lola shivered. "Do you suppose she realized what was happening?"

"I doubt it. She might have simply fallen asleep."

"Who would want to harm an elderly woman who pretty much kept to herself? At least according to Dale," Lola said.

"Get this." I relayed the information from Ruby's scrapbook and Lola's reaction mirrored mine.

"Our Ruby? A world-famous concert pianist?" she asked doubtfully.

"Yep. Same one."

"Hard to visualize her playing for royalty. With that mouth!" Lola said.

"Ditto," I said.

Tucking my jacket around my midsection, I urged Lola to hang in there, finished my coffee, and headed next door to the municipal building. June weather in Jersey—humid and hot one day, cool the next. I stopped in the foyer and checked out the latest additions to Etonville's ego wall of mementoes and trophies. There was a new photo of the mayor receiving a certificate from the Chamber of Commerce for who knows what.

Edna trundled down the hall towards me. "Have you heard? Oh my. I can't imagine…"

"Hi, Edna. Yes. Very sad. I'm glad Lola is putting something in the program to acknowledge Ruby's contribution to the show, and her passing."

Edna's face crumpled. "I figured someone was out to get her."

That's what murder meant. "But why? Who?"

"Well, this is a 10-36…" Edna whispered.

"A 10—?"

"Confidential information." She hesitated. "I was on my headset and I overheard the medical examiner say '10-50.'"

"Edna, you're going to have to be more specific with your codes."

"Influence of drugs." She walked past me. "Gotta make a coffee run. What's Henry's special today?"

"Gazpacho!"

"10-4."

Drugs? There were drugs in Ruby's system? Someone was definitely out to get her.

I'd been so pre-occupied when I entered the building, I hadn't noticed Bill's missing police cruiser. Officer Shung greeted me in the outer office, indicating she'd take my statement. Suki was unique—a Buddhist cop— serene, solemn, and usually silent. We'd bonded while pursuing bad guys during the ELT production of *Arsenic and Old Lace*.

"The chief said you spoke to the victim the night she died?" Suki tilted her head. Her straight, black hair swished to one side.

"That's right. Ruby and I talked a bit before the run-through."

"What about?" Suki's pen was poised above a notepad.

"Let's see…how Walter was a 'horse's patoot' and how she thought the co-production was a recipe for disaster, and how she hated the food at the Windjammer. Said it made her sick."

Suki coughed and tried to hide a smile. "Anything else? Did she mention anyone connected to the theater?"

"No." I paused. "But she did give me relationship advice. About how you can't trust anyone because you don't really know them." I left out her vehement recommendation that I stay single. Suki scrutinized my face. Was *she* thinking *I* was thinking about Bill? "Ruby said they'd only get you in the end."

"Who would get you?" Suki asked.

"I have no idea, but she emphasized she spoke from experience."

"Then what happened?"

"She went over to her piano and rehearsal began," I said.

"Was that the last time you spoke with her?"

"Yes, but I did see her leave the stage at intermission," I added.

"Oh?"

"I assumed she was heading to the loading dock. She tended to take smoke breaks back there. She also took drink breaks with the flask she carried," I said.

"Yes, the flask." Suki made notes on her pad, and I waited. "Anything else you can remember?"

"She said an odd thing as she walked away. 'It's not what you know about them. It's what you don't know.' What do you think that means?"

Suki closed her pad. "It's hard to tell. Some painful event in her past?"

"That's what I thought," I said.

Suki's mouth twitched as if she was holding something back, but all she said was, "Great minds…"

We locked eyes and laughed.

"Thanks for coming in, Dodie. I'll pass this on to the chief. If you remember anything else…"

"Right." I reached for my bag. "Oh! I nearly forgot!"

"What?" Her cop face all business.

"I saw her for about ten seconds at the end of intermission too. I was in the lobby getting ready to leave and she popped in looking for her bag. It wasn't in the lobby, so she went back into the theater." I stopped.

Suki studied me. "What? Something else?"

"Well...I remember thinking: How could she have lost her purse that fast?"

* * * *

Georgette from Georgette's Bakery—supplier of the Windjammer's desserts—was hosting her cousin Rebecca from England last month when the food contest got underway. Georgette insisted on entering Rebecca's favorite recipe, and I insisted that we needed to be good citizens by supporting her entry. Henry reluctantly agreed. The result: steak and ale pie was on the menu tonight. I'd never had it, and neither had Henry, but the Windjammer could always do with a dose of international cuisine.

"Hey, Benny," I said as I hung my jacket on a coat hook by the restaurant's entrance. I placed my bag on a barstool.

"The excitement never ends," he said, and pointed to a copy of the *Etonville Standard*.

"I know."

"Sounds pretty mysterious. Older woman dying in her car by the side of the road—no clues or witnesses. The chief has his work cut out for him."

"The Creston police are also involved," I said.

"Oh yeah. I keep forgetting you have the inside track when it comes to the Etonville PD," Benny said.

I swatted him playfully with the newspaper. "Wise guy." I could feel heat creeping up my cheeks.

"Cheney Brothers called to say they're delivering the snack boxes in the morning. Should be a wine delivery then also."

"I ordered extra cases of white and red, and I'm taking Wilson to the park tonight so he can get the lay of the land and check out the concession stand." I glanced at the kitchen doors. "Kind of quiet in there."

"When I got here, Henry and Wilson were already wrestling with the steak and ale pie. It was the pastry part they were...discussing," Benny said. I could hear the air quotes.

"Morning guys," I said as I entered the kitchen. "What's cooking?" Wilson and Henry, bent over a scrap of paper, looked up. Wilson broke out in a grin and Henry, per usual, glared. What now? "Smelling good in here."

"*Do-dee*, we are having our heads together over *ze* steak pie." He looked at Henry.

"And ale. Don't forget the ale," I said cheerfully.

Henry regarded the case of Guinness on the center island as if there weren't enough bottles in the universe to compensate for his having to create the winning dish with Wilson as sous chef. "Maybe you should work on the gazpacho," he said to Wilson who immediately waltzed to the side counter where he blended chopped parsley and basil to add to the pot of tomatoes, cucumbers, bell peppers, and onions.

Wilson hummed as he worked.

"I don't get it," Henry mumbled. "What's with that guy?"

"It's called a good mood, Henry. You should try it some time," I said sweetly and headed to the freezer to do a seafood inventory for the weekend. We would serve our last winning entrée Saturday night.

I felt arms around my waist and a familiar tug as Wilson lifted me up, catching me off guard. "*Do-dee*, I am so happy to go to *ze* park for *ze* show tonight!"

He swung me in a semi-circle, my flexed feet clipping the shelf that held the herbs and spices. Jars and containers tumbled to the floor followed by a piece of the wooden shelving. The crash no doubt sounded catastrophic. Henry and Benny were at the door of the pantry.

"Wilson, down!" I landed on the floor, kneeling, while Wilson ended up in the midst of the condiments.

"What the—" Henry's eyes popped.

"All good, here. Not to worry!" I said.

Benny stifled a grin. I'd speak to him later.

Wilson apologized, and I assured him there was no real harm done. I suggested that he return to the gazpacho while I cleaned up the messy pantry. There had to be a way to channel Wilson's passion for life.

* * * *

The gazpacho was a hit even though I had to explain to the Banger sisters that cold soup was a staple of a Mediterranean diet. "It's a Spanish dish—"

"Andalusian, to be specific," said Vernon, as he and Mildred sat down at a table next to the sisters.

"Why, Vernon, I didn't know you were so cosmopolitan," Mildred said with a giggle.

The Bangers stared at him blankly. "Cold or hot. It doesn't matter. We like our soup room temperature," one sister said.

"Give it a minute and it will warm up. Meanwhile what about a sandwich? Or salad?"

"Oh no. Watching our waistlines, don't you know," the other sister said. "We're getting our head shots taken tonight."

Poor Pauli.

I circled the dining room, accepting comments on the soup and recommending Henry's grilled chicken wrap. While customers were polite as I strolled around, they were more interested in chewing over the facts of Ruby's death than any of Henry's dishes.

"Who do the police think killed Ruby?" asked Mildred knowingly. She winked at me.

"I have no idea," I said politely. Everyone assumed I had more information than the *Standard* reporter had gleaned from the Etonville police department. It didn't matter anyway. What the town didn't know factually, it would create fictionally.

"Well, you could ask...Bill," one of the Bangers tittered.

That was enough. "Let me send Gillian over with the coffee pot." I gritted my teeth and hurried away.

That might have been the end of the murder speculation, had Bill not walked into the Windjammer two minutes later. Interested customers followed our progress to my back booth.

"Lots of rumors today," I said and set a menu in front of him.

"Whatever's special," Bill said dismissively and waved the menu away.

"Soup and a chicken wrap." I placed his order in the kitchen and drew a soda.

"Suki said you stopped by." Bill took a drink of his Coke. "That was a cryptic conversation you had with Ruby."

"Nothing that provided any hint of a looming crisis in her life. Have you interviewed the cast?"

"Suki's working on it. So far, nobody has much of anything to say. The Creston people never socialized with her. I guess she kept to herself. The Etonville contingent had less to say. Ruby had a smart mouth on her, but most folks ignored it or laughed it off." He scowled and tugged on his blond spikes. "Not a lot to go on. Her car is clean. No prints inside or out—except Ruby's."

I reached in my bag. "You might want to see this." I handed him Ruby's scrapbook.

"What's this?" he asked.

"The scrapbook I mentioned?" I said lightly.

"You never mentioned a scrapbook." A light scowl creased his forehead.

"I didn't? I picked it up the day Lola and I visited her apartment," I said.

"You removed evidence from a murder victim's home?" Bill's face reddened. "You're not going off on your own and—"

"Calm down. She wasn't a murder victim when I borrowed the scrapbook. I intended to return it, but then you discovered her death was a homicide. So there it is."

Bill regarded me warily. "What's in it? Because I know you've gone over everything."

"I paged through it. Some family photos and a ton of clippings. Did you know Ruby was a world class concert pianist?"

Bill said, "No, I didn't."

"She played for royalty and at the White House and won every award in the book," I said.

Bill studied the scrapbook in his hands. "Doesn't sound like the woman everyone is describing to me."

"I know, right? What do you think happened to her career?" I asked.

"I have no idea and, more importantly, neither do you, so let's keep it that way," he warned gently.

Gillian brought his gazpacho and chicken wrap. Bill dug into his lunch.

"Any other news?" I asked innocently. Had Edna overheard the ME conversation accurately?

Bill hesitated, and then lowered his voice. "Ruby had an overdose of Ambien in her system. Enough to knock her out in no time. There was a half-empty bottle in her purse."

Edna was right on. "She was drugged as well as asphyxiated?"

"Possibly. Unless she was so inebriated she took them by mistake. There were half a dozen vitamin bottles in there too—like a pharmacy. Keep all of this under your hat for now."

Penny said Ruby was an insomniac. *Someone made certain she would fall asleep before she began to notice the effects of the carbon monoxide.*

"What?" Bill said.

"If someone wanted to make sure Ruby swallowed the Ambien, they might have put it in her flask."

Bill's soup spoon halted halfway to his mouth.

7

I sifted through my conversation with Bill over lunch. Drugging Ruby felt, somehow, more premeditated than asphyxiation. I gave him a nudge about the final dress rehearsal tonight. He half-heartedly agreed to show up.

I took my three o'clock break in the back booth and fanned a stack of mail I'd stuffed in my bag yesterday and had yet to open—utility bill, cable bill, cell phone bill. Ugh. There were offers for hearing aids, window washing, various medical services, and an appeal from my alma mater's alumni association. It had been a while since I'd sent even a minimal amount. I promised myself once I got ahead of my bills and stashed a bit in my savings account I'd be more generous with requests like these. Alumni... Something was gnawing at the back of my brain.

* * * *

By five thirty, the early birds were arriving to sample tonight's food contest winner. Word was out that it was an English specialty. *All* of Etonville would feel more continental.

"I like beer with my meal, so steak and ale is right up my alley," said Jim, Abby's husband and a big teddy bear of a man.

"Not sure you'll actually taste the beer," I said.

"It's a pie, Jim, in a pastry," said Abby as she dug into Henry's flaky crust. "Not bad. Kind of a beef stew pot pie with mushrooms and carrots."

I was happy with the verdict. Bless Georgette's cousin Rebecca. That was three out of three for the food contest. *One more to go.* "Enjoy your dinner."

"Need to get my energy up for this dress rehearsal," said Abby. Then she continued, darkly. "All these murders. Someone's jinxed the ELT."

"You think so?" I asked, noncommittally.

Abby considered me. "Mostly since you arrived in town."

Jim scooped up the end of his steak pie. "Now that's what I call a dinner." I hurried away.

I'd arranged for Benny to take over at seven so that Wilson and I could skip out. Henry was fine with giving Wilson—and himself—a break. Beginning with tomorrow night's opening, Wilson would be responsible for organizing the snack boxes and drinks. I'd hang around to supervise in case of any mishaps. Gillian would pitch in at some performances as well. Former sous chef Enrico and his wife Carmen, a part-time server, worked weekends so Henry was happy to see Friday come.

I parked my Metro on a side street near the park and Wilson and I got out. I inhaled the scent of new mown grass and lilacs. The Etonville public works crew had cut the lawn, trimmed the bushes, spruced up the flower beds, and generally beautified the natural elements surrounding the newly created theater. "I love that smell."

Wilson inhaled too. "*Ze* smell of nature."

"Takes me back to my summers down the shore. I spent most of my time on the beach. My aunt Maureen had a lovely yard and lots of trees and flowers. Crab apple trees and blueberry bushes. Her flower beds were the talk of the neighborhood: lavender, hydrangeas, wildflowers...I hung out with her a lot."

Wilson hugged me. "You love your aunt!"

"I did love her. She's passed away." I missed my favorite great aunt. Her legacy to me was a philosophy of life, a terry cloth robe, a ceramic lamp, and tons of fun memories. She made me laugh harder than anyone else in my life, and she taught me how to play poker.

"I am sorry for you," Wilson said forlornly.

I gestured for him to join me, and we cut through the seating area on the sloping lawn to the portable concession stand. "Here's where we'll sell the snack boxes and drinks."

Wilson nodded somberly. He was taking his job seriously. "*Do-dee*, I am ready to take charge!"

"Good. We'll bring the coolers and drinks here tomorrow afternoon so you can open the concessions at six. That will give the audience plenty of time to nibble before the curtain."

Wilson's attention had shifted to the stage where the small band was tuning up and Lola and Dale—already in costume—were getting set to rehearse a number. Alex played the introduction to their duet "Rosie." Dale was singing about how his girl was sweeter than any other flower around, and Lola, twirling in and out of his arms, was singing about how her life would be rosy and happy and how they'd set off to find a preacher. The number captivated Wilson. His head bobbed, and his foot tapped in time to the music. It was sweet to see him so engrossed—

Suddenly he grabbed my arm and spun me into his chest, then flipped me out again. "Whoa! Wilson! Back to work—" I released his hand, intending to rotate away and end our dance number, but I didn't see Walter walking up the path behind me. I rotated right into him.

"Oof," he said, flinching.

I rebounded off his chest. Walter was the last person I would want to get up close and personal with—accidentally or on purpose. I rotated back into Wilson.

"I love to dance, *Do-dee!*"

"I can see that," I said, catching my breath.

Walter regained his dignity, adjusted his sunglasses. "We don't have time for fooling around."

He glared at the stage as the number ended. Dale laid a big smooch on Lola and she responded accordingly. Talk about method acting. Was that in the script? Were the two of them rehearsing the kissing scene offstage as well?

"Penny?" Walter roared, drowning out the applause of Wilson, Edna, and the Banger sisters, who were watching the duo perform. "Get the cast onstage for warm-ups!"

"I'm on it." She signaled that it was time for another of Walter's bizarre pre-show workouts. I didn't get it. Most of his exercises left the cast in stitches, less, not more, focused. Walter was oblivious.

The actors proudly displayed their 1950s costumes while Chrystal, fiddling with accessories, and Carol, waving a can of hair spray, ran hither and yon. The teenagers were the last—and loudest—actors to make it onstage. At least they wouldn't have to create the circle—

"—of light," Walter said.

Not that again. Walter used it to create trust in the cast. I'd participated once and the thing I learned was *not* to trust the cast. The Creston Players looked confused while the ELT members reluctantly formed a circle, and allowed themselves to collapse into each other's outspread arms, assuming the company would catch them. It took three minutes for the discipline to break down and the cast to dissolve into giggles. Penny tooted three or four times but to no avail.

Lola confronted Walter, who submitted to the hilarity, changed tactics, and motioned to Alex to continue the warm-up. Now that made sense. After a few runs up and down the scales, he had them work through various numbers. I leaned against the counter of the refreshment booth as the actors settled down and their voices wafted into the night air. It was going to be a beautiful production, marred only by Ruby's death. I wondered how many of the cast had been down to the municipal building.

"*Do-dee*," Wilson whispered, "I am going there." He pointed ahead to the seating area.

"Sure," I said. Henry wasn't expecting him back tonight. His sous chef was really into the musical and I was planning to stay for the entire run. I'd seen Act One several times this week, but had yet to see Act Two. The overture began.

Pauli fell into a seat next to me, his digital camera slung around his neck. "Hey."

"Hey yourself. Saw you taking photos of actors," I said slyly.

He ducked his head. "Like yeah. Some people need headshots."

Like the Banger sisters. "Janice?"

Pauli adjusted the camera lens. "Yeah. It was awesome."

"And did you talk to her like I suggested?"

"Sort of. We might hang out after the rehearsal."

"All right." I raised my hand to high five him.

Pauli giggled like a little kid and smacked my palm. It was cute to see him in high spirits. He stopped giggling and leaned closer. "Like, I, uh, heard about the piano player."

"Ruby. Yeah. Really unfortunate."

"Murder, right?" he asked.

"Uh-huh."

"If, like, you need help with digital forensics or whatever..."

Most of the time Pauli was a typical teenager—a nice kid with raging hormones—who was preoccupied with his cell phone. When it came to the digital world, Pauli was a skillful practitioner of Internet investigation. He could find anything on the web.

"I'll let you know," I murmured.

"Cause I'm only working part-time at the Shop N Go until September," he added.

Pauli was graduating from Etonville High in two weeks and attending college in the fall. He wanted to continue with his online digital forensics courses, but Carol and her husband insisted on a liberal arts education. They compromised on a local community college for the next two years.

Besides the Shop N Go, Pauli was staying busy with his website company, keeping area businesses online. Including the Windjammer. "You'll be an Etonville High alum in a couple of weeks."

"Totally," he said, straining to see if Janice and the athlete from Creston High were onstage yet.

What was it about alumni that caused a twitch on my neck? First my college, then the idea of Pauli graduating, then…Ruby! Ruby was a graduate of the Maynard Institute. The alumni office probably had information on her. People often kept in touch with their colleges even while ignoring the people they went to school with. I knew that from personal experience. I told Bill I had no interest in Ruby's murder investigation, but something about the elderly woman struck me. Was it because she was about the same age my aunt was when she passed away? Was it because I wanted to know why someone of her talent walked away from a brilliant career? My aunt walked away from a successful banking career when she was fifty. She moved down the shore and took a position at a local newspaper as an advice columnist. I hadn't thought about it much over the years—until now. Why did she leave her job as a financial officer—only to dish out guidance to the lovelorn?

On the other hand, maybe it was Ruby's warning that jabbed at me: *You can't trust anyone…they only get you in the end.*

The *Bye, Bye, Birdie* overture ended, the lights rose on the stage, and Lola entered, looking smashing in a form-fitting, black and white checked 1950s suit and updo. Carol's specialty. She glided across the stage to Dale, teasing and insisting that he leave the music business and return to teaching English. Albert, handsome in a beige suit, listens to Rosie hatch the publicity stunt to have Conrad Birdie sing "One Last Kiss" with a teenager from an Ohio fan club. That teenager would be Janice. Pauli's love interest.

The band hit the first notes of Lola's song. I watched Alex take them through their musical paces, while keeping up on the keyboard and directing Lola and Dale via head nods. Whew, Alex was one busy guy, but he seemed up to the task. Had Ruby shared her past with him?

The sun set over the Etonville Park, its last rays streaked the sky with blues, reds, and purples. The moon rose through a light cloud cover. Night sounds emerged from the dark whenever the stage went still for a moment: crickets, an owl hooting, and the *zzzt* of the bug zapper.

Cavorting teenagers danced with period phones for "The Telephone Hour," while Edna, having a ball playing the Mayor's overwhelmed wife, fainted again and again at the sight of Conrad Birdie's hip-thrusting pelvis. I laughed out loud, and Wilson joined in. He was having a ball too.

A shadow flitted off to my right and a figure materialized out of the dark. "Hi," Bill said.

I shifted in my seat and murmured, "You made it!"

"Taking one for the municipal public relations team," he grumbled.

His costume looked surprisingly like his everyday uniform—except for the billy club attached to his belt. I'd never seen Bill with one of those. Guess he was right. He *could* have worn his own cop regalia.

"Any word on the whereabouts of Ruby's flask?" I asked.

"We've checked the theater, her car…no sign of it. It would have been the perfect means for delivering the drug," Bill said softly.

"Whoever killed her had to know about the flask in advance."

"Like someone in this crowd," Bill said grimly.

"I haven't noticed anything out of the ordinary lately. It's difficult for me to believe someone in the production is responsible for murdering that elderly woman," I whispered.

"I'm visiting her apartment in Creston tomorrow morning," Bill said.

"There's not much there. Lola and I went over everything."

"That's what I'm afraid of," he said ruefully.

"The only thing of importance seemed to be the scrapbook, and her laptop, which we didn't touch," I added hastily.

Act One was drawing to a close rapidly—with a cascade of hijinks: Conrad Birdie singing "One Last Kiss" on the Ed Sullivan show, getting ready to plant one on Kim; a jealous Hugo punching Birdie in the face; Rosie breaking up with Albert; and the panicked Albert leading a reprise of "A Normal, American Boy."

I had to admit it; Walter had done a nice job with the staging. The last notes flowed into the makeshift house, and the onstage lights dimmed. Wilson, Pauli, Bill, myself, and crew members applauded loudly.

The house lights rose and the usual disorder broke out. Crew ran onstage to set up Act Two. Actors, giddy with the success of the run-through, ran into the house to chat with each other—while a handful searched for Chrystal to complain about ripped hems, broken zippers, and missing accessories.

"Penny! Get the cast out of the house!" shouted Walter.

"I'm on it. Performance conditions!" she cried shrilly, blasting her whistle. But the actors were either too excited to pay attention, or so used to the whistle they ignored it.

Chrystal ran past us. "Get those pants off, Romeo! I need to sew the seam."

Lola waved from the stage, giving me a thumb's-up. I gave her one back. Bill gawked. "What the…?"

"Another night in ELT land," I said. "Organized chaos. Actually, it's pretty much theater in general from what I can tell."

"Uh-huh," Bill said, unconvinced.

"You'd better head backstage and check in with Penny. Don't want to make the stage manager crazy." Any crazier than she already was...

Bill heaved himself up, and stood awkwardly by my seat. "Do I look okay? This outfit is tight." He yanked on the collar of his shirt.

I was a sucker for a tight uniform—especially one that emphasized Bill's former football physique. "What do you mean okay?"

"You know, like a cop?" he asked.

"Sure. But you look like a cop all the time so..."

"Here goes nothing," he said.

"Go get 'em, Stanislavsky."

"Who?" Bill asked.

"A Russian actor Walter's always quoting."

"I'd like to see him in this cop suit," he grumbled.

"Too late. He's dead."

"Lucky guy." Bill marched off as if to his doom.

I stood and stretched, mentally ticking off tomorrow morning's to do list. Wilson approached. *"Do-dee, c'est fantastique! Formidable!"*

My French was minimal, but I got the gist. Wilson was more than impressed. "I agree. Can't wait for Act Two. I'll be right back."

Post-show notes required the entire company's attention, so any chance to speak with Alex one-on-one would have to happen now. He bent his head over the score. "Alex? Sorry to disturb you."

He looked up, took a moment to register my presence. "Hi Dodie. How's the show looking out there?"

"Great. Very nice."

He turned back to the score. "Can I do something for you?"

"I know your mind is on other things, but I wanted to ask you something about Ruby."

"What about Ruby?" He continued to examine the score.

"When Lola and I were searching for the cue sheet, I found a scrapbook. It had a lot of family photos of Ruby and her parents and a bunch of clippings. Did she ever mention her past to you?"

"Her past?" His face was a question mark.

"The fact that she was a concert pianist who'd won a ton of prizes and awards when she was young," I said. "She graduated from the Maynard Institute."

Alex grew quiet. "She did?"

"Yes, but it all ended in her late twenties. I wondered why. What happened that she suddenly stopped playing and touring?"

Penny tramped over. "Places in five," she said with as much authority as she could muster. "Hey O'Dell."

"The show's going well, Penny. Good luck with Act Two," I said.

"You know what they say: The show's over whenever the fat lady sings. No names." She cackled and moved on.

Geez.

"Sorry, I have to get back to work," Alex said apologetically.

"Right. I didn't mean to distract you."

"By the way, Ruby never talked about her career. I'm as surprised as you are," he said. "Of course, she kept to herself a lot. You seem very interested in her. Were you friends?"

"No. I'm just curious about her background. Studying at Maynard then giving it all up? I'd like to know more about her." I made my way back to my seat. Wilson was texting and beaming as I passed him. Yep, he was in a good mood, all right.

8

By ten thirty, I was slapping mosquitoes as quietly as I could. Lola and the ELT better put the word out to the public that bug spray was *de rigeur*, especially if it rained before or between performances. I intended to hang on. Bill's big scene was approaching rapidly. At the climactic moment, frantic parents, accompanied by Policeman Bill and a couple of ELT actors, rescued the wayward kids, arrested Conrad Birdie, and generally restored peace to Sweet Apple, Ohio. Lola and Dale sang the "Rosie" number they rehearsed last night, and the company took its final bow. We gave *Bye, Bye, Birdie* a standing ovation, which thrilled the cast who broke ranks and delivered a series of war whoops, much to Walter's chagrin.

"Decorum! Decorum!" he bellowed.

Penny picked up her whistle, and then threw it down. The stage manager had given up. I supposed the cast deserved to celebrate. It had been a grim week what with Ruby's death and police interviews. Lola and Dale attempted to reestablish order, while Chrystal flew here and there begging actors to hang their costumes on rolling racks before the notes session began.

Bill, still in his costume, ran off the stage. "What did you think?" He was sweating and panting.

"Bravo!"

He grinned. "Another day on the job."

"Told you it would be exactly like policing Etonville. Same bedlam."

"Yeah. Hey, those lights are bright. And hot," he said.

"You gotta suffer for your art," I said.

Bill inclined his head. "Coming over later?"

"I don't know, you being a big star and all," I teased.

"I have to get a note from Walter and get out of this thing." Bill pulled the sticky shirt away from his chest, loosened his tie, and darted backstage.

I smiled at the confusion. While I had no greasepaint in my blood, I was learning to appreciate what it took to create such pandemonium.

"*Do-dee!*" Wilson's cheeks were wet. "It is beautiful. I must cry."

"Come on. You'll have a lot of chances to cry again this weekend and next." I touched his arm and he followed me to my car.

I dropped Wilson off at the Windjammer so that he could retrieve his bike. Most days he pedaled from a room he rented in the south end of Etonville on Ellison Street. I offered to load his bike into my trunk and tie it down with bungee cords, but Wilson was firm. He preferred to ride it home. He cycled off.

I peeked in the front window of the Windjammer. Benny was wiping down the bar. Gillian and Carmen were cleaning tables. I left well enough alone and backed my Metro out of its parking space. I was feeling restless, and knew I had twenty minutes or so before Bill would be home. As if it had a mind of its own, the Metro turned right on Anderson, past Georgette's Bakery and Snippets salon, toward the highway instead of left down Bennington toward Bill's. I found myself crawling past Timothy's Timely Service on the access road to State Route 53. The spot where they'd found Ruby's car was just ahead. I slowed down.

Was someone else restless tonight? A car had pulled onto the shoulder, headlights and taillights visible. The driver's side door opened and a person, dressed in dark clothing with a baseball cap on, stepped out. I was too far away to determine gender, but I eased my Metro to the shoulder and switched off the engine. I slinked down in the seat, barely able to see above my dashboard. The figure walked around the exact place where Ruby had parked her Toyota, stopped, looked down, and moved again. Then, suddenly, the figure looked in my direction, jumped in the car, and took off.

What was there to see at the location? The person definitely appeared to be searching for something. I waited five minutes, then cranked my engine and rolled to the same spot. I flicked on my cell phone flashlight and swept it over the area. Nothing but gravel on the edge of the road that crunched as I walked back and forth. I retraced my steps several yards in each direction. Again, nothing that might pique someone's interest. Besides, I told myself, Bill or his CSI techs had no doubt combed through this area as soon as they realized Ruby had been murdered. If there were anything unusual, anything that might be evidence, they'd find it.

I froze. Or would they? I stooped down and flicked my flashlight off. A tiny piece of something was illuminated. I scraped away small pebbles and unearthed a speck of tape, a quarter inch by a half inch. Seemingly insignificant, except that it wasn't. I'd heard Penny harangue the crew time and again that they were wasting the expensive tape used to mark placement of props and furniture on the various sets of the Etonville Little Theatre: tape that would glow in the dark. She said they only needed to use a bit of it. When the lights were out, the actors would have no issues navigating the set. Someone had left a fragment of the glow tape in the gravel—probably attached to the bottom of a shoe. Possibly the murderer—or the individual who had driven away from the crime scene?

Suddenly, I was anxious. I jumped into my Metro and locked the doors. I examined the glow tape. If it came from the set of *Bye, Bye, Birdie*, it had to be someone connected to the theater. In the far reaches of my mind, I'd been holding out hope that Ruby's death was somehow unrelated to the Etonville Little Theatre and the Creston Players. The tiny object in my hand dashed that optimistic perspective. I had to hand it over to Bill.

I stomped on the gas, made a wide U-turn, and drove to the north end of town. I'd barely reached Bill's neighborhood when I had the spooky feeling that a car had been tracking me for several blocks. I turned onto Bennington, and it kept a safe distance. My hands clutched the steering wheel tightly as I caught a glimpse of it in my rearview mirror. When I hung a right onto his street, the car continued down the road. Bill would chalk up my uneasiness to my overactive imagination.

* * * *

"Glow tape?"

"Right. They use tiny pieces of it to mark the set so the actors don't kill themselves in the dark. Makes sense that this is so small." The bit of tape was now nestled inside a plastic baggie, on the coffee table in Bill's living room.

He uncorked an expensive cabernet and poured two glasses and set them beside a tray with white cheese and artisanal crackers. I'd been too busy to eat much today, what with the steak and ale pie, the news of Ruby's drugging, accompanying Wilson to the park, and the dress rehearsal of *Bye, Bye, Birdie*. I bit into the creamy stilton, which was pungent enough to tickle my taste buds. *Nothing like the contents of the snack boxes that the Windjammer would be delivering to the park tomorrow.* The audience would be eating cheddar, Ritz crackers, salted cashews, and assorted candies. I picked up the bottle of wine.

"What are we celebrating?" I was not the red wine connoisseur that Bill was, but I was developing a more discerning palate. This one was definitely out of my financial league.

"Thought it would be nice to treat us." He took a sip.

"We deserve it because this has been some kind of a—"

"What were you doing at the crime scene? You didn't mention that," Bill asked carefully.

I took a swallow of wine. In the past, questions like that would have required a sustained tap dancing effort on my part to dodge the truth. Been there, done that. At least I hoped so.

"I dropped Wilson off at the Windjammer to get his bike, and then I was coming straight here. I knew it would be a while before you got home, so I took the long way."

"Past the crime scene on the access road?" The corner of his mouth ticked upward in a familiar crooked grin.

"Well…yes. My Metro has a mind of its own. Anyway, I thought you'd want to see this. It confirms that the murderer is a theater person."

"Let's don't jump to conclusions," he said and held up a hand.

"But it seems likely, right?"

"We'll see. Based on the interviews, there might be persons of interest— people who were not too fond of Ruby. She got on a lot of nerves, even if she was talented," Bill added.

"Did you have a chance to read her scrapbook? Talk about talent."

"Not yet. We have to finish questioning the cast and crew. According to them, Ruby kept to herself, unless she was insulting someone or badmouthing their work. The only people who were at all positive about her were the musical director and Penny." He bit into a cracker. "We'll have to continue the meetings after the musical opens."

"What about her laptop?"

"The Creston PD picked it up. With a search warrant, they can access her email and Internet searches without her passwords. Digital forensics," Bill said dryly, "but I guess you already know that."

I certainly did thanks to Pauli. Hacking email accounts, specialty search engines on the Internet, and facial recognition software had all played a part in my previous investigative adventures. Playing noncommittal was my best defense at the moment.

"That's good." I skated over his implied accusation.

He leaned in, brushing a stray hair off my face. My pulse pounded, as it always did when Bill got playful.

I melted into his new, plush, off-white sofa. An excellent addition to the early American theme of his home furnishings. "This is comfy. Cushier than the last one."

"Yeah. Makes for a nicer place to relax." He made a beeline for my lips. *Yowza.*

* * * *

I juggled my caramel macchiato, keys, and *New York Times* as I ducked under awning after awning, making my way down Main Street. Of all days, I had to park a block away and was trying to avoid the light mist that had been falling for the past three hours. Opening night and the weather gods were having a good time at the expense of the ELT. The rain would mean soggy grass in the picnic area, and the possibility of delaying or postponing the production. I should have expected a messy day. I'd taken to reading my daily horoscope in the run up to my birthday. Today's horoscope warned that it *was not a good time to be out and about*, and advised to *stay indoors and commune with a good book or a good friend.* Too little, too late.

I unlocked the front door of the Windjammer and my cell phone chirped. I deposited my bag, drink, and newspaper on the table in my back booth and checked the text message. It was Lola: *Freaking out with the rain. Call me.* I checked the weather app on my cell and then tapped her number.

"Dodie!"

"Hi, Lo—

"I can't believe it. Walter called me four times, Penny keeps texting, and I can't reach Dale. What are we going to do if this keeps up?"

"Slow down, girlfriend. First of all, it's barely drizzling and second, the weather app says the precipitation will end by two this afternoon." I didn't have the heart to add that it also looked as though the rainfall might start again about nine or ten tonight. "You'll be good to go."

"We've invested so much in this show. Time, energy, our budget… Walter and I are counting on a huge box office. The Creston Players, too, of course." Lola paused. "I wish I could locate Dale. I want to run some things by him before tonight."

"When's the last time you saw him?" I asked. I didn't want to pry into Lola's love life, but she'd said enough in the past weeks to confirm a romance that was steadily growing.

"He was in a grumpy mood last night after the run-through, so I said good-bye and went home. I needed a good night's sleep."

"Why was he upset?" I asked.

"Dale's very fussy about timing and cues. Walter has him doing a dance routine during the second act that he hates, and last night Alex was a mite late with the downbeat of several numbers. Anyway, he was not a happy camper."

Camper…the word sent my mind spiraling down the rabbit hole of our summer vacation. Bill was already fantasizing about a camping stove he'd seen advertised in *RV Living*.

"What do you think?" Lola asked.

"Uh…sorry, I got sidetracked."

"I was saying I saw a different side of Dale this last week. Moody, angry, on the attack."

"Pre-show jitters?"

"He's a stage veteran. He's done professional work in the city, and has performed with the Creston Players for years. I don't think this is stage anxiety."

"Speaking of anxiety. How is Walter holding up?" I asked.

"Oh brother. I told him directing and choreographing were too much for one person, but he insisted. I hope he has enough Xanax to last through the weekend," Lola moaned.

The bell at the back door rang, signaling a delivery from Cheney Brothers. "Lola, gotta run. Fingers crossed, kiddo. I'll check in later with you."

As I double-counted the cartons of snack boxes and signed the requisition sheet from the food distributor, I mused over Dale's behavior. He was so romantic during the past several weeks—taking Lola to the theater, bringing her to the Windjammer after rehearsal, going to dinner on the weekends…maybe there was something in his private life that was forcing a personality transplant.

"Guess that's it. Tell the Brothers I'll be calling with next week's order," I said to the delivery guy. I was used to him by now—Yankees cap, chewing gum, pencil behind one ear.

He gave me his yada, yada, yada expression and stuffed the signed sheet into his shirt pocket. "Whatever."

Where did they find this kid?

Henry walked into the restaurant, brushed off a windbreaker, and jerked his thumb in the direction of the front window.

"I know. Don't say it. If the show is cancelled this weekend, we'll be stuck with four hundred snack boxes." I stopped. "They could be tomorrow night's special?"

Henry grunted and put on the coffee.

I settled into my back booth with inventory sheets and went to work. My cell clanged.

"Hey there," I said in my sexy voice. "You ran off early this morning— didn't put on the caffeine. I had to make a run to Coffee Heaven—"

"Sorry. Listen, have you spoken with Lola today?" Bill asked. "I know she often texts you first thing in the morning."

True. So sweet of Bill to pay attention. "Very observant of you."

"I saw your text messages last week."

Or not.

"I'm trying to reach Dale Undershot. He's not picking up his landline or cell phone. I thought Lola might know where he is?" he said.

"Funny you should ask. She called minutes ago, and said she was looking for him, too."

The line was quiet. I recognized Bill's police chief pause. "Oh? Is that all she said?"

"Also that he's been testy lately and got into it with Alex and Walter last night."

"I saw a little bit of that. He was gesturing wildly and pointing at various spots on the stage floor. I figured typical dress rehearsal stuff," Bill said.

"Is there a problem?"

"No. Standard investigative practice," he said guardedly.

I could hear a shroud of vigilance in his voice.

"Speaking of Dale's testy behavior…"

"What?" he asked abruptly.

"The night I spoke with Ruby at rehearsal? At intermission, she crossed the stage to go to the loading dock for a smoke and Dale…well they had a conversation," I said.

"What kind of conversation?" Bill's voice was tense.

"Intense. Dale grabbed Ruby's arm and appeared to be angry."

His vocal register rose. "And you didn't tell me?"

"I didn't think too much of it at the time. I assumed it was an argument about musical cues, but now…" Sometimes, I had a tendency to read more into a situation than was actually there. "You're the one telling me I have an overactive imagination," I said in my own defense.

Bill exhaled loudly. "If you hear anything about Dale, text me?"

"Sure."

He clicked off.

In the kitchen, Henry was studying the recipes for tomorrow night's final food contest winner: pistachio crusted chicken and cauliflower steaks. I wanted to go with a more exotic entrée, but Henry assured me that choosing a dish submitted by the mayor was good for business and for the town. Meanwhile, Wilson mixed the ingredients for the salmon burgers. We featured them a few times in the last year, and they were always a hit with the customers. Our Haitian sous chef was creating his own version of the burgers. Wilson kneaded the red and yellow bell peppers, panko bread crumbs, and garlic into the chopped fresh salmon, adding eggs, soy sauce, and lemon juice as he worked.

"Can't wait to try them," I said.

"*Do-dee*, I will make one *especial* for you!"

"Thanks, Wilson." He really was a nice guy, thoughtful and—

A clatter succeeded a bang, as a bowl with seasoned mayonnaise tipped over and tumbled to the tile floor.

"Wilson!" Henry exclaimed.

The young man looked stricken, dropping his eyes to the puddle of soy sauce and sesame oil, as it slowly spread in an ever-widening circle.

"Got it covered!" I said and darted for a mop and bucket.

* * * *

It was all hands on deck—loading the snack boxes, wine, and soda into the Windjammer van. I'd already prepped the plastic cups and napkins.

"Sure you've got enough help at the park?" Benny asked. Hooray for the weather app—the sun was shining, the air was thick with humidity. I pushed the thought of showers tonight out of my mind with a vengeance.

"All good," I said. I'd enlisted the aid of Pauli and some of the teenagers in the cast to help set up. Pauli asked Janice, who had asked a few others, and soon I had a working contingent of half a dozen kids. Probably more than I needed, but never mind. It was nice to have them involved. "Ready Wilson?"

I drove the van onto the path used by the Public Works Department to deliver landscaping equipment to the park and pulled up next to the concession stand. My crew was already waiting.

"Hi, guys. Thanks for helping out."

Pauli opened the door of the van. "Like, easy peasy."

He unloaded the hand truck, hopped on the back of the van, and shifted the cartons of snacks to Wilson, who stacked them up on the hand truck for the teenagers, who wheeled them to the concession stand. It was a coordinated effort.

Within half an hour, the food and drinks were neatly stowed inside the stand, the bottles of wine and soda tucked under a shelf for safekeeping. Good thing Wilson was now guarding the stash of concessions!

"Is that it, Dodie?" asked Janice. She was a pretty brunette with dimples. No wonder Pauli was smitten.

"That's it. You've all been great."

Because they had a couple of hours before the curtain rose, the cast members drifted away from the refreshments to the stage to hang out where everything—the floor, lighting instruments, curtained dressing rooms, and orchestra pit—had been covered by JC with heavy duty tarps. The audience, however, could arrive at any time to picnic, eat the snack boxes, or drink wine. I glanced longingly at a bottle of chardonnay.

"So uh, like, Janice might come to my graduation party," Pauli said confidentially, his eyes shining.

"Nice!"

"Yeah. Epic."

Out of the blue, his smile faded. He was fixated on Janice. The athlete actor from Creston High had joined her, laughing, making the other girls laugh, sucking the air out of Etonville Park and deflating Pauli's balloon.

"Hey, don't let him intimidate you. Get in there and fight for Janice." I gently nudged his shoulder.

Pauli shrugged. "I gotta bounce anyway." He took off.

Geez.

I left Wilson in charge of the concession stand with a cashbox. I posted a sign for the Etonville and Creston patrons, which listed what they would pay for a snack box, wine, or soda. Some of them might bring their own picnics; however, there would be folks who wanted to sample the Windjammer fare...or so I told Henry. I moved away from Wilson and cut across the damp, sloping lawn. I hoped people would be sensible enough to bring lawn chairs as well as bug spray. I wiped some sweat from my face and sat down on a large rock. On it was a plaque that proudly proclaimed this spot as the site of town founder Thomas Eton's log cabin. I hoped I wasn't defiling the founding father's living space. My cell buzzed, indicating a text. It was my mother, asking if I intended to spend a week at the shore in August. Though they were now permanent citizens of Naples, Florida, I had the sneaky suspicion if Bill and I were down the shore, my parents might join us. They still had friends there and talked about visiting to catch up. I texted back: *Not sure yet. I'll call.*

I mulled over family and how mine kept in touch via email, texts, Facebook, and Skype. I wondered about Ruby. Was there anyone she was in touch with? Family or friends in Indiana? Her apartment was so spare, so lacking in personal touches that it was impossible to know.

Lola's Lexus parked behind my Metro and she alighted dressed in running shorts and trotted over.

"Hi. Sorry I was such a mess this morning. The sun is out and Dale's meeting me here for a run around the park before our call." She stretched, testing the limits of her lime green spandex tank top.

The jogging was a new pastime: Dale's influence.

"I'm glad you caught up with him. Did he say where he was?" I asked

"Oh, you know. Running last minute show-opening errands. Join us?"

"Thanks, but I'll pass. Need to keep an eye on the concessions." Besides, I get enough exercise just pushing my luck.

Lola waved and ran to meet Dale, who'd parked his dark sedan behind hers. He was similarly dressed in jogging gear. They sprinted off, and I whipped out my cell and tapped Bill's number in my contacts.

"What's up?" He sounded frazzled.

"Thought you should know. Dale Undershot is here at the park. He and Lola are jogging around. Don't know why given the humidity, but—"

"Thanks for letting me know," he said, a mite more personal. "I actually reached him earlier. He was very cooperative."

That last word hung in the ether between us.

"Is there any reason he wouldn't be cooperative?" I asked.

Bill hesitated. "Not really. We have Ruby's laptop and are checking her emails and search history…"

"What about social media and credit cards and bank accounts? Maybe she posted things or had a spending or saving pattern that would tell you something. What about a cell phone?" I was trying to be helpful.

"Already covered."

He was being more cryptic than usual. "Oh."

"She didn't have a cell phone. At least we haven't found one." Silence for a moment. "Look Dodie, I know I can trust you…we've discovered some weird things."

I waited.

He lowered his voice. "We found a lot of cash stashed away in a bank account that isn't consistent with her lifestyle."

"You mean…she had money…but where did she get it and why didn't she spend it?"

Bill said, "Something like that." Then more seriously, "This is really confidential stuff until we can figure out what was going on with her."

"Got it. See you later—all tricked out in that fifties cop get-up," I said.

He chuckled. "I should have told the mayor to play the cop."

"Bye, Bill!" I said brightly and clicked off.

Ruby Passonata had been a wealthy woman who wore the same rumpled clothes, drove a well-used, modest car, and lived in a bare efficiency apartment. Bill was right...something odd was going on. Someone had to know more about who she was.

9

The applause following the teenagers' "Telephone Hour" grew and reached a crescendo as the kids posed with the old-fashioned equipment. Not sure who enjoyed the number more—the sold-out crowd or the performers. Never mind, the rain was holding off despite a light wind that had kicked up and gentle rolling thunder that punctuated a song every now and then. The patrons were game—bringing chairs to avoid the wet grass, scarfing up their own picnics as well as our snack boxes and downing multiple alcoholic and non-alcoholic drinks. Wilson had nearly sold out the food, and cases of empty bottles were stacked counter high in the refreshment stand. Even the mosquitos took pity on the ELT and Creston Players. The spraying and body slapping were minimal.

"Bravo!" Someone screamed later as the young girls fainted over Conrad Birdie, falling and standing and falling again. It was a riot and Walter had obviously settled the swoon versus squeal issue.

The combo played their hearts out, Alex shifted his focus from the piano to the musicians to the cast as if he was juggling balls. Finally, we made it to intermission. The only mishap was a wardrobe malfunction for Conrad Birdie: his gold lamé could take only so much hip thrusting, and Chrystal had to stitch a pivotal seam. When the lights dimmed for the end of the first act, folks hurried to the portable bathrooms and purchased the remaining soda stock. Wine was off-limits for the second act: the Public Works Department wanted everyone to get home safely.

"*Do-dee*, it is *ze* last of *ze* drinks," Wilson said, emptying a container and putting it into a carton.

"Good work, Wilson. Let's close up, and you can watch the second act from out there."

"Beautiful!" He clasped me before I could brace myself and fend off his affection.

"That's fine. You head on over." I kindly pushed him in the direction of the grassy slope. I needed to have a talk with him one of these days. I appreciated his warmth and friendliness but—

"Hi." It was Bill in his work clothes.

"What are you doing out here? It's performance conditions!" I sounded like Penny. "You have to get into costume."

"I know." He was out of breath.

"Did you jog here from the municipal building?" I asked.

"Almost. Parking's full around the perimeter of the park."

"Well, mister, you better head backstage," I said, playfully reprimanding him.

"Yeah. I'd better go before Penny blows her whistle."

"As if." Penny materialized behind us. "I can't blow my whistle with the house open. Get going."

Bill looked at me. "I have no idea how she does it," I said. He ran off.

Penny smirked. "Rookies. They never get the theater drill."

"Right. Even if they are veteran cops in real life."

"O'Dell you kill me. Real life doesn't matter in the theater. It's all fake."

"What about the magic?" I asked. I'd heard Lola wax poetic on the mystery of the stage often enough. Anyway, I loved to stump Penny.

"Magic?" Penny chortled. "Haven't you ever heard about breaking the walls? Third wall, fourth wall? Unwilling inspection of disbelief?"

I was so caught up in Penny's lecture on theater lingo, neither of us saw Walter until it was too late.

"Penny!" he hissed. "It's five minutes until places." His forehead was furrowed, his jaw tight with tension.

"I'm on it." She scurried off.

He took one disdainful look at me and followed her.

* * * *

Toes were tapping, heads bouncing to the music. We'd reached the second act reprise of "Lot of Livin'" with Sweet Apple, Ohio's teenagers and all was well. I felt a sprinkle and my heart plummeted. The cast was oblivious, singing and squirming around the stage. Ten minutes to go, and two more numbers. Lola was about to begin "Spanish Rose." Raindrops splattered my face. I moved inside the concessions booth.

The drizzle must have distracted the combo, because a musician missed an entrance and the instrumentation tangled between stop and go. Alex motioned frantically, and Lola stood stock-still waiting for her cue. It never came. Always a pro, Lola bravely started off singing a capella. Alex followed her with the piano and urged the rest of the combo to join the party. By the end of Lola's number the rain was coming down at a steady clip. Dale dashed onstage to wrap up his scene with Lola, his hair matted to his head. They attacked the lines, trying to make it to their last song. The band picked up the tempo, playing "Rosie" double-time, while Lola and Dale rushed through their final love ballad, singing as speedily as they could.

The audience valiantly attempted to remain faithful, but now gathered up kids and belongings. A mass exodus ensued. The orchestra had barely played the last note when the cast sprinted onstage for a curtain call; insisting on their moment of glory. Most of the combo gave up—but Alex played on as actors slipped and slid around the wet platform. The teenagers were hysterical, Abby bumped into Romeo, whose gold lamé pants were dangerously close to an R rating. Edna, Mildred and the ensemble of townspeople huddled as one, bowed swiftly, and scampered off. Bill tried to maintain some propriety—Walter must have been proud—and bowed stiffly. When he saw the mayhem around him, he gave up and sauntered off. The actor playing Hugo picked up Janice and carried her away. I fervently hoped Pauli wasn't in the house tonight.

The only one who remained completely undisturbed by the weather was Wilson. He stood in place, clapping enthusiastically until the last actor was out of sight as the downpour drenched his head and soaked his clothes.

It was an opening to remember.

* * * *

After closing up the refreshment stand, dropping Wilson at the Windjammer, and depositing the cash from the concessions in the night depository at the Valley Savings Bank, I limped home, wet, cold, and looking forward to a warm bath and my terry cloth robe. Bill had an early appointment with the medical examiner in the morning, so I texted my congratulations to him, happy to hunker down by myself. I was fantasizing about the luxurious bubble bath when my cell rang.

"Hi Dodie."

"Lola, sorry I missed you after the show. I got busy."

"What a disaster! I don't know how they manage the Central Park plays in the city. It's nerve-wracking...this weather thing."

I debated, then pushed the bubble bath fantasy out of my mind. "Where are you? Want to stop by?"

"I'm in the car. Be there in five."

I changed into a dry sweat suit, retrieved a bottle of chardonnay from the fridge, and opened two snack boxes that I'd stashed away before the crowd hit the concessions. It would have to do. Lola appeared in my driveway exactly five minutes later. Though she'd barely survived the downpour onstage, Lola coped well with emergencies from a wardrobe standpoint. She tucked her blond hair, still wet, neatly into a bun at the back of her neck. Her sweater was immaculate and her jeans crisp. How did she do it?

"Congratulations," I said, holding the door wide for her to enter.

"At least we made it through opening night, but did you see the curtain call?"

I laughed. "I did."

"Quite the tadoo!"

I was thinking train wreck. "The kids had a good time. Not sure about Walter, though."

"Walter was tearing his hair out backstage."

"Dale didn't want to celebrate tonight?"

Lola glared. "He was his moody self after the curtain call. Kind of standoff-ish. Something's going on."

"I'll bet he calls you tomorrow to smooth things over," I said with optimism. "Anyway, I saw Jocelyn tonight. Wonder if she made contact with Walter?"

Lola snickered.

"I'd like to chat with Dale too," I said.

"Really? Why?" Lola asked.

"I'd like to ask if he knew anything about Ruby's past. The Maynard Institute, her awards."

Lola's cell chirped and she read a text. "You're in luck. He asked me to join him for breakfast. Want to come along?"

"I don't want to be a third wheel," I said.

Lola tossed back the end of her chardonnay. "He owes me one after his temperamental act tonight."

"Fine. I'll stay a few minutes. Then you two lovebirds can get back to...whatever."

A serene smile spread over Lola's face. *Yowza!*

* * * *

After a good night's sleep—minus any camping or contestant dreams—I awoke bright-eyed and ready to pounce on the day. In between setting up the refreshments for *Bye, Bye, Birdie* and calming the kitchen yesterday, I'd made a couple of phone calls. The first to the alumni organization at the Maynard Institute to see if they had anything archived on Ruby.

The operator said the receptionist was out but would be back in the morning. The second call was to Greenburg, Indiana information to see if any of Ruby's relatives still lived in the town. I figured Bill would also be searching for Ruby's family, but his focus right now was on the medical examiner's findings and the carbon monoxide tampering. Bad luck on the second call—there were no Passonatas in Greenburg. There could be Passonatas in other parts of Indiana, or the rest of the country for that matter. I had to admit I was less interested in Ruby's killer than I was in her past.

I showered and dressed in a lightweight pair of slacks and a pale, blue, sleeveless blouse that flaunted my upper arms nicely. Not too shabby. I decided that I would zip into Manhattan after meeting with Lola and Dale and speak with the alumni office. They wouldn't need me at the Windjammer until lunch—plenty of time to interview the receptionist. Besides, Enrico and Carmen worked weekends, easing the pressure on Henry and the dining room.

My neighborhood was sleeping in this morning. No lawn mowers or sprinklers. I backed out of the driveway and headed to State Route 53. Dale and Lola were breakfasting at a café on Main Street in Creston that I had frequented in the past whenever I needed some time away from Etonville. It was certainly more private than Coffee Heaven and far removed from the town's ever-nosy citizens who would, no doubt, have opinions on last night's near-washout of a performance. Those opinions were probably more than Lola and Dale could handle this morning. I'd declined Lola's offer of a ride to Creston since I needed to get to New York as soon as possible and didn't intend to overstay my welcome.

Traffic was light on the highway, and I eased into a parking space in front of the café at nine. I peered in the front window and saw Lola and Dale already cozy in a booth by the door. They made a good-looking duo. Dale had the looks of a cartoon character: a chiseled face, muscled upper arms, and a cleft chin. I entered, and when the waiter at the counter looked up I pointed to the occupied booth.

"Hi. Hope I'm not intruding."

Lola tore her attention away from Dale. "Dodie! What a nice surprise! Whatever are you doing in Creston?"

Huh? What was Lola doing? "Uh…well…I had an errand in town and thought I'd stop in for coffee—"

"Have a seat," Dale said smoothly. He showed no sign that he might be upset that I was joining them.

Lola shifted over, moving her coffee cup and table setting and gave me a sideways glance. She wasn't a diva for nothing…I read the subtext. Mum's the word on my invitation to meet with them.

I sat down. "Thanks. You two must be pleased with the show last night. It went well."

"Until the rain," Lola said, a trifle mournfully.

I ordered coffee and refused a menu. "Good news on tonight's weather. The skies look clear."

Dale scowled slightly. "Not too bad for an opening. There were some hits and misses."

I couldn't afford to waste time. I had to swing this conversation into Ruby territory soon. "I guess Alex had some trouble with music cues?"

"Some?" Dale hooted. Lola smiled wanly.

"Must be difficult juggling the piano and the musical direction," I said.

"Real professionals can manage both," he said.

Professionals? It was a community theater production during a rain shower.

"Alex did his best," Lola interjected.

I dove in. "So unfortunate about Ruby. She was a genius at the keyboard, right?"

Dale hesitated. "A genius? She was competent."

Whoa. Some salt in that wound. There *was* something to their offstage spat. "I heard she went to the Maynard Institute."

Lola studied the dregs in her coffee cup. Dale became frosty. "Where did you hear that?"

I sneaked a glimpse of Lola's face: totally noncommittal. What was going on with her? She knew about the scrapbook too. Obviously, Dale had no more idea of Ruby's background than Alex had. "One of the Creston Players might have mentioned it," I said.

Dale snorted. "Why would someone who attended the Maynard Institute play the piano for a community theater?"

"It does seem unusual," I said.

In a bid to move the conversation to safer territory, Lola grabbed a non-sequitur out of thin air. "Speaking of unusual, did you know Dale is a financial advisor? He's giving me fantastic portfolio advice." Lola put on her dazzling smile.

"I didn't know. If I had any money to be advised about, I'd sign up."

Dale relaxed into the seat back and graced us with a short chuckle. "It's a good time to be in the stock market."

"Right. Well, I should be going." I stood up and grabbed my bag. "See you tonight. Here's hoping the weather holds."

I waved good-bye, and Lola rotated in her seat to give me a pointed stare intended to communicate something. But what?

* * * *

Trucking into Manhattan on a weekend morning was nothing compared to rush hour on a weekday. I cruised onto Route 3 East past the Meadowlands and the stadium where the New York Giants played, the strip malls and outlets that lined the highway. I made my way to the mouth of the Lincoln Tunnel within fifteen minutes.

The Maynard Institute was located on New York's Upper West Side, but my best bet was parking in Midtown. With the pleasant weather, I was tempted to walk the thirty blocks to the school, but given my schedule, a taxi was a better solution. I flagged one down and we zigged and zagged through city traffic. Before I could formulate an opening salvo for the alumni receptionist, the cab pulled up in front of the Institute.

Wrought iron gates encircled a quad that fronted the main administration building. I'd checked out the campus map online, so I felt somewhat familiar with the layout. I walked through the gates, past a cluster of ivy-covered structures dating from the eighteenth century. The Maynard Institute was an oasis of serenity in the midst of the bustling city—a kind of artistic paradise. It was not surprising that tuition, fees, and room and board topped fifty thousand a year. Of course, when Ruby entered the school in 1958, her scholarship would have been worth far less.

As I approached Ostracher Hall, where the alumni office was located, the music of a string quartet poured out an open window. Students hustled in and out of buildings. I considered the setting, trying to imagine a young Ruby making her mark here, which still felt odd—knowing the Creston Players accompanist as I did. The building directory pointed me to room 132. The floor tile sparkled, the walls overlaid with mahogany-stained wainscoting. The atmosphere reminded me of the hushed reverence of a church, except for the bone-chilling air conditioning.

I pushed open the wooden door to room 132 and faced the receptionist, who was on the telephone. Martha Bissel, according to her nameplate, had gray hair styled in a pageboy, wore a crisp white blouse and deep red lipstick. Her lined face suggested she was probably in her early seventies. Martha looked up and gestured to me to "hold on." I moved away from her desk and sat on a stuffed chair out of the range of her conversation. When my cell pinged, I surreptitiously withdrew it from my bag as if I was involved in illicit activity and stole a glimpse. It was Lola: *I can explain!* I hoped so.

"Now then, young lady, what can I do for you?" Martha asked politely.

I approached the receptionist. "Hello. I'm wondering if you can help me."

"It depends." A jovial grin creased her face. I'd bet she was fun on a night out with her girlfriends.

"I'm trying to find some information on an alum of the Maynard Institute."

"Oh? Who might that be?" she asked.

I had already resolved to play it straight. Less complicated. "Ruby Passonata."

Martha frowned. "I've been here fifteen years. I don't recall anyone by that name," she said, her fingers poised above her keyboard. "How do you spell her last name?"

"P-a-s-s-o-n-a-t-a. But she would have graduated well before 2000," I said hastily. "Around 1962."

"Our database doesn't go back that far. There might be paper records, but they're stashed away in the basement."

I apparently didn't do a terrific job of concealing my disappointment. "Oh."

The receptionist laced her fingers together and leaned forward. "If you tell me what you are looking for, I can offer some assistance."

How much information to share? Odds are Ruby's murder hadn't been broadcast in the New York media. "I met Ruby recently…she was accompanying a musical production at a community theater in New Jersey. She died…suddenly."

"I'm so sorry to hear that." Martha Bissel was genuinely sympathetic.

"When I was helping to sort through her…personal things…" Mostly true. "…we found a scrapbook that mentioned the Maynard Institute and contained dozens of clippings from concerts and tours after she graduated from here. She was an international celebrity pianist."

Martha beamed like a gratified parent. "Many of our graduates have gone on to stellar careers. Maynard has a very proud tradition."

"I was hoping there would be some record of her time here," I said. "Someone who remembered her."

The receptionist studied me quizzically.

"I'd like to…I don't know…know more about her." Is that what I wanted?

"Well, as I said, records from that far back, over fifty years, have been archived and locked away in dusty old files that no one ever searches. I don't have access to them."

I nodded and shifted my purse from one shoulder to the other. "Thanks for your help. I really appreciate it."

"But there may be one other source of information." She scribbled on a Post-It note. "Professor Yurkov was on the piano faculty in the sixties. He's nearly ninety now and retired for several decades. But he comes around and keeps in touch. He might remember Ruby."

My heart skipped a beat. "That's wonderful."

"And he lives right around the corner on Amsterdam." She handed me the note. "I have to warn you. He's a tad gruff at first, but after a while, he warms up," she said with a twinkle.

I nodded. "Got it."

"By the way, he loves cannoli from the bake shop next door to his apartment building."

* * * *

On the sidewalk beyond the wrought iron gates, I checked my watch. I'd intended to buzz into the city and buzz out again, arriving at the Windjammer by noon. It was ten thirty. I still had time to call on Professor Yurkov. Martha graciously offered to call and give him a heads-up so I could stop in the bakery and pick up his favorite dessert. By ten forty-five, I was ringing the buzzer for B. Yurkov, apartment 2C, and climbing the stairs to the second floor.

I knocked on his door and it immediately opened four or five inches, the chain in place. A wild halo of white hair surrounded a pudgy face, which filled the gap. "Yes?" he said brusquely.

"Professor Yurkov? Martha Bissel in the Maynard alumni office suggested I speak with you."

"Why?"

The receptionist was spot-on. The professor would require a little wooing. "I'd like to ask you about Ruby Passonata. She was a student there in the sixties and Martha thought you might remember her."

The professor released the chain from the door. It clattered against the jamb. "Ruby? You know Ruby?" he asked, excited.

"Yes, I do." Did.

The door opened wide and he stood on the threshold. His face was clean-shaven, his starched shirt collar dug into the folds of skin on his neck. He sported a bow tie, sweater vest, and neatly pressed trousers. Professor Yurkov was all dressed up. Did he have any place to go? He stared at me. "Come in. Come in."

"Thank you." I lifted the cake box. "Martha also mentioned you are a fan of cannoli, Professor Yurkov," I said.

"Please call me Boris, and don't put much stock in what Martha says," he grumbled, but took the box and inhaled the scent of the cannoli. He pointed to a settee covered by a colorful afghan. "Please sit."

He disappeared into the kitchen where I could hear him moving about, probably making coffee. I glanced around the apartment. Not much larger than Ruby's, but with tons more personality. Reading materials and tchotchkes crammed the bookshelves. Photos decorated one wall, and a lace doily covered an end table. The end table, next to a recliner, held reading glasses and a coffee cup.

"Do you take milk or sugar?"

"Black is fine," I said.

The professor reappeared with a cup of coffee for me and the plate of cannoli. He set both on a coffee table and settled himself into the recliner. "Now what about Ruby?" He bit into the crispy shell of a cannoli, savoring the sweet creamy filling.

"You remember her?" I asked eagerly.

He gave me a withering look. "What? A teacher should not remember his best student? I taught for over forty years—students from every state and many countries." He halted as if seeing a lineup of four decades of pupils. "No one...Ruby was the most promising musician I ever taught. Eat!" He pointed to the plate of cannoli.

I took one. "When I knew her, she seemed like a genius."

His bushy eyebrows shot upward. "Genius? Yes! You say you knew her?"

I explained how I'd met Ruby, that she'd passed away, and that her scrapbook had intrigued me. After a moment to absorb her passing, Boris described her talent, the awards, and concert tours—much of which I'd already read about.

"Community theater? *Bye, Bye, Birdie*?" Boris looked aghast. "I had no idea she was in New Jersey."

"Were you in touch in recent years?" I asked, nibbling on the pastry.

Boris picked up another cannoli. "The last time I heard from her was in...1969."

The last year there were clippings in the scrapbook. "Do you know why she stopped performing? Did something happen?"

He took a sip of his coffee. "I have no idea. I was astonished to learn she had retired at such a young age. I called her and asked why? She said she never wanted to play again. I was astounded! I pleaded with her to see me. Tried to talk sense into her. Tried to persuade her to go back on tour." He dabbed at his eyes. "But she hung up the phone. We never spoke again."

Silence for a moment.

"But you never forgot her," I said.

"Never."

"Boris, I'm wondering...was there anything about Ruby or her past that you would consider...unusual? Remarkable?" I asked.

"Unusual?" His brow puckered as he finished off the cannoli, wiping stray crumbs from his lips.

"I know she came from a town in Indiana. Ending up at the Maynard Institute must have seemed unusual."

"I don't know about that. Ruby was a private person," he said.

I finished off my coffee and stood. "Thank you for seeing me on such short notice." I held out my hand and Boris shook it.

"Thank you for the cannoli." He bowed slightly.

I turned to leave.

"Wait!"

I swung around and faced the professor again. "Yes?"

"In her final year, a month before she graduated, we had a meeting set. I was waiting for her to arrive. It was not like Ruby to be late. I was more impatient in those days," he said sadly.

"Something happened?" I asked.

"My office window was open, and I heard loud voices in the quad. It was Ruby and a young man. I don't think he was a Maynard student." He gazed upward as if trying to retrieve the moment from his memory. "The man...he was explaining something, I think. He said, 'Ruby, I'm sorry,' over and over."

"What did Ruby say?"

"She screamed. 'If you think you are sorry now, just wait.'"

"A lovers' quarrel?"

"That would not have been so surprising. I looked out the window. They sat on a bench. The young man was in great distress, but what shocked me was the rage on Ruby's face. I had never seen anything like that from her before."

"Did you speak with her?"

"Ten minutes later she knocked on my door in good spirits, as though the fight had never happened."

"Ruby never mentioned it?"

"Never."

"I wonder who the guy was?"

"She shouted his name but…" Boris shrugged, then rose from his recliner and crossed to the bookshelf. He rummaged around a stack of albums and returned with a photo. He held it out. "Ruby's final concert at Maynard."

Ruby and Boris were side by side, she in an evening gown, he in a tux. Both beaming. "She looks so happy here."

"She played like an angel that night…Chopin and Bach."

I wrote my cell number on a piece of paper and Boris agreed to call if he remembered anything else.

As I opened the door, he said, "Her voice was full of vengeance."

10

Lunch was crazier than usual. Much of Etonville was taking advantage of the pleasant weather, and the Windjammer was standing room only. All anyone could talk about was *Bye, Bye, Birdie*, the rain, and the wacky ending.

"I laughed myself silly," said Vernon. "That curtain call was the best part of the evening."

Mildred thumped his shoulder. "Don't let Penny or Walter hear you. The cast is supposed to take their bows with respectability, regardless of the weather."

I filled coffee cups and cleared tables as Gillian and Carmen ran from the kitchen to the dining room. Benny's forehead was moist, a testament to his hard work.

"Can I freshen up your coffee?" I asked the Banger sisters.

They bobbed their heads in unison.

"Dodie, we're so excited, don't you know," said one sister.

"Our first musical!" said the other.

"Keep your fingers crossed on the weather tonight," I said.

They raised their chins defiantly. "Neither rain nor snow will stop the swift completion of our appointed rounds," they said in unison.

Snow? "That's the motto of the post office. You know, mailmen?"

"Yes. Our performance is like a special delivery." They beamed.

"Right." I zoomed off before I had to think about it. I plunked down on a stool at the bar.

"Seltzer?" Benny asked filling glasses from the soda taps.

"Sure." I tallied checks, sipped my drink, and scanned the dining room. Though all of the tables and booths were full, the waiting line had dwindled. "It's like the town came out of the woodwork."

"They're not so hot on Henry's cold cucumber soup," Benny said.

"Or Wilson's Haitian quiche," I added.

"I'd say the jury is out on both items." Benny looked at the customers busily eating. "This was a burgers-and-fries day."

Benny was right. Folks were avoiding the specials and ordering the tried and true standbys. As long as they were ordering something…

"Hi."

I looked up into Bill's usually dazzling blue eyes, which were now cloudy. "Hi yourself. You hungry? I can recommend the soup or quiche, though neither is selling out—"

"Can we…?" He angled his head in the direction of my back booth.

A little isolation wouldn't be so bad. Benny followed us to my booth, writing up Bill's takeout order.

"What's with the mystery?" I asked.

Bill lowered his voice. "We got a search warrant to dump Ruby's computer."

I didn't like his concerned expression. "And?"

"Nothing much in her email, but she had an Excel spreadsheet in her documents," he said.

"That's all? I have budget spreadsheets for work and home, though trying to keep myself on a monthly budget hasn't exactly been an easy job—"

"Dodie!" Bill said hoarsely.

I blinked at the abruptness of his interruption.

"Ruby had a list of entries and dates," Bill said, his voice tight.

"What kind of entries?" I asked slowly.

"Payments. A thousand dollars a month."

"Where would Ruby get that kind of money? Social security?"

"No. That check was direct-deposited into her bank account." Bill stopped. "By each entry were the initials DU and a check mark. First notation was a year ago and the last entry was May."

"DU." I wondered. "Could it be Dale Undershot?"

"It's a distinct possibility. Unless there's another DU in her life."

"Maybe Dale was her financial advisor and she was receiving monthly checks from her portfolio," I said.

"Maybe."

"You don't look convinced," I said. "Did you ask Dale about Ruby's investments?"

"He didn't have much to say, and definitely didn't volunteer any information about Ruby's financial situation."

Did the spat during the technical rehearsal have any connection to the spreadsheet entries?

Bill studied my expression. "What?"

"What?"

"I know that look. What occurred to you?"

"I was thinking about their argument in the theater the other night," I said. "And Dale's quick temper. I guess you'll have to speak with Dale again?"

"ASAP."

"Could it wait until after tonight's performance? I mean, there's no show tomorrow, and the cast has some days off before next weekend. Plenty of time to grill him then," I pleaded. "You don't know for certain that he was involved with anything illegal."

"Dodie, it's a murder investigation. The wheels of justice are moving forward."

My heart sank as Lola walked in the door of the Windjammer. Bill followed my eyes and muttered, "Keep this to yourself until I can sort it out."

"Got it." I gestured to Lola to join us.

"Hi Bill," Lola said and flipped her blond hair off her face. "Nice job last night."

Bill smiled sheepishly. "I have to admit it was fun. Even running around the stage getting wet."

"Bit by the acting bug," I teased. "Onstage drama suits you."

"I get enough offstage drama in Etonville," he said wryly. "Take my seat, Lola. I'm heading back to work." He slid out of the booth. "See you tonight."

Lola watched Bill stride to the register and pay for his lunch. "He gets hunkier by the day." She settled onto the bench.

"So, what was with this morning?" I asked.

Lola looked stricken. "Dodie, I'm sorry I had to play that little charade. I was about to tell Dale you were joining us when he said he needed to speak to me in private and he was so serious that I couldn't tell him I'd invited you. Did you get the information you wanted?"

"Yeah. He apparently doesn't know anything about Ruby's background." I eased into my next question. "What was so important he had to see you privately?" I asked casually.

"I'm not sure. He talked about his company and gaining the trust of his clients and then you arrived. After you left, he continued on about how he'd never want me to think he was taking advantage of me or anyone, and I said I trusted him completely and would never entertain the thought that he might be...oh, I don't know, dishonest?"

Gillian brought Lola a cup of coffee and she smiled her thanks.

"And then what?"

"His cell rang and he checked the caller ID and said he had to take it and he'd call me later. He just got up and left the café. It was the strangest thing," Lola said.

"That is strange." I had to bite my lip to keep Bill's findings from spilling out of my mouth. "Was he trying to tell you something?"

Lola shrugged. "I have no idea. Anyway, I'm going to go to the park later this afternoon to meet with Walter so I'll see him there." Lola fiddled with a teaspoon on the rim of her saucer. "You know, Dale has been moody and withdrawn ever since they discovered Ruby's death wasn't an accident. He wasn't close to her. They were barely acquaintances."

"Was he her financial advisor?" I asked.

"Why would Ruby need a financial advisor?" Lola asked skeptically. "Where would she get enough money to need advising?"

Where indeed.

"The stress of the weather getting to Dale?" I asked.

"Whatever it is, I hope he shapes up soon. We have a show to run."

* * * *

Usually, Etonville Little Theatre reserved curtain speeches for opening night when Walter dramatically took the stage, often in costume, and delivered commentary on the upcoming season or an appeal for donations. He'd quote Shakespeare, or some other famous writer, and end with sweeping gestures to a sometimes-confused audience. Walter saved his eulogies for actual funeral services. He'd delivered two of them in the past two years. Either his ego needed a massaging, or the Xanax was making him way too chill, but at the last minute Walter decided to eulogize Ruby at tonight's performance. Ruby...whom he pretty much disliked.

"I know. Ruby drove him crazy," Penny chuckled.

"Penny," I said sweetly, "Could you please stay out of my head for the night?" I had no desire for Swami Penny to read my thoughts on Dale.

"O'Dell, you kill me." She tapped a pencil against her clipboard. "This is going to put us behind schedule," she said importantly.

"Maybe Walter will only speak for several minutes." I was attempting optimism. "After all, this is a co-production. Someone from the Creston Players should deliver the speech. Dale?"

Penny pushed her glasses up a notch on her nose. "Walter is the *real* artistic director around here—"

"Actually, that would be Lola—"

"—and Dale is a *temporary* artistic director for the Creston Players. Anyway, Dale might choke up. He and Ruby were..." Penny crossed two fingers to indicate the intimacy of their friendship.

"They were? What makes you say that?" I asked.

Penny sighed patiently. "O'Dell, how many times do I have to tell you? I'm the PM. Got to keep eyes and ears on the ground. Ever seen anything get by me?"

"Uh, well..."

"I know." Penny cackled.

"What did your ears and eyes tell you about Ruby and Dale?"

"Until she...uh...you know..."

"Died? Go on," I said.

"She and Dale used to meet backstage before rehearsal. One night he had his arm around her." Penny gave me a knowing look.

"What did they talk about?"

Penny straightened her back, adding an inch to her five foot two height. "I don't eavesdrop on actors backstage unless I have to deliver a message or something. It would be unprofessional."

"Right. But I'm sure you had to give them a message from time to time. After all, you are the PM," I said.

Penny squinted at me. "O'Dell, are you yanking my chain?"

"Who me? No!"

"Well, one time I heard them talking about financial stuff. Deposits, payments, debts. It was all pretty hush-hush," she said.

I'll bet.

"He's a financial wizard," Penny said. "He can't be blasting stock tips over the loud speaker."

"I guess not."

"Penny!" Walter whined from the stage. "I can't find my notes for the curtain speech!"

"I'm on it," she said. "Keep that info out of your bonnet," she called over her shoulder.

I saluted Penny as she hurried away. Dale and Ruby having a backstage tête-à-tête concerning financial matters. Interesting...

* * * *

The weather was holding nicely at seven thirty, with light clouds scudding across the bluish-gray expanse of sky. The sellout crowd had availed themselves of the snack boxes and drinks from the concession stand where

Gillian was on duty, happily texting and Instagramming photos of herself at work.

I planned to see the show underway, and then sneak out. I'd return at the end of Act Two to pick up the cash bag for the nightly deposit and see Bill perform without the rain. The illumination onstage dimmed and a spotlight hit Walter as he marched forcefully to center stage. His favorite place. He was looking the part of the suave director: seersucker suit, white shirt, an ascot around his neck. The audience took this as a sign that the show was beginning and settled in, cutting off conversations and shushing one another.

Walter waited, one hand in a jacket pocket, the other resting on his chest. He wore his funeral expression: Life is short and we've lost another member of our theater family. Unfortunately, I had come to identify his memorial bearing.

"Dear friends…I come to you tonight not as the director of our little play…"

I heard a few titters from the offstage area where the teenagers gathered.

"…but as a colleague and collaborator of our currently deceased accompanist." He waited to let interest build. "Ruby Passonata."

A hush fell over the crowd.

"She departed from us much too soon…" he said mournfully as if Ruby's passing were all her own idea and not the result of murder. "But we are left with fond memories of her nimble fingers plying her trade at the piano."

I wondered what Ruby would make of Walter's describing her work at the piano, considering she thought of him as a "horse's patoot." Walter went on to define Ruby's character—gracious and warm, more titters; work ethic—considerate of her coworkers, I swore I heard a snort from Penny's stage manager's box; and love of the theater. Really? How could someone who had the career Ruby had, give it all up to find herself accompanying voice lessons and playing the piano for a community theater. Even one as good as the Creston Players. A rustling from the seats suggested folks were getting restless. From my vantage point near the refreshment stall, I could see part of the curtained, offstage area where Lola was shaking her head and, I imagined, rolling her eyes. I watched Lola and didn't notice the silence on stage. Walter was still, head bowed, the audience leaning forward in their seats. Was he finished? Had he lost his place? Was he overcome with emotion?

With a jerk, Walter lifted his head, and thrust his arms wide. "Tonight, we dedicate this performance of *Bye, Bye, Birdie* to one of our flock who has flown away. 'Good night sweet princess, and flights of angels wing thee to thy rest.'"

I sincerely hoped Shakespeare hadn't tuned in tonight. He'd be appalled to hear Walter editing *Hamlet*. Audience members applauded enthusiastically, probably as much for the end of Walter's speech as for Ruby. The stage went black; Alex lifted his hand to signal the combo for the start of the overture. The music vaulted into the park.

I had about two hours before Bill made his entrance; plenty of time to go home and do some digging on Ruby's life in Indiana. The last rays of the sun were sinking behind the houses that outlined the park, leaving a wash of color as remnants of the day's light stole away.

Streets around town were empty, with several houses lit up. Either everyone had gone to bed early or *Bye, Bye, Birdie* had crushed the box office tonight. That would make Lola happy. Financial security for the Etonville Little Theatre for another year. Financial security reminded me of Ruby's Excel spreadsheet. Dale was a financial advisor, an authority according to Penny. Had his and Ruby's relationship included his fiscal expertise?

I pulled into my driveway and ran into the house. There was no time to waste. In order to find missing persons in the past, I had used the Internet's White Pages. I set myself up at the kitchen table with my laptop and a glass of chardonnay—way more comfortable than sitting in the park, fending off the mosquitos, and desperately hoping that the weather held.

I entered Ruby's name, assuming that something would pop. Her Creston address appeared, but there was nothing for Indiana. Though her parents would no doubt be deceased, I input both Edward and April and found nothing in Indiana, though there was an April Passonata in Denver, Colorado and several other Passonatas scattered around the country. I called information for the Greenburg, Indiana area, and requested phone numbers for any Passonata still living there. There were only three numbers, all of them located outside the town of Greenburg. I left a message at one, the second had been disconnected, and the third belonged to Ruby's third cousin. He had not seen or heard about her in decades. James Passonata knew about Ruby's musical prowess from his father's side of the family, but he was twenty years younger than Ruby, and had met her only once when he was a child. He wondered why I asked. I had no idea if word of Ruby's death had reached Greenburg, and I didn't want to tread on the toes of the investigative work undertaken by the police department. I rambled on about how I'd met her in New Jersey at a local community theater, what a talent she was, and how much I appreciated speaking with him. Then I ended the call. After an hour of burrowing into Ruby's background, I learned practically nothing— only that she had a third cousin in Indiana who couldn't remember her.

I leaned back in the seat and sipped my wine. It was time to call in the big guns. I texted Pauli: *Got a job for you. Call me.* I had seen Pauli earlier at the park taking production pictures of the cast and crew before the performance. He was no doubt hanging around, tailing Janice or the athlete actor from Creston. My cell rang.

"Uh, like, you need something?" Pauli whispered.

"Yeah. Where are you?"

"Like, watching the show. Janice is on again in a minute."

"Got it. Anyway, could you help me think outside the digital box?"

"Like what?" he asked eagerly.

I loved his Internet enthusiasm. "I want to do some research into Ruby Passonata."

"The piano player, right?"

"Right."

"Like, you're going after her murderer?" he whispered softly.

"Nothing like that. I'm curious about her background."

"Oh," Pauli said, disappointed.

"Can we talk tomorrow?"

"Uh-oh. Gotta bounce. Janice is on."

"I'll text you in the morning."

Pauli clicked off. I had about twenty minutes before I had to return to the park. I typed Dale Undershot into my computer's search engine to see what would show up. Apparently, Undershot was an unusual name because, aside from our Dale, there was one other individual with that name and he was a dog trainer who lived in Manchester, England. Dale had a LinkedIn profile, a Facebook page, and a Twitter account. His profile described the services provided by Undershot Financial, such as wealth management, planning for retirement, investment options—stocks, bonds, and mutual funds—and annuities and insurance. Dale was a one-stop shop for anyone looking to broaden his or her financial understanding and security. What aspects of his business did Ruby utilize? It was a challenge to visualize her healthy bank account and steady investment income. Her lifestyle felt like a square peg in a round hole. What exactly was her lifestyle? What did she do away from Creston Players productions?

My cell binged. It was Gillian, antsy because the show was ending and wanting to know when I was returning to close out the cash box. I downed the rest of my wine, grabbed my bag, and headed back to *Bye, Bye, Birdie*.

I needed another visit to Ruby's neighborhood.

11

We lounged on stools at the center island in Bill's kitchen. "You outdid yourself." I swallowed the last bite of his Mediterranean omelet.

Bill peered over the top of the front page of the *New York Times,* the corner of his mouth ticking upward. "No big deal: eggs, some tomatoes, scallions, feta cheese, black olives, a dash of oregano."

Our Sunday ritual had become a regular event: brunch at Bill's where he'd captivate me with a gastronomic treat, while we shared the *NYT* and hashed over the latest Etonville antics or crime spree. "Did you see my horoscope for today?" It was a not-so-subtle hint that my birthday was right around the corner, and Bill had yet to offer any sort of plan for the big day.

He stuck his face back into the paper. "Nope."

"Nice to have a day off. Glad the Windjammer's closed on Sunday and the show is dark today."

"Me too. I need a break from the greasepaint."

"I don't know. You might be going all rogue on me. Looking pretty comfortable up on that stage chasing the teenagers of Sweet Valley, Ohio. I like that bit where you catch the mayor's wife as she faints at the end."

"Yeah. Edna gets a kick out of it too," he said wryly.

"How about Walter's curtain speech?" I chuckled.

"The cast sure enjoyed his tribute. Walter has a knack for bending the truth to serve his needs."

"Bending Shakespeare too." I moved to the counter to retrieve the coffee pot, ruffling Bill's already ragged, bed-head on the way. "At least the standing ovation at the end of the show was well-deserved."

"I need a haircut." Bill tugged on his brush cut.

"Why don't you stop by Snippets? I could give Carol a call." Bill would rather tread on hot coals than step foot inside the gossip center for a trim. "Vernon gets his hair cut there."

Bill groaned. "That's all I need. To listen to that crew offer opinions on everything from Ruby's murderer to the dangers of carbon monoxide to potential suspects."

"Are there any? Suspects?"

His face took on a guarded police-chief-expression. "We're working on it."

"Working on it" likely meant both the Etonville and Creston forces were stumped at the present. "Did I mention that I visited the Maynard Institute yesterday?" I asked casually.

Bill looked perplexed. "Maynard Institute?"

"Where Ruby went to school."

He dropped the newspaper on the table. "No, you didn't. Why did you go, and what did you find out? You're out of the investigative business. We agreed—"

"Rein it in! I'm not investigating anything. I'm wondering about her, that's all."

"Yeah," he said, unconvinced.

I poured us both a second cup of coffee as I recounted my trip to New York and conversation with Boris Yurkov. "I can't get over it—how someone so talented could throw away a career."

Bill shrugged. "It's been done before. Someone walking away from a lucrative contract. I've seen plenty of NFL players choose to call it quits at the height of their careers."

"Okay, but that's not the same."

"Why not? Because football players aren't talented?" he asked, testing me.

"No, because football is a dangerous game. Playing the piano is a lot safer profession."

"Really?" Bill said.

I got his drift. To quote Walter, were Ruby's "nimble fingers plying her trade at the piano" connected to her death?

"Anyway, don't get carried away about Ruby," he warned, shaking a finger playfully in my face.

"Fine but if you need my instincts…" I let the offer hang tantalizingly in the air.

"I'll let you know. Besides, there is enough growing evidence to investigate persons of interest."

"Really? Who—?"

Bill stood and stretched. "I have to run into work. I'll catch up with you later. Making my spaghetti carbonara for dinner."

"Oooh…you forgot. Tonight's poker night at my place. Last month I decided that we needed a girls' club. We were looking for something looser than a book club so we settled on poker."

"Poker? I know *you* can play…

Bill and I had taken a day trip to Atlantic City in April. I shocked him by winning at blackjack and three-card poker.

"…but what about—"

"Lola, Carol, Mildred, and Edna? I'm teaching them. Anyway, we only play for pennies and nickels."

"I was looking forward to cooking for us. Cracking open a nice red wine, and catching up on Netflix." He pouted like a little kid.

"You could always broaden your horizons to include the poker crew—"

"No," he said hastily.

"It'll be fun. Like being in Snippets without the dryers and hair spray. Maybe you'll learn something about Ruby," I said.

Bill chuckled. "You're going to owe me."

"Mmmm…I can taste the calories already."

"I'll need a lot of wine," he added.

"My treat."

Bill showered and left for the Etonville police department. I lingered over my coffee, texting Pauli to see if he could come to my place for internet reconnaissance later. I doodled in the margin of the Arts and Leisure section of the *Times*. Whatever became of the young man who argued with Ruby in the quad near Boris Yurkov's window? It sounded like a significant fight. Did they ever make up? Were they a couple while Ruby was on tour for the next six years or so? Did they marry? Is it possible Ruby had a love life before she exited the concert scene? My cell pinged. Pauli: *Hey. I'm in.*

* * * *

"Any update on Janice?" I asked as Pauli went to work at my kitchen table, Slurpee and a bag of barbecue potato chips in hand.

He flipped open his laptop. "Nah."

I tiptoed into sensitive territory. "Is she still coming to your graduation party?"

"Dunno. Would be epic if she did."

"I hope you're not letting that kid from Creston cramp your style."

"Nah. He's like kind of a bozo." He looked in my direction. "You think he can act?"

Actually, yes. "He's okay. You have other talents. Photography, digital forensics..." I poured myself another cup of coffee.

Pauli sipped his Slurpee. "Like, yeah. So what about Ruby?"

"Right. I want to dig into her background."

"Awesome," he said. "Like what do you want to know?"

It all boiled down to her abandoning her talent. Why was I fixated on that? Never mind. "She had this great concert career. Traveled around the world. Met celebrities here and abroad."

"Sweet." Pauli's brow puckered. "You sure that's the same Ruby who played the piano for *Bye, Bye, Birdie?*"

"I know what you mean. But yes, same person."

I explained to Pauli that I'd checked phone listings for Greenburg, Indiana looking for relatives to no avail, except for one. And that Ruby had had no social media presence that I could find, which was odd. Mostly everyone was on Facebook these days. My parents joined to keep up with my brother Andy, and to see photos of his wife, Amanda, and son, Cory.

There were, of course, the newspaper clippings in the scrapbook, but they dated from the sixties. It was as though the young Ruby vanished at the age of twenty-nine, only to emerge in New Jersey as a seventy-something older woman who played for the Creston Players.

"We gotta think outside the box," Pauli said.

"Right. A deep Internet search? One of those lesser known search engines or databases you've used before? Here is some info on her: full name, age, place of birth, last known address in Creston." I placed a sheet of paper in front of him.

Pauli cracked his knuckles. His fingers hovered above the keyboard. "Yeah. Gotta dive deeper." He paused. "But like we have to do some lateral thinking."

Lateral thinking? Where did the kid come up with his ideas? "Like what?"

"Like we had this creativity class at school last month, and we worked on stuff that challenges preconceptions." He waited for me to catch up.

"Right."

"Yeah, so like we solved puzzles by spinning problems around. You know like here's one. It's about a murder," he said knowingly. "The police come to a house to arrest a suspect named John. They don't know anything else about him but he's definitely in the house. They bust in and see a truck driver, a firefighter, a mechanic, and a carpenter. They're all playing poker. The cops arrest the firefighter. They totally got their man." He stopped.

"I'm supposed to solve this by thinking laterally..." The poker playing comment reminded me I was hosting the game tonight, and needed to spruce up my home before everyone arrived. My place wasn't as large as my house down the shore, but its five rooms suited my lifestyle: small enough to keep presentable; large enough to entertain friends, like tonight's poker party.

Pauli slouched down in his seat.

"Don't tell me!" I played with several possibilities, then conceded. "I give."

"The firefighter's the only man. The rest of them are women." His eyes sparkled in triumph.

"I see what you mean. We come at Ruby from another direction?"

"Like what if you forgot about Indiana and focused on New Jersey or other places? Like what if she was living here all the time after her career tanked or whatever?"

The hairs on the back of my necked tingled. "Like hiding in plain sight." I had been so stuck on Indiana I hadn't entertained the possibility that Ruby had been living in other locations—including the New Jersey area—during the past decades. My great aunt Maureen would be proud. Many years ago, when my middle school science fair project bombed—my lab partner and I were measuring the effects of Coke on raw meat, when her puppy saw his chance for an early dinner and devoured our experiment in one bite—she said, *"Dorothy dear, if you can't change the direction of the wind, adjust your sails."* We did a poster board on photosynthesis and won third prize.

"Yeah or like what if she had jobs playing the piano for other places?" he said enthusiastically.

My mind was buzzing. The kid was onto something. I jumped up and planted a kiss on the top of his head. "Pauli, you're a genius!"

He ducked his head and blushed. "Whatever."

Pauli never ceased to amaze me. "Maybe we should check those search engines with New Jersey in mind?"

Pauli was way ahead of me. I left him to his own devices—crosschecking obscure databases with Ruby's information—and prepared a couple of chip dips. I planned to leave the culinary heavy lifting to Bill. I needed to text the poker players and tell them about dinner. They would be thrilled to taste test Bill's recipe.

"Awesome!"

I gazed at Pauli, shaggy brown hair hanging over his forehead. "What?"

He shoved his laptop across the table so that I could see the screen. There was a picture of a younger Ruby from 1990. She was not quite fifty, but her facial features were shocking for a young woman: deep lines around her mouth, sagging eyelids. Pauli's lateral thinking was close, if not exact. Ruby hadn't been living in New Jersey at the time the photo was taken. She was living in a town in western Ohio, and the article described a high school choral performance accompanied by Miss Veronica Passonata.

"Pauli that's great work!" Finally, something concrete. Ruby had lived in Ohio after her touring ended. She'd gotten work as an accompanist.

"And like, yeah, her real name was Veronica. Believe that?"

There was no mention of "Veronica" in the scrapbook. I guessed that name was relinquished in favor of Ruby when she was growing up.

My cell phone chirped. It was Carol texting to see if Pauli was here working on the Windjammer website. Our cover, whenever I needed Pauli for some covert digital detective work. "Better call home," I said. "Your mom's checking in."

Pauli grunted, tapped Carol's number, and carried on a monosyllabic conversation with his mother. "Uh...yeah...okay. Now?" He handed his cell phone to me.

"Hi Carol."

"Dodie, I'm so excited. I've always wanted to learn poker. What can I bring?"

I thanked Carol for the offer. I explained that Bill had agreed to serve as chef tonight, and was serving one of his favorite pasta dishes. Carol gushed over Bill's thoughtfulness and insisted she contribute dessert. I agreed, and told her I'd send Pauli on his way soon. I clicked off. "Time for you head home."

"Yeah. Gotta bounce. Want to do more searches tomorrow?" he asked. "Like there are some cool police and government databases I can access."

Pauli was raring to go! "I'll let you know. Meanwhile, let's keep quiet about our discovery."

"Like, I never forget the first rule of digital forensics," he said.

"Confidentiality. Thanks Pauli."

"Yeah, cause like even dead people deserve their privacy."

Sensible words from someone barely legal.

* * * *

"I call it Captain Jack's spaghetti carbonara. The recipe came from an old precinct buddy of mine from Philly." Bill laid out the ingredients for his dinner, and politely accepted the oohs and aahs of the poker gang as they observed him working.

"I've wanted to make this dish for years, but Vernon has high cholesterol," said Mildred.

"I'd love the recipe...Bill," Edna said and tittered. The others snickered. Edna was off duty, as was Bill, and calling him by his first name was a new experience—one that made her slightly self-conscious.

Bill was undoubtedly rolling his inner eyes, but all he said was "Sure."

"What's the secret, Bill?" asked Lola brightly.

"Two kinds of bacon." He cut the Canadian variety into thin strips. "And whipping cream."

"Yummy," Carol said.

I felt certain Bill needed a break from the admiration society, but to my surprise, he seemed both amused and flattered by all of the attention. Who was this guy and what had he done with my boyfriend? "Let's go into the dining room and I'll explain the basics of poker until the food is ready," I said easing my way into the center of the group. No one budged; all of them were consumed with Bill separating egg yolks from egg whites.

"I had this dish once. It's kind of like bacon and eggs on pasta," said Penny, who had joined us at the last minute to replace Jocelyn who'd heard that Walter, a realtor when he wasn't presiding over the Etonville Little Theatre, had an open house this afternoon in Bernridge. Pretending to want to purchase a home was a good way to get Walter to notice her, or so she thought. How Walter would react when he caught wind of what Jocelyn was up to was anybody's guess.

"...you fry both until they're cooked, but not crusty." Bill lifted the skillet and poured bacon grease into a can. "You want to keep about three tablespoons in the pan."

"Just three?" asked Carol.

"Uh-huh, and then you add whipping cream and simmer. Keep one eye on the pasta." He scanned his audience.

Had I created a cooking class monster? I finished setting the table. I'd splurged on an expensive bottle of red wine. I'd thought Bill might deserve extra consideration tonight. Although judging from the concentration of his rapt spectators, extra consideration was the last thing he needed.

* * * *

"Simply delicious," said Mildred and the others nodded, mouths full.

I passed the bread and poured the wine. "So I'll explain basic poker rules while we eat. That way we can get into the game sooner."

"I'm going to need something a little more physical after this," said Carol, taking a bite of her spaghetti.

"Me too, but it's worth every calorie," said Lola.

"I'd say the chief has performed a 10-61," said Edna. "Miscellaneous public service!"

Everyone agreed.

"So O'Dell, what're we playing? I say five card draw, jacks or better to open, progressive," Penny said.

The group looked startled.

"We'll begin with easy games, Penny. Dealer's choice. The buy-in will be a dollar—"

"Is that all?" said Mildred. "I expected to lose my shirt," she giggled.

"You can always buy more chips later." I shuffled the cards. "We'll play seven card stud. That's three cards down and four up."

"Low spade in the hole splits the pot?" Penny asked.

"Let's keep it simple for now—"

"Can you pass me the cheat sheet?" asked Carol.

I'd written out the list of hands in order from a single pair to a straight flush. *Little chance of that.*

"How's the meal, ladies?" Bill stuck his head into the dining room.

"Delicious!" Mildred said, and the rest of the table chimed in.

"Join us?" asked Lola.

"No thanks. Wouldn't want to interrupt the game. I'll eat in the bedroom."

There was a beat as everyone registered Bill's familiarity with the layout of my house. He must have realized how it sounded, and his normally ruddy face turned a deeper shade of crimson. "I'll just go…there," he mumbled and beat a hasty retreat.

As soon as he was out of sight, everyone focused on me.

"Such a nice guy." Carol.

"So thoughtful." Mildred.

"And hunky." Lola.

"You are one lucky gal." Edna.

"O'Dell, you know what they say…" Penny.

I couldn't imagine.

"Love makes the world go underground."

Geez.

* * * *

Within the hour, we had cleared the dishes, distributed the chips, and I'd introduced the poker neophytes to seven card stud and Texas Hold 'Em.

"I forget. Which is higher, three of a kind, or two pair?" Mildred asked.

"Three of a kind," I said and shuffled the cards.

"Is there a wild card this time? I like wild cards," said Lola. "They always give you an extra edge."

"Wild cards are for newbies. Real poker players don't need 'em," said Penny, and she pushed her glasses up her nose.

"Well, I'm a newbie so bring on the wild cards," said Carol, and she took a bite of tiramisu. When she'd learned what Bill was cooking, she'd insisted on keeping with the Italian theme. She stared at Lola. "With your hair like that, swept over one shoulder, I'm seeing Veronica Lake."

"Who?" asked Penny.

"An actress from the forties. She's in a lot of late night classic movies," I said.

"I see the resemblance," said Mildred.

Lola smiled serenely. "I've been told that before. Whose deal is it?"

Before I could stop myself—must have been the wine—I blurted out today's finding. "Did any of you know that Ruby's actual name was Veronica?"

"What?" asked Lola.

Penny attempted to put a lid on this particular bit of trivia. "She never said anything to me about her real name. If her name were Veronica, I'd know about it. It would be in the production notes."

"Well, looks like she kept a secret from you," I said.

"Dodie, how do you know that?" asked Lola.

Mentioning Ruby had the effect of a wet blanket. It brought everyone back to the harsh reality of the murder, and they gawked at me, waiting for an answer. "I was fooling around on the Internet, and when I Googled Ruby's name...up came some links that led me to an article about her life in Indiana. It referred to her as Veronica R. Passonata. I guess the R was for Ruby," I finished lamely.

Carol whistled softly, Mildred and Edna jiggled their heads, and Penny adamantly refused to believe that something as important as an actor's name had gotten past her clipboard. Lola was silent, her face full of questions. They would have to wait until later.

"Were there other things about Ruby we didn't know?" Mildred wondered.

"Like what?" I asked.

"She tipped the shampoo girls with a twenty dollar bill once," said Carol.

"Really? She didn't look like she had money to spare," said Mildred. "Anyway, she kept to herself."

"One time, during a rehearsal break, I caught her typing on an iPad. She thought I was looking over her shoulder and turned it over. Told me to mind my own business," Penny offered. "As if I cared that she was surfing the Internet for investment websites."

"So you *were* looking over her shoulder?" Lola asked.

Penny sat up straighter. "As PM I gotta keep eyes and ears on everything and everyone," she said sternly.

"Investments? Ruby never seemed to have more than two pennies to rub together," said Carol.

"She certainly could be starchy," said Edna. "Might have been the..." Edna tipped her hand upward to mime Ruby and her flask.

The game was on hold. "Is that all we know about Ruby? Her drinking, her finances, or lack thereof?" Never mind that I was privy to Bill's discovery of her Excel spreadsheet with the record of regular thousand dollar payments.

"Ruby could play the ivory off the piano keys," said Edna.

"Dodie and I searched her apartment for the cue sheets. It was so clean and neat. No full ashtrays or empty liquor bottles." Lola said. "It didn't seem like Ruby at all."

"She gave me vegan recipes," Penny blurted out.

We all gawked at her. "You're a vegan?" Lola asked.

"Not yet. But I'm thinking of becoming healthy," Penny said defensively.

"Ruby smoked and drank but was a vegan? Talk about a mystery," I said. Everyone nodded in agreement.

Edna stood. "Have a code 8." She hurried off to the bathroom and poker night ended.

As I cleaned up the dining room, I mulled over one piece of information. Penny's snooping confirmed Ruby's interest in investments. My cell rang. I didn't recognize the caller ID.

"Hello?"

"Is this Dodie O'Dell?"

"Professor Yurkov?" I said.

"Yes. I hope I am not calling you too late," Boris said apologetically.

"Not at all."

"I remembered the name of Ruby's young man. It was Otto."

We talked another minute, Boris repeating his surprise at Ruby's state of mind the day he overheard the argument. He thanked me again for the cannoli, and extended an open invitation to drop in whenever I was in Manhattan. He was a thoughtful man.

I turned off the lights. Otto was an unusual name. Where had I seen it before?

12

The clanging alarm yanked me from a deep sleep. I reached out and slapped the snooze button, one eye peeking out from under a tired lid. I'd been restless until three a.m. Thoughts tumbled around my mind like wet clothes in the dryer. I finally surrendered to sheer exhaustion. Ruby had taken up residence in my brain and every fact I knew about her kept replaying on a mental loop. I rolled over and extended my arm to the pillow where Bill's head should have been. It was empty. I didn't have a chance to discuss Boris's phone call last night, as Bill was already snoring when I dragged myself to bed. Apparently, he rose early. I slipped on a sweat suit and headed to the kitchen where I could smell fresh coffee. Yes! A shot of caffeine would do the trick.

"Thanks for the coffee," I said as I rounded the corner into the kitchen.

There was no sign of Bill but a scribbled note on the table, indicated that his presence was required in the department at eight a.m. this morning. I drank a cup of coffee, and jumped in the shower, letting the warm water stream off my head and neck. I needed some oomph to face the day and complete my to do list. That meant two things: dressing for comfort in capris and a lightweight cotton blouse, and stopping by Coffee Heaven for a caramel macchiato.

My street was empty for a change; no need to share trivia with the neighbors or hear them ask how Bill was doing. The day was bright and sunny, a clear, beautiful, summer morning with a gentle breeze and puffy clouds sailing across the blue expanse. On days like this down the shore, my mother used to call the clouds heaven's cotton balls.

I traveled over Ames and down Fairfield. Etonville was just waking up, a line of cars inched down Main, herky-jerky, grabbing parking spots. I took a chance and crept into a space by a hydrant. I only planned to be a minute in Coffee Heaven, and sent a request to the parking gods to keep the town's meter maid busy until I returned.

As I opened the door, the tinkling of the welcome bells mingled with the chatter of patrons creating a pleasant blanket of white noise. I stepped to the counter. Jocelyn looked up from a booth where she was pouring coffee and hurried to my side.

"Dodie, am I glad to see you," she said, breathless.

"Hi Jocelyn. I'll have my regular—and extra icing on the cinnamon roll."

"Sorry to miss the poker game, but yesterday I was a woman on a mission," she said confidentially.

"It was fine. Penny filled in. How did it go?"

She wrote up my ticket. "That Walter can be thick. Know what I mean?"

Oh yeah. "What happened?"

"I hung around the open house until everybody else was gone, then kind of edged my way to where Walter was standing, staring off into space." She mimicked Walter's stance. "He can be a little quirky too."

Takes one to know one. "Sure," I said.

"So I said, 'I'm interested in this house.' And he said, 'Jocelyn?' Like that. 'Jocelyn?'" She seemed overwhelmed by Walter's attention.

"Then what?"

"What do you mean 'then what'?"

"I mean, what happened next? Did he say anything else?" I asked.

"He didn't need to. He said my name. That was enough." Jocelyn floated off to get my order.

All it took for Jocelyn to walk on air was Walter saying her name...I wanted to laugh, but then I remembered the first time Bill said "Dodie." I got it.

* * * *

I unlocked the door of the Windjammer. There was an hour before anyone would show up, and I relished the quiet. My caramel macchiato and warm cinnamon bun kept me company. I sat in my back booth with vegetable and meat inventory sheets and Henry's menu for the week, attempting to reconcile the two. He planned to serve his traditional meat loaf tonight as a special, but decided to let Wilson have his way with it. Both the Windjammer and the regular customers of the Windjammer relied on the old standbys; sometimes folks needed food they could count on. Wilson was not into old standbys.

Fajitas and shrimp with pasta were on the menu this week as well, along with an experiment suggested by Wilson for tomorrow: a tapas menu featuring a variety of small plates. It seemed like a good idea at the time, but his lineup included various flatbreads, chorizo-filled dates wrapped in bacon, lamb meatballs, fingerling potatoes, vegetable skewers, and simple small salads. They sounded delicious, but preparation-heavy. We'd need all hands on deck, which meant confirming that Enrico and Carmen could work that night.

I made notes on the meals, and found myself scribbling in the margin of the inventory sheet. *Ruby: thousand dollar deposits, twenty dollar tips to salon girls, Ruby and Dale discussing finances*…money issues swirled around her. What did it all mean? Finally, there was Boris's memory: *hers was a voice full of vengeance.*

My cell binged. It was Lola texting: *Veronica? What was that about? What are you not telling me? I'll stop by WJ.* Today would be a good time to fill Lola in on my trip to New York.

The front door opened in a whoosh. Henry, frowning, his shoulders stooped, tromped in and plopped onto a barstool. He looked completely defeated.

"Hey, it can't be that bad. Is it Wilson? He's coming along and by the way, your Saturday night contest winner was a hit. I overheard audience members raving about your chicken and cauliflower."

Henry waved me off. "It's not the restaurant."

"Oh. So…?"

"My future son-in-law's parents are meeting us in New York tomorrow. My wife has this whole day planned."

"Nice," I said hopefully.

"I told her I can't close down the restaurant for the night," he said darkly. He raised his chin. "The only option is Wilson."

Wilson would be chef for the day. In my nearly four years managing the Windjammer, Henry had closed the restaurant only twice: once for a week in August last year giving everyone a summer holiday; and once to repair leaks in the roof from ice damage. He rarely took a day off, and when he did, Enrico took over and we simplified the menu. To suggest that Henry was a control freak was an understatement. "Uh-huh," I said impassively.

"What do you think?" Henry asked.

My opinion? Shut down. But that was unfair to Wilson—after all, he was the sous chef. He was responsible for several evening specials. How much damage could he do? *Don't answer that*, I told myself. "I say give him a chance. We have small plate night planned for tomorrow…we'll need Enrico and Carmen to come in anyway."

Henry harrumphed.

"It will all work out. Good for Wilson, good for you to get a break."

Henry slumped his way into the kitchen.

Lunch was well underway. Henry's crab bisque vanished rapidly. The black bean burger—another attempt to expand the palates of Etonville—received a mixed review. Most of the patrons didn't understand why Henry didn't serve his "regular" special burgers, and leave well enough alone.

"Who needs beans on a bun?" one of the Banger sisters asked.

"They're not exactly beans, in the normal sense. They're mashed up with spices and herbs and formed into burger patties," I said. My explanation fell on deaf ears. "They're delicious."

"I'll take one," the other sister chirped. "I'd like the cheese, tomato, lettuce, and onion, but hold the beans."

"Right." I motioned to Gillian to take their order.

"Hey, O'Dell," Penny waved a menu. She was on her lunch break from the post office. "Good poker game last night. I won fifty cents," she cackled.

"High stakes," I teased. "Next time we'll have a two dollar buy-in."

"You know," she said seriously, "we should have a tournament. Like Wide World of Poker?"

"That's a thought."

"BTW, I was cleaning up the theater yesterday and I found this." She withdrew an iPad that had Ruby's name spelled out in stick-on letters, like the scrapbook.

"That's a…"

"Same one I caught Ruby surfing the web on."

The air around me shifted. "Where did you find it?" I asked.

She cleaned her glasses with the tail of her postal uniform shirt. "In the piano bench."

"Penny, you should have taken it to the police department. That might be evidence," I said, my pulse quickening.

Penny looked stricken, her mouth forming an O, and thrust the notebook at me. "You're in bed with the chief—" she caught herself. "I mean, you see him a lot so you can, you know, pass it on." She checked her watch. "Gotta get back to work." Penny jumped up and darted out of the restaurant.

Ruby used the iPad to surf the Internet! I hurried to my back booth and stuffed the notebook in my bag.

Benny rushed over. "Trouble in paradise. We ran out of crab bisque, half a dozen people returned their bean burgers, and Henry is throwing a hissy fit over Wilson's meatloaf recipe. You better get in there."

"On my way," I said and bounded into the kitchen.

* * * *

Lola picked at her Cobb salad dumbfounded. I'd recounted my trip to Maynard Institute on Saturday, and swore her to secrecy regarding Pauli's poking around on the Internet. She was, after all, my BFF. I had to unload my findings on someone besides Bill, who was appreciative but not as fascinated as I was about Ruby's background.

"Dodie, about Ruby…you are…" She searched for the right word.

"Obsessed?" I offered.

Lola nodded.

"I know. But I can't get her life story out of my mind. Now that I know her real name was Veronica, I'm more intrigued than ever."

"But what does her background have to do with her murder?"

"Nothing, probably. Bill and the Creston police are investigating everyone she had contact with at both theaters, but I don't know what they've discovered. I'm out of the loop." Not completely, I thought. After all, Bill did share details of her death and his finding the Excel spreadsheet. But, so far, no mention of persons of interest. "I'm not a part of the investigation."

"But you are looking into Ruby's life," Lola said.

I was. We chatted awhile longer, and then Lola left. She was meeting Walter at the theater to review notes before Wednesday's brush-up rehearsal—also to review Lola's relationship with Dale…

It was nearing three o'clock, the usual time for my late afternoon break when the Windjammer was most quiet. I needed some fresh air and a breather from the chaos of the day before the evening mayhem began. I had just enough time to complete my plan of action.

I placed my lunch plate in the dirty dish bin. "Benny, I'll be back in a while."

"I'd like to leave early tonight? Need to put the princess to bed."

The princess was Benny's six-year-old daughter. His wife worked some nights, and when she did, Benny did solo parenting.

"When dinner is up and running, you can take off."

"Appreciate it." He lowered his voice. "Heard about Henry leaving the kitchen in Wilson's hands tomorrow."

"I think Wilson is up to it." I crossed my fingers.

The humidity had increased from this morning, I noticed, as I climbed into the driver's seat of my Metro. The brilliant blue sky was overcast with gunmetal-gray clouds. Never mind, I'd deal with the raindrops. I backed out of my space and hit the gas. By my calculation, I could drive to Creston, revisit Ruby's apartment, and be back in an hour or so. I kept my plan to myself. I didn't even share my intentions with Lola. How could I explain that my instincts were in a tug-of-war with my common sense when it came to the accompanist? I had the intense feeling that if I could find the correct piece of her life's puzzle, I'd have Ruby figured out. Bill and his colleagues could arrest whomever for her death; I'd have deciphered her life.

Traffic was light on State Route 53, and I hit the outskirts of the city in twenty minutes. My GPS Genie helped me retrace the route that Lola and I took on our first visit: Barrow Street to Hamilton Avenue. I parked my Metro down the block from Ruby's apartment building, walked past the tavern and post office, and stopped at the door of the deli. On a whim, I walked in. Behind the counter, a young man with a cheerful countenance, curly brown hair, and a full beard acknowledged my presence.

"Can I help you?" he said.

"I'll have a regular coffee, black," I said, and smiled back.

"Coming right up."

While he fixed my drink, I looked around. The store was empty, the shelves half full, the floor tile was worn and grimy. I was willing to bet this deli had seen better days.

"Here you go." He set my cup on the counter and I handed him a five dollar bill.

While he made change, I took a sip of my coffee. "Um. Good. You make this?"

"Yeah. I do everything," he said, a tad ruefully. "My uncle owns the store, but he's been ill lately. Anyway, not much business around here." He handed me some change.

"I wouldn't know about that. I'm from Etonville."

"Never been there," he said.

"I get over here a lot. In fact, the Creston Players are doing a show with the Etonville Little Theatre. You heard about it? *Bye, Bye, Birdie*?" I asked.

"Not much into theater. Usually here anyway."

I was starting to feel for the guy. A deli that was ready to go out of business consumed his life. "A friend of mine used to live across the street. Ruby Passonata? She was the accompanist for the Creston Players." I paused to see if her name rang a bell.

The clerk frowned. "Don't know her."

"She died in Etonville a week ago. Really tragic. She was—"

"Murdered! Yeah, I read about that. She used to come in here."

My radar system freaked out. "She did?" I asked.

"I didn't know her name. I saw her picture in the paper," he said. "She was one nice lady."

Again, a description that was at odds with the Ruby I knew. "Why do you say that?" I was truly curious.

"She always asked how I was doing. Ordered the same thing. Coffee, cream, two sugars, and a bagel with cream cheese. And she always left me a great tip." He nodded at the tip jar by the register.

Oops…I was still clutching the change from my bill, which I deposited in the glass container. "That's nice. I felt bad about her being all alone," I said sincerely. "I don't think she had many friends. I never saw her with anyone."

"Me neither. Except for that one time last week."

"One time?"

"Yeah she came in with this guy. He looked a little tense while she ordered, didn't say anything. She looked like she got a kick out of him feeling uncomfortable."

Now *that* was the Ruby I knew. Was Dale the man she made so uneasy?

"I think I know who he was. An actor from the Creston Players…leading man type, handsome, broad shoulders," I said, and then added, "Black hair."

The guy considered my description. "Not sure."

"Do you remember what day Ruby came in here with him?"

He stared at the ceiling. "Last Monday morning. A week ago."

The morning of the last rehearsal that Ruby attended. A cold chill ran down my spine, though the deli was warm and stuffy.

"Why are you asking about her? Are you involved with the police?" His friendly, open face shut down, replaced by a wary, suspicious one.

"Me? No. I'm a friend…who feels terrible about her death. She went too soon," I said.

The guy relaxed a bit. "Yeah. I agree."

I stepped into the gloom of the late afternoon and checked my watch. I had to hustle if I was going to get into Ruby's apartment and then back to the Windjammer in time for the dinner rush. I hurried across the street and through the courtyard, with its fractured walkway and patchy brown grass. Nothing had changed since Lola and I were here a few days ago. I pressed the super's button, tapped my foot impatiently as I awaited a response. Nikolas might be away, or doing repairs in someone's apartment.

I hadn't thought of that. Now what? I was about to give up when a voice boomed out of the speaker.

"Yes?"

It was the same Eastern European accent. "Nikolas? Hi, I'm Dodie, Ruby's friend. Could I speak with you?"

There was a moment of silence. "Come in."

The buzzer sounded and I opened the door. Nikolas met me in the lobby within seconds, dressed in a similar plaid work shirt and tool belt, as before. He was reluctant to let me back into Ruby's apartment, especially since the police had been there and, apparently, had scrubbed the place for evidence. What could I possibly want to see now? What indeed. But I was prepared.

"Ruby had some books she'd been meaning to give me. And then she died before she could."

"You were her friend?"

"No" was ready to hop out of my mouth, but if a friend was someone who was concerned about your welfare—dead or alive—then maybe I was becoming Ruby's friend. "Yes," I said, and it didn't feel like I was lying.

Nikolas beckoned me to follow him into the elevator. Again, we rode in silence to the third floor and walked down the hallway to Ruby's unit.

"I will be back in ten minutes," he said. It was an order.

I entered the apartment, and, as Nikolas kept me under observation, beat a straight path to Ruby's bookshelves, touching several volumes until Nikolas shut the door. I looked around. Everything was much as before except that the investigators searched the bookshelves—tossing books on their sides. They left the cupboards in her efficiency kitchen open. Ruby's laptop was missing.

I thrust my hand into my bag. In the rush to get to Creston, I'd forgotten I had Ruby's iPad. I needed to get it to Bill. I scanned the room again. Was there anything else here, besides the scrapbook, which might provide a clue to Ruby's life? I skimmed the books, opened and closed drawers and the cupboards. Nothing but a minimal number of dishes, silverware, assorted packaged foods, and canned goods. I dashed into her bedroom. The bed was unmade, the wardrobe door ajar, with clothing pushed to one side. I assumed the police had done a thorough search. The dresser drawers were half-filled with underwear, socks, sleeping gear, and tee shirts. "Speak to me," I whispered.

As if some otherworldly spirit had heeded my call, I walked over to a bedside table. I yanked on the drawer but it was empty except for a pack of cigarettes and a flashlight. I felt around the inside of the drawer, and then yanked it out. I reached into the opening and my hand touched paper. I carefully withdrew a yellowed newspaper article. Folded in half, it was from the *Greenburg Chronicle* dated August 1986. Ruby's hometown paper...

Nikolas's voice in the hallway jerked me out of my reverie. "You are the second person to come to Ruby's apartment today. I left a woman here before."

Instinct told me I didn't want to meet whomever was in the hallway with Nikolas. Maybe it was the police. I'd told Bill I'd sworn off murder investigations and I'd meant it.

Nikolas's key turned in the lock. I panicked and dove under the bed. It was a tight squeeze and I struggled to inch my way toward the wall. I shut my eyes hoping that if I couldn't see them, they couldn't see me. I heard the thud of footsteps as they entered the apartment.

"Hello?" Nikolas said. "She must have left." He sounded peeved. "You see the size of the piano. It's gonna take four guys to get it out of here. You want to measure it now?"

The other party must have given his assent, because Nikolas continued to talk about the piano, the difficulty of removing it, Mets baseball, and the weather.

Though the rest of the apartment was neat and orderly, someone had neglected to mop under the bed. Dust bunnies were everywhere, my nose so dangerously close to inhaling one; I had to bury my face in my arm to stop a sneeze. Not a smart thing to do, according to Aunt Maureen. *Stifling a sneeze could cause the brain to explode*, she'd told me. Her warning gave me nightmares as a kid, so I sneezed regularly. I edged forward until my head was near the frame of the bed. I craned my neck to see around the half open door, but all I could spot were Nikolas's work boots and the hem of his jeans. Nothing of the other person in Ruby's living room.

A cell phone rang. "Hello?" said Nikolas. Silence. "Okay. Be right there." He must have ended the call. "Hey, have to go. When you finish, shut the door behind you. It'll lock on its own."

The apartment was eerily quiet, except for the pounding of my heart. Footsteps thudded again and now, from my location beneath the bed, I could see white sneakers for a moment before they disappeared. In my sight and out of my sight as though the man was walking back and forth. Was the person searching for something? All of a sudden, the sneakers vanished. Had he left? I heard a soft bump like a cabinet door closing and the outer door slam shut. He was gone.

I waited a full ten minutes, and then scooted out from under Ruby's bed. My back was sore from holding myself at an odd angle; maybe it had been silly to hide from them. After all, Nikolas had given me permission to be there. Who was the other person?

I inspected the living area. Nothing was out of place. I grabbed two books off a stack on the shelf, crept to the door, cracked it open an inch, and scanned the corridor. Then I remembered the "soft thud." The bathroom! I looked inside the medicine cabinet. The Ambien was gone. My neck hairs danced in a frenzy. Had the police taken it? Or the visitor to Ruby's apartment?

In the hallway, the coast was clear. I sprinted to the Exit sign and ran down the stairs to the first floor. I hesitated as I grasped the handle, composing myself. I'd have to be convincing if I bumped into Nikolas. I would have to explain how I checked Ruby's books and left the apartment. Needing the exercise, I walked down the stairs but then I sprained my ankle and I had to sit down and...blah, blah, blah.

I casually limped into the lobby. Nikolas was nowhere to be found. I race-walked to the exit, flew out the door, and shuffled my way to the Metro, in case Nikolas happened to see me. My heart was doing double time as I dove into the front seat. It was ten minutes to five. I was running late so I cranked the engine and pulled away from the curb, blowing down Hamilton, hitting every green light. I barely slowed down as I sailed through intersection after intersection. The entrance to State Route 53 was half a mile down the road.

My trip to Creston was very successful. I discovered that Ruby had contact with a man the morning of the day she died; that Ruby kept an old hometown newspaper article tucked away for safe-keeping—instead of pasting it in her scrapbook; that someone was in her apartment measuring her piano for removal; and that that someone *might* have taken her Ambien. How did it all add up?

I darted onto the highway, my mind mulling things over. Traffic was heavy, but in the past, I'd usually keep my Metro in the slow lane and maintain the speed limit. Tonight was an exception. I put the pedal to the metal and stayed in the passing lane. Things were dicey enough at the Windjammer with Henry taking off tomorrow and Wilson experimenting with his small plate menu. They didn't need me waltzing in later than usual—

A black Honda Civic in the slow lane whizzed by me, and a pick-up truck began riding my back bumper. I veered into the right lane and tapped the brakes—nothing happened. The brake pedal hit the floor, but my Metro maintained sixty miles an hour. My breath caught in my throat. What was wrong with my brakes? I was approaching an SUV in front of me and now the Honda Civic zipped back into my lane, squeezing itself between me and the SUV. I pumped the brakes ferociously knowing, rationally, that there was something drastically wrong—no amount of applied force would stop my car. I kept my foot off the accelerator, held the steering wheel steady, and frantically surveyed the shoulder ahead for a place to stop. I flicked on the emergency flashers. The car behind me grew impatient, as I slowed and I wound down the window and gestured for it to go around me. Meanwhile, the Honda zoomed out of my lane again, and harassed a much larger automobile in the passing lane. Where were the state police when you needed them? The shoulder was a narrow strip of tarmac, with a drop off down a steep embankment. Not promising. There was an exit ahead. If I could make it to that spot, I could coast onto the ramp and off the road.

I sat forward and gripped the wheel with clammy hands, my breathing ragged, my pulse throbbing. The exit was coming up. I eased my Metro to the shoulder, then steered off the highway onto the ramp. I turned the wheel gently, rolling into a patch of dirt and gravel, and jammed on the emergency brake. My car shuddered to a halt.

13

Timothy scratched his head and replaced his ball cap. "What you got here is a failure of the brake system. Your brake fluid moves from the pedal to the brake-line system." He gazed at the underside of my car which was perched atop his hydraulic lift. "Liquids can't be compressed so they move around." He whooshed his hands back and forth, and shifted his gaze to make sure I grasped his automotive explanation.

"So what caused the brakes to fail?" I asked.

"Well, the movement pushes against the instrument that stops the vehicle. When the fluid…"

"The brake fluid?"

"That's right. When the brake fluid runs low, you got a problem," he said. No kidding. "How low was my brake fluid?"

Timothy formed a goose egg with his thumb and forefinger. "Zilch."

How did that happen? I drove to Creston with no problem. What had occurred in the time I was in Ruby's apartment? "I don't understand. I didn't see anything leaking."

"I'll take a look and figure it out. Meanwhile, I'll get you a ride back to the Windjammer. You gotta stay on top of car maintenance," he said, reminding me of my father.

"Thanks Timothy." I'd texted Benny and Henry while I'd waited for the tow truck back on Route 53 to let them know I would be late. That was five thirty. It was now seven o'clock.

Timothy assured me that I could pick up the Metro in a couple of days, and that it would be safe to drive. Meanwhile, he'd drop me off at the Windjammer since I declined his offer of a loaner until tomorrow. My cell rang and I checked the caller ID.

"Hi stranger," I said, deepening my voice. "You slipped away early this morning."

"I had an appointment with the Creston department at eight a.m." Bill was irritated.

"Anyway I was about to text you. I had a—"

"I received a call from them half an hour ago. They got a call from the super in Ruby's apartment. Evidently, a woman, whom he'd met before, stopped by and asked to get in to the apartment to take some books. He got suspicious when she disappeared."

Geez. Why did Nikolas have to rat me out to the Creston police?

"Her description sounded familiar."

His unspoken accusation filled the silence.

"I can explain," I said.

"Dodie, you promised you would stay out of the investigation."

I didn't exactly promise…

"And now the Creston police are getting their noses out of joint." He exhaled loudly.

"Sorry."

"What were you looking for anyway? We'd already gone over her place. There was nothing to find."

What about the newspaper article? "I'm not sure. I have this feeling about Ruby—"

"And the sudden end of her career. I know."

I'd always believed that the best defense was a good offense. "Did the Creston police mention that someone else was in the apartment? A guy measuring the piano for removal?"

"How do you know that?" he asked.

"I was there." Oops…how was I going to explain my time under Ruby's bed inhaling dust?

"What?"

"Look, I was in Ruby's apartment. As I was leaving, the super and another guy arrived. I overheard the super mention measuring the piano." Partly true. The part that mattered most, anyway.

"Dodie, that doesn't make sense. How did—"

"But do the police know that? They should be investigating this piano-measurer. Maybe he was a friend of Ruby's who knows something."

I had a sudden thought. Could he have been the same guy who accompanied Ruby to the deli? I heard muffled speech, then Bill came back on his cell. "I gotta go."

"See you tonight?" I asked.

"I doubt it. Might be a late one here." He ended the call.

Might be a late one here...what kind of a romantic sign-off was that? I had pushed one too many of Bill's law enforcement buttons.

* * * *

"Sorry, sorry," I said hastily as I rushed into the restaurant. "Benny, you can take off."

"Are you okay? What happened to your car," Benny asked as he whipped off his apron.

"I lost my brakes." I inspected the dining room, which was half full at the moment. "Apparently, I ran out of fluid."

"On the highway?" Benny asked aghast. "You could have had a bad accident. Or worse."

I avoided contemplating the obvious. "Yeah, I was lucky."

Benny grabbed my hand. "Are you shaking? You'd better sit down. I should stay. I can call the babysitter—"

I tugged my hand away, gave him a gentle shove, and pointed toward the door. "Go. Take care of the princess."

Benny left and I collapsed onto a barstool.

Lola texted: *I heard you almost got killed and your car is totaled!!!* I texted back: *All good. Can you pick me up at closing?* Lola agreed to be here at eleven.

Gillian had the dining room in hand and Carmen was picking up the bar, so I took a moment to let reality seep in. I could have been killed. I could have killed someone else. Goosebumps emerged on my arms. Something was going on.

* * * *

"*Do-dee*, I hear you have *ze* accident?" Wilson said dramatically. His brown eyes concerned. He reached for me.

I backed off. "Oh...uh...I'm fine."

"You need *ze* bicycle instead of *ze* car," he said.

That wasn't a bad idea. Carmen was closing the bar and Gillian was wiping down the tables. Henry had offered to lock up since he would be off work tomorrow. This meet-the-in-laws event was taking a toll on his mood which was iffy under the best of circumstances. Wilson was making some last minute edits to the tapas menu.

"All set to run the kitchen tomorrow?" I asked him.

"It is my dream!" He hummed "A Lot of Livin' to Do" from *Bye, Bye, Birdie*, and when he couldn't contain himself, he burst into song. He had a deep, rich baritone.

"Wow, you have a lovely voice, Wilson."

He leaned closer. "Thank you *Do-dee*. When I am growing up in Haiti, I see American musicals on DVD. I learn English that way."

"And you know all the lyrics to that song," I said. "Impressive."

"I know words to *all* songs," he said soberly as though we were two conspirators discussing plans for a bank robbery.

"You know all of the songs in *Bye, Bye, Birdie*?" I asked, surprised.

"Dances too. I see once…" He snapped his fingers. "…and learn." His eyes twinkled.

"Amazing."

Henry bounded out of the kitchen as Lola rushed in the door.

"How are you? Are you hurt?" Lola asked, examining me.

Henry snapped, "Dodie, I need to see the final draft of tomorrow's menu."

"I'm fine," I said to Lola, and pivoted to Henry who needed to get a grip.

"Time to let go, chef. Wilson has everything under control," I said with more confidence than I felt. After several words to Wilson, and a demand that Henry enjoy himself tomorrow, I trailed Lola outside to her car.

"Are you really okay?" Lola asked, as she backed out of her parking space.

I surrendered to the luxury of her Lexus. I was loyal to my Chevy Metro, but after a day like this, Lola's ride was soothing to my weary body. I reassured her that I was perfectly safe, that Timothy was checking out the brakes and missing fluid, and that all I needed was a glass of wine and a good night's sleep. Lola agreed to join me for the nightcap.

We sat on the sofa in my living room, glasses in hand, shoes off. I'd recounted my trip to Creston, conversation with the kid in the deli, and escapade hiding under Ruby's bed. Lola's eyes expanded with each bit of information. Instinct told me to keep quiet about the newspaper clipping I'd pinched from Ruby's nightstand.

Lola asked, "Who are these men?"

"I don't know but I'm going to have a talk with Bill about them tomorrow." *When I hand over Ruby's iPad.*

The open windows invited the evening air and the comforting night song of the cicadas.

"Where's Bill tonight?" Lola asked.

"Working late in the municipal building. What about Dale?"

"He said he has meetings with clients. All of them seem to be in the midst of financial crises." She fluttered her arm dismissively and took a big gulp of her wine. "Dale's so irritated and unpredictable lately. I'm beginning to think I was mistaken about him."

"Meaning?"

"That he was serious boyfriend material," she said.

"I'm sorry to hear that." *Looked like the bloom was off this particular rose.* Love *was* blind, despite the perspective of Great Aunt Maureen. She asked, on one occasion, *if love was blind, why was lingerie so popular?* I didn't have a good answer.

"I'm staying off dating sites forever," Lola said firmly.

"Hey, it's not over 'til it's over. Dale needs to get his head out of the world of finance and back into the theater universe. When the show is up again, I'll bet you'll have his full attention."

"I hope he's in a better mood for Wednesday's brush-up rehearsal."

We finished off the wine; Lola gave me hug, and told me again how worried she'd been. I thanked her and reminded her that's what BFFs were for. I closed the door after she left, shut the windows, and headed to my bedroom. I grabbed my bag to remove the article I'd found in Ruby's apartment. I silently bemoaned the fact that I was spending the night alone when my hand touched her iPad. I withdrew it and stared at Ruby's name on the cover. What was it Penny said? Ruby was surfing investment sites. I opened the lid and stared at the keyboard. It wasn't a brand new device. In fact, it looked well-used. I tapped on the Internet icon, and noticed that a password wasn't necessary. I was curious about Ruby's browsing history. You could tell a lot about a person by what they investigated on the Internet. I didn't know how to access it. A light bulb went on…Pauli! It was too late to text him now, but first thing in the morning.

* * * *

I gasped for air, struggling to squeeze through an opening in a tunnel, sneezing nonstop. I panicked; afraid I'd never get out. Suddenly, I burst onto a highway like a rocket, running and tripping until I found myself in a car jamming my foot on an unresponsive brake. "Help!" I yelled. "I'm going to crash!" The car kept moving. I kept screaming until an older, gray-haired woman floated in front of me. She played a piano and laughed hysterically. "Get out of my way! I'm going to hit you!" I bellowed. She ignored me and continued to pound the keys.

I thrashed back and forth to stop the car and awoke with a jerk. My body was damp, my heart throbbing. I sat up, fighting for air—another scary nightmare—a mashup of my time under Ruby's bed and the loss of my brakes. I lay down again, and plucked the sheet up to my chin. My subconscious was working overtime. What was so terrifying about the dream? It wasn't the tunnel or the brakes: it was the old lady's laughter. Ruby was hysterical at my expense…did she think my exploits on behalf of her history were ridiculous? If she were alive, she'd have choice words for me, sticking my nose into her past. I tried to picture her the last time we talked the night she died. She had the same caustic, mocking, honk of laugh as in my dream, asking if I was married, offering relationship advice. I didn't care, I told myself. Ruby wasn't here to stop me, and I didn't intend to let the murder investigation stop me either. I "had a stubborn streak," to quote Bill.

I hopped out of bed and snatched my cell phone from its charger on my bureau. I texted Pauli to see if he could meet me before he went to work at Shop N Go. *Coffee Heaven in an hour*?

I got into the shower to wash off yesterday's grime and this morning's nightmare, and reviewed my day—a meeting with Pauli, a visit to the Etonville police department to deposit the iPad and, I'd hoped, run into Bill. He had to be over his pique from my visit to Ruby's apartment. After all, that's what people in a relationship did, right? They got over things…

Pauli texted back that he'd meet me at nine. I dressed in a hurry, slipped into tan slacks and a green knit top that complimented my green eyes and auburn hair. It wouldn't hurt to give Bill a reason to stare.

Pauli was already at Coffee Heaven looking like he'd been up late, his eyelids drooped, and one arm supported his head while his other hand texted.

"Hey. Sorry to get you out this early," I said, and signaled to Jocelyn.

He snapped to attention. "No problem. Gotta be at the Shop N Go by ten. It's coupon day and everybody in town, like, goes crazy."

I could imagine. "I won't keep you long." I placed the iPad in front of him and lowered my voice. "I'd like to take a look at the browsing history."

Pauli hunched forward. "Did this belong to…?"

"Right. But mum's the word on that."

"You two look like you're doing some heavy duty business," Jocelyn said.

I jumped back, leaving my arm to cover Ruby's name on the lid of the notebook. "Hi Jocelyn. I'll have my regular. Pauli?"

Pauli ordered a soda and two cinnamon buns—plenty of sugar to get him through the havoc of coupon day.

"Any word on the 'house hunting'?" I asked. Code for her pursuit of Walter.

"I might need to put in an offer soon." She strolled away.

"So…like…uh…the iPad?"

I removed my arm and, in a flash, Pauli was tapping on the iPad keyboard. "Easy peasy if you, like, know what you're doing," he said confidently.

I clearly didn't. Jocelyn brought our breakfasts and we munched on the buns. I checked email while Pauli worked. He flipped the iPad around so that I could see a list of the topics Ruby had browsed most recently.

"Wow, thanks Pauli," I said, studying the fruits of his labor between sips of my caramel macchiato.

"Like, uh, is it there?" he asked.

"What?"

"Whatever you're looking for." He wiped icing off his mouth.

I had no idea what I was looking for. "I'm not sure but I want to see what she was up to."

"I'm checking on 'Veronica Passonata' on another search engine."

"Thanks for taking the initiative! Let me know if you find anything."

He blushed. "Yeah. Anyway...gotta bounce."

"Between us...you should show up at the *Bye, Bye, Birdie* rehearsal tomorrow night."

Pauli brightened. "Huh?"

"Let Janice know you're still in the picture," I said.

* * * *

I savored the last dregs of my coffee, and studied Ruby's browsing history. Sure enough "investing" was first on the list, followed by the *Greenburg Chronicle*. Ruby obviously wanted to stay on top of hometown news. There were also searches for stock market analyses, investment opportunities, and articles on a piano competition won by a student at a high school in Ohio. Maybe where Ruby had taught decades ago. There were also some vegan recipes. That last was a revelation despite Penny's disclosure about recipe sharing. It didn't look as though anyone had made use of Ruby's kitchen recently. I was about to close the iPad when I caught two searches at the bottom of the list: financial scams and investment fraud. It looked as though Dale had been advising her on investments, but what did these searches reveal and, more importantly, why had she done them? I glanced at my watch. It was ten-fifteen and I had to be at the Windjammer by eleven, which didn't leave much time to see Bill.

Outside, the day was already humid, the sun hot on my face. We were expecting the temperature to nestle in the mid-eighties. I strode through the municipal building, down the hallway to the dispatch window where Edna was on duty. She removed her headset.

"Hey there Dodie, heard you had a run-in on the highway? Glad to see you don't have a neck brace. Getting rear-ended is nothing to sneeze at. It could have been an 11-79…ambulance call."

"Edna, I wasn't rear-ended. My brake fluid leaked out and…" I gave up. "Is Bill in?"

Edna's console lit up and she replaced her headset, holding up a finger to indicate I should wait a minute. "Etonville Police—" She paused. "Right here." Another pause. "Copy that, Chief. 10-4." Edna looked up from her console. "That was the chief. He said to wait in his office."

"Got it."

Edna leaned out the dispatch window. "Good luck at the Windjammer today. Wilson is going to have a lot on his plate. No pun intended," she said and chuckled, jamming a pencil into her bun.

"Right." I said good-bye, continued down the hallway past Suki's desk, which was empty at the moment, and tentatively opened Bill's office door. I had been in here by myself once before. On that occasion, I peeked into a file on his desk that was, strictly speaking, off limits. My intentions were good, and the information that I had seen helped crack a murder investigation. Today, I had no ulterior motives for being here.

I marveled at how organized Bill's office was. The desk was empty—except for a neat stack of manila folders, a cup holder of pens and sharpened pencils, and a desk calendar. My attention wandered to a modestly full bookshelf. It had a Buffalo Bills pennant, and other memorabilia from his NFL days. On the wall behind his desk were team photos from his years in Cleveland. A door to my right opened to the room where Bill stored cartons of evidence from ongoing and past investigations. Yep, this place was a reflection of Bill's uncluttered state of mind—so unlike my own.

I checked my watch again. Edna didn't mention where Bill was, or what time he would show up, only that I was to wait in his office. My cell binged. It was Henry prompting me to call Cheney Brothers for the weekend's vegetable and meat order. I removed the iPad and placed it on Bill's desk. I remembered the article I'd stashed away yesterday. I pulled it out and unfolded it carefully. The paper gave off a musty odor. The article was brief, and described the death of a man from Greenburg, Indiana who had apparently committed suicide. Where had I seen this before?

My radar was on high alert. I hesitated. I might be crossing a line, but I couldn't let this opportunity vanish—besides, neither Bill nor Suki were present to ask permission. I hurried to the evidence room. It was unlocked. I inspected the metal shelving and brown boxes. Everything was dated and titled. I saw evidence from previous murder investigations in Etonville—James Angleton, Antonio DiGenza, Gordon Weeks, and now Ruby Passonata. I lifted the lid of her carton. There wasn't much to see. Her computer—bagged in plastic—and the scrapbook at the bottom of the box. I flipped to the last page of clippings. I found it—an article that was identical to the one I found in Ruby's apartment. What made this story so special—that Ruby had kept two copies of it? I reread the clipping, looking for any clue to its importance. Bingo! Now I understood why Boris Yurkov's recollection of Ruby's fight with a young man named Otto rang a bell. The name of the man in the article was Otto too. I pieced the information together. Ruby argued with someone named Otto in 1962 at Maynard Institute. Then, most likely, the same man committed suicide in 1986 and Ruby kept the clippings…as what? A memento? A regret? I replaced the scrapbook, put the lid on the evidence box, and slipped back into Bill's office where I sat down on the settee in a corner and tried to calm my whirling mind.

"You look frazzled," Bill said, standing in the doorway, jacket and cap in hand.

"H-hi," I said smoothing my slacks and adjusting my knit top.

Bill hung his cap on a coat hook, and draped his jacket on the back of his desk chair. "Apparently, I can't leave you alone for one day," he said and sat behind his desk.

"Look, I'm sorry about Ruby's apartment. I had an instinct—"

"I'm talking about the highway incident. What exactly happened? I've heard everything from 'you were rear-ended on State Route 53'—"

"Nope."

"—to 'you lost control of the steering and rebounded off a guardrail.' Were you hurt?" he asked.

Any leftover irritation from yesterday was replaced with genuine concern. I was touched.

"I'm fine. Timothy said the brake fluid must have leaked out. When I pumped them nothing happened," I said.

"That's dangerous stuff. You could have had a life-threatening accident."

"I coasted off the highway onto an exit ramp. Timothy is checking out the Metro," I said off-handedly.

"You know, that car is getting old. It's time to consider trading it in for a newer model." He loosened his tie.

I gawked at him. "Give up my Metro? Not a chance. We've been through some tough times together." I was thinking of several car chases…

"At least stay on top of the maintenance." He sounded like Timothy. "What's this?" He finally noticed Ruby's iPad.

"That's why I'm here."

"This belonged to Ruby?" he asked, surprised. "Where did you get it?"

"Sunday night at poker, Penny mentioned that she'd seen Ruby on an iPad during rehearsal breaks. In fact, Penny caught her surfing investment sites."

"So?"

"Yesterday, I saw Penny at the Windjammer, and she gave it to me. Said she found it in the piano bench. Not sure why Ruby would store it there."

Bill looked wary. "What's on it?"

"You're the investigator," I said. "I'm running late. I'd better scoot."

"I'll have the tech guys at the state lab look it over. Thanks." Bill walked around the desk and joined me at the door. "One more thing. The reason I wanted to see you—remember the flyers we posted around Etonville and Creston last week? Hoping someone saw something the night of Ruby's murder? We got a hit this morning. An eyewitness."

"Wow! Someone from Etonville?"

"From Creston who happened to be in Etonville that night eating at La Famiglia," he said wryly.

Bill and I had a history with La Famiglia—one romantic-but-ultimately-dreadful dinner.

"Why are you telling me this?" I asked quietly.

"This is strictly confidential," he said.

"I know the drill."

"This is preliminary, but the description of a man seen arguing with Ruby that night fits Dale Undershot," he said.

"Oh no." Could Dale have murdered Ruby? Would that explain his bizarre behavior lately, according to Lola? Lola! How would she take this news? "Where were they? What time was it?"

Bill cut me off. "That's all I can say for now. Just thought I'd give you a heads up. We'll keep this under wraps for another day but when the word gets out, there's going to be hell to pay."

"Etonville will be beside itself—"

"Not to mention the cast and crew of *Bye, Bye, Birdie*," Bill said.

Yikes! The show. "He's not under arrest is he? I mean he can rehearse and perform this week, right?"

"For now, he's a person of interest," Bill assured me. "So no leaking anything to the ELT." Bill kissed me on the cheek—on another day, I might have turned the other one...

14

I struck a hard bargain with Wilson. Normally, as master chef he would have final approval of the day's menus. Knowing the intricacy of his small plates dinner specials, I persuaded him to simplify lunch. We'd focus on our standard sandwiches—three cheese, Henry's special burgers, chicken salad—and cut the soup. My one concession was Wilson's beet salad with avocado and fried goat cheese. He was insistent that it remain on today's menu. I agreed since I loved beets prepared any way—pickled, roasted, curried in soup.

"Dodie, what's the soup du jour?" asked a Banger sister.

"No soup today. We're offering a special beet salad, though. It's delicious. Want to try it?" I asked.

"I'm not fond of beets," said her sister. "But they are good for digestion, I've heard."

"I've eaten them instead of prunes," said the other sister.

Whoa. I was dangerously close to learning all about the gastrointestinal habits of the Banger sisters. "That's nice." I headed to the kitchen.

Enrico was busy at the grill, flipping burgers and creating the three cheese sandwiches. "Dodie, it's nice to be back during the week," he said.

"It's nice to have you back."

Enrico looked over his shoulder to the center island, where Wilson was humming and creating beet salads. "Our chef is happy today," he murmured.

"He's happy *every* day."

As if he knew we were discussing his temperament, Wilson glanced up when he saw me. "*Do-dee*! My beet salad is special. *Ze* customers love it, yes?"

For the most part. No point in mentioning the Banger sisters' evaluation. "Absolutely."

"I will go to *ze* dining room now and speak with *ze* customers." He wiped his hands and set the salads aside.

"What? No! You need to stay in the kitchen and keep things moving. After all, you're in charge in here. Maybe tonight you can greet the customers."

* * * *

I'd been holding my breath for three hours, waiting for one shoe or the other to fall. To my amazement, all went well during the lunch rush—and Wilson demonstrated surprising competence in the keep-the ball-rolling department. We had one meal down and one to go. Henry texted half a dozen times to see if the Windjammer was still standing. I assured him that all was well, and encouraged him to have a good time with his daughter's future in-laws—fat chance.

"Benny, I'm going out for a minute."

Most tables and booths were empty. Only a few stragglers remained. Wilson and Enrico were hard at work—prepping for tonight's menu. We were keeping the potato and mozzarella croquettes, lamb and beef meatballs, fingerling potatoes, vegetable skewers, and small salads. We eliminated the chorizo-filled dates and flatbreads.

"Go ahead." Benny wiped down the bar with a sudsy cloth. "No accidents in the kitchen today. Wilson did a great job."

"I agree. Henry will be proud—or feel competitive," I said.

Benny understood. "Game on."

I exited the restaurant and sat down on the loading dock out back that faced Henry's herb garden. I had about an hour before I needed to ride shotgun on the kitchen, and one important task on my to do list. Earlier, I'd searched the Internet for the *Greenburg Chronicle's* phone number. I was relieved that it was still publishing, and hoped I might find someone in the obituary department with a recollection of the details of Otto Heinlein's death in 1986. I tapped the numbers and waited while the phone rang on the other end. I lifted the hair off my damp neck, whipping it into a ponytail. The temperature was in the high eighties, but the humidity had dropped a little.

"*Greenburg Chronicle*, Stanley Felten speaking," said a crisp voice with a Midwestern twang. I envisioned suspenders and spectacles.

"Hello, I'm calling from Etonville, New Jersey. I'm looking for some information about an article published in the paper in August 1986."

"What kind of article?" the voice asked politely.

"It's about the death of an Otto Heinlein. A kind of obituary. He lived in Greenburg."

"1986 you said? Obits…about thirty years ago. I wasn't here then, but I might be able to connect you with someone who was. What's your interest in the story?" he asked.

"I knew a friend of his and I'm trying to track down information on his death." Did that make sense?

It passed muster with Stanley Felten—because he stepped away from the phone after asking me to wait a minute. I listened to musak while I was on hold, running through the potential challenges facing the restaurant during the next five or six hours.

"Obituary department, Helen Woziak." The voice was female and throaty.

"Hi, I'm not sure if Mr. Felten explained what I was looking for. I read an article in the *Greenburg Chronicle* from 1986 about an Otto—"

"Heinlein. That's right. I wrote it. What can I do for you?" Also no nonsense.

"As I explained to Mr. Felten I knew a friend of Otto's and I was wondering about his death."

"What about his death?" A note of impatience crept into her voice.

"Did you know him personally?"

"No, not really. I live outside Greenburg. I saw him back in the eighties. With his wife and son. They ran a music store. Sold instruments," she said.

Like Ruby, Otto was also in the music business. "He was married?"

"Of course," Helen said as though it was a rule if one wanted to live in Greenburg, Indiana.

"Are his wife and son living in the area?"

"His wife Ellie died shortly before Otto. She'd been ill a while."

"I'm so sorry to hear that. And his son?"

"Not sure where he is today. He left town after Otto died." There was a pause on the line. "It was a suicide."

"Yes, I read that in the paper."

Something shifted in the conversation because when Helen Woziak spoke again, the edge had faded and her inflection had softened. "He was a nice man. And to think he had to go that way."

I gulped. "What way was that?"

Silence for a moment. "Carbon monoxide poisoning."

* * * *

A short line had formed at the door, as Gillian ushered a couple to a table near the front window. Benny poured drinks and delivered them to customers. Carmen hopped from booth to booth. I was monitoring everything. Word spread that Wilson was in charge tonight, and that the special menu consisted of small plates. Though some customers weren't certain what that entailed, it was a change of pace and that was enough to stimulate the appetites of Etonville. Curiosity was the lifeblood of this town.

"Love these meatballs," Mildred said, spearing the lamb variety.

"Me too," chimed in her husband Vernon, "but why the heck do we have to eat them off of these little plates. And why is the portion so tiny?"

Mildred nudged him. "Vernon, that's the whole point of small plates."

"Well, I like regular plates. And normal amounts of food."

"Here, try the croquettes." Mildred said and plopped two on his plate.

"What's that?"

"A fried roll with potato and mozzarella," I said. "Really tasty."

Vernon took a bite. "I generally like my potatoes and cheese separate. But this isn't too bad." A rave review coming from Vernon.

Lola, at the door, motioned to me from behind Georgette and Edna. I walked over.

"It looks like most of Etonville has come in for dinner tonight," Lola said.

"Tables and booths are full, but I could set you up at the bar," I said.

"The bar is fine."

Lola settled onto a stool, ordered dinner from Benny, and buried her face in her cell phone.

Half an hour later, as she nibbled on a vegetable skewer and toyed with a green salad, I led the last of the waiting patrons to a table. Things were beginning to calm down.

"Whew," I said and drew myself a seltzer. "Be careful what you wish for. I was hoping we'd get through the night without any major mishaps, but I didn't anticipate this. Big crowd and great reviews. Wilson is ecstatic." I sipped my drink. Lola was preoccupied. "What's up?"

"It's Dale again."

"What now?"

"We had a date tonight…sort of like a do-over from last week when he was out of sorts, and this week when he had these nightly meetings with clients. I was so looking forward to it. I bought a new outfit. Macy's at the mall had a sale and then an hour ago he called and canceled. I am so upset that I could—"

"Stop the presses, Lola," I said. "What was his reason this time?"

She panted. "He *said* he had to take care of a sick friend. Doesn't that sound like a trumped up excuse?"

It was like all the times my grade school classmates and I claimed the dog ate our homework. Even if we didn't have a dog. I didn't dare breathe a word of Bill's eyewitness evidence and the implications for Dale's future. I needed to change the subject. "Maybe he'll call later. But speaking of calls..." I shared the phone conversation I'd had with the *Greenburg Chronicle*.

"Isn't that strange? Ruby and a guy she knows from the past both die of carbon monoxide poisoning?" I said.

Lola was totally engrossed with my story, Dale forgotten for the moment. "Yes, it is strange except that one was a suicide and the other a homicide."

We sat in silence.

"Interesting that music was his business, too," Lola said.

"But not surprising if he was Ruby's friend from school days in Greenburg. It's possible that's how they met...in a high school music class."

"And fell in love...and then she went away to Maynard—" Lola said.

"And he was left in Greenburg until he came to New York—" I added.

"Where they had a terrible argument and a falling out."

Lola and I had created a fantasy love life for Ruby and Otto. I needed to do some Internet digging on Otto Heinlein. Either that or get a hobby.

Wilson burst through the swinging doors that led into the dining room and addressed the Windjammer crowd, arms outstretched in a welcoming embrace. "*Bon soir, mes amis...*" he sang in his full-throated baritone.

Etonville diners looked up. Lola's jaw dropped. "What the..."

Wilson was taking me up on my suggestion that he greet the dinner crowd instead of the lunch bunch. "I thought a few words here and there. Not a concert," I muttered.

Wilson proceeded to move from table to table, asking patrons how they liked the dinner. Did they have any comments? He smiled and embraced them when he received compliments, usually ended with another round of "*merci*" and "*bon soir.*" After five minutes of this, I gently interrupted and escorted him back to the kitchen on the pretext that Enrico needed his help. Wilson was gracious in his departure, air-kissing customers whose reactions ranged from mild amusement to eager applause. I escorted him off the stage.

I needed to put this Windjammer fire out—before things went too far. I was prepared to apologize for the interruption to the diners' meals. Instead, an excited buzz greeted me.

"That Wilson is the nicest man..."

"I hope he stays in Etonville…"

"I hope he cooks more meals…"

"Henry should come out of the kitchen too…"

Uh-oh.

By eight o'clock, Lola said good-bye, and promised to keep me posted on Dale. I promised I would try to get Bill to the brush-up rehearsal tomorrow night. The throngs of customers thinned, and Gillian was cleaning tables. The door opened, and musical director Alex walked in. I motioned for him to join me at the back of the dining room.

"Hi, Alex. You just made it."

"I hear the special is a variety of small plates. I'll take one of everything."

"Hungry, are we?" I teased.

"I spent the day cleaning out my garage and dumping trash."

I realized that I had no idea where Alex lived or what he did for a living. "In Creston?"

He paused. "Actually Bernridge."

Bernridge is a community next door. More blue collar than Etonville, its residential neighborhoods sit side-by-side with manufacturing areas.

"Lived there long?"

"Long enough to know I'd like to move elsewhere. Etonville's a nice, quiet community," he said.

I flashed on Snippets on days when gossip was at its peak. "Sometimes."

"I was sorry to hear about your accident. I guess it was a close call," he said sincerely.

"Not really. Loss of brake fluid. It happens," I said.

"You must have been terrified," he said.

"I was. But I had to react so fast I wasn't really frightened until it was over and my car was off the road."

"Reacting fast. Like improvising," he said.

"Right."

"Sometimes I felt that way working with Ruby. I had to react quickly. She liked to adlib musical phrases, and I had to adjust so the actors could keep up. "

"Wow. That's a talent."

"Not really. I'm just good at working fast. But Ruby was a…creative challenge." He smiled. "A rare bird."

* * * *

"Woohoo!" Gillian sang out as the champagne cork hit the ceiling.

We closed down the Windjammer half an hour ago. Wilson, Benny, Enrico, Carmen, Gillian, and I collapsed into seats, proud of the way everyone functioned without Henry at the helm. Wilson was especially thrilled. He sang a Haitian melody in French.

"What we need is a toast!" I said. It was unusual for the staff to hang around after closing and celebrate, but it was equally unusual for Henry's sous chef to take over for the night and perform so well. I chose a mid-priced bottle of chilled champagne—there was hardly any call for it among the Windjammer's regulars—and Benny eagerly popped its cork and poured.

We held our glasses aloft. "To Wilson. Well done!" I said.

We drank.

"To the entire staff," Benny added.

We drank.

Everyone chimed in with their own tribute to the night—small plates, the Windjammer's customers, the entire town of Etonville, the island of Haiti that spawned Wilson…a second bottle was required, and the party continued. In the middle of it, Henry texted that his neighbor had driven by the restaurant and saw lights glowing. I reassured Henry that we were merely late cleaning up—and all was well. Enrico and Carmen persuaded Wilson to sing another song, and he obliged them with show tunes: "There's No Business like Show Business" and "Hello Dolly," with a napkin-waving chorus consisting of Enrico and Benny!

The mini-concert was in full swing when I heard a knock on the front door. Please God, let it not be Henry. The staff had worked hard and deserved to celebrate, but Henry might not appreciate the fact that we'd liberated champagne from his stock. I planned to replace it tomorrow.

I stole to the door and cautiously eased it open. "Yes?"

It was Bill. "What's going on?" He peered around me. "Who's singing?"

"It's only you," I said relieved.

"Only me?" he asked, displaying his crooked grin.

"We're closed." I hiccupped. Champagne did that to me.

Bill smirked. "I don't have to run any of you in for disturbing the peace, do I?"

"Nope. Just a little celebration because the night went so well." I hiccupped again.

"I'm glad. I wanted to stop by…but things got nuts at the station," he said ruefully.

"I'd fix you a small plate but we actually sold out. Henry will be in seventh heaven though he'll grumble about…" Bill turned away and ran a hand through his spiky blond hair. He was agitated. "Need to talk?"

"Yeah. In your office?"

Bill followed me into the Windjammer. Everyone looked up.

"Hi Chief," Benny said and lifted a bottle of champagne. Bill declined his offer and accepted a beer instead. "Have you eaten?"

"Kind of forgot about food tonight," Bill said. "I guess I am hungry."

"What's left in the kitchen, Wilson?" I asked.

Wilson saluted Bill. "Chief Thompson, I will bring you a delight *zat* will tickle your taste buds!"

"Never mind the taste buds. How about something simple and quick?" I asked.

Wilson ran off while the rest of the crew, giggling happily, wiped and mopped and generally made the restaurant presentable for tomorrow's lunch service. Bill joined me in my back booth and took a big swallow of his beer.

"Tough day, huh?"

Bill lowered his voice. "Things are moving quickly with the investigation."

"That's good, right?"

He fidgeted with the beer bottle. "We brought Dale in again today. He's one smooth talker. Had an answer for every question."

"The Excel spreadsheet?"

"Says he was Ruby's financial advisor and paid her monthly dividends. Perfectly legitimate. Unfortunately, Ruby's not here to contradict his statements. But his alibi's shaky. Says he was driving around Etonville and Creston after the rehearsal and then he went home. No one can corroborate. The first substantiation came when his neighbor got up early at three a.m. and saw his car in the driveway. But according to the medical examiner, Ruby could have died anywhere between one a.m. and four a.m."

Wilson waltzed to our booth with one of Henry's special burgers. "Henry says *ze* burger is *ze* chief's favorite meal." He beamed.

Bill laughed appreciatively. "Henry's right."

"It is *ze* avocado and *ze* sauce." He kissed his fingertips, one of Wilson's favorite ways of expressing his pleasure.

Bill bit into his sandwich while I drilled *my* fingers on the table.

"So you have means...Dale had easy access to Ruby, but what do you think is his motive? I know they argued backstage, but that could have been about anything. The show, her accompaniment, the cue sheet..." My instincts were whispering that Dale's conflict with Ruby was about finances.

Bill unfolded a napkin. "Not clear yet but it might have something to do with the spreadsheet and the monthly payments. After all, Ruby died with a decent amount of money stashed away in a bank account."

"Did she have a will?" I asked.

"Haven't located one yet. Only living relative is a third cousin in Indiana."
I'd spoken with him. "What about the eyewitness?"

"Shh," Bill said and peeked over his shoulder.

He needn't have worried. Benny and Gillian chatted, Enrico planted
a kiss on his wife's face, and Carmen tittered like a schoolgirl. The two
of them headed to the kitchen, arm-in-arm, to help Wilson close up for
the night. Maybe we needed a champagne party every night. "No one's
paying us any attention."

"I told Dale we had a witness who'd seen him with Ruby on the access
road—"

"You didn't tell me that!"

"Shh. It's—"

"Confidential. I know. That is incriminating, but it was dark. Could the
witness see them well?" I asked.

Bill's face was impassive. Deliberately not reacting or offering a hint
to the person's identity.

He leaned across the table murmuring. "The dome light was on. Their
faces were illuminated."

My heart sank. "It doesn't look good for Dale."

"He agreed to join a lineup at some point to see if the witness can
identify him."

"But he wouldn't do that if he was guilty, would he?" I asked hopefully.

"Maybe. Maybe not. If he felt cornered, he might see this as the best
strategy. Or he's counting on the fact that the witness didn't have a good
view," he said.

Benny and Gillian sidled up to our booth. "We're heading out." Benny
said. "I'm dropping Gillian off. Enrico and Carmen are gone. Wilson too."

"Great work tonight."

The restaurant was still, except for the hum of the refrigeration cases
behind the bar. I grabbed my bag, clicked off the lights, and locked the
door behind us. We drove to my place in Bill's squad car, parking in front
of my bungalow. Never mind what the neighbors might think.

"I'd like to hear more about this accident with the brakes," Bill said as
he sat on the bed and wrenched off his shoes.

"I'm picking up the Metro in the morning. Timothy might have found
something."

"You need a new set of wheels." He yawned and walked to the bathroom.

"Could be a birthday present from myself," I called after him.

No response.

I whipped out my cell phone. There was one more item on today's to do inventory. I texted Pauli, asking if he'd found anything on Veronica or Ruby Passonata, and requested that he add Otto Heinlein to his deep search list. He'd probably see the text in the morning.

Bill tumbled into bed and I cuddled next to him. As he dozed off, my cell binged and he woke up.

"Who's that?" he asked groggily.

I bounded out of bed and checked the message. Pauli: *Nothing on Ruby yet. Will check out Otto. Gotta bounce.*

Me too. It was 1 a.m.

15

"Well, this baby's pretty old. She's got a lotta mileage on her." Timothy smoothed his hair and replaced his ball cap.

Tell me about it. Over a hundred and twenty thousand.

"So it coulda been worn brake pads," he said.

"Yeah?"

"But it wasn't."

"Coulda been the master cylinder," he added.

"Yeah?"

"But it wasn't."

"Timothy, did you find anything?" I was tired and edgy.

"Well, you got your rubber hoses, your valves, your cylinders, your pistons and everything operates like a heart. Pumping blood to all the parts of the body. In this case the brake fluid is pumped to all the parts of the braking system." He waited to see if this was registering with me.

"Got it."

"Every part of the brake system can leak," Timothy said and crossed his arms confidently.

"The Metro?"

"Had a puncture in a brake line," he declared in triumph.

What? "How did that happen?"

"Brake lines get worn out. Or you run over something in the road. Road debris could do it."

Road debris? I didn't remember running over anything from the time I left Etonville until I arrived in Creston.

"I fixed her up. Replaced the brake line and refilled the fluid," Timothy said. "But if I was you…"

"I'd get a newer model," I finished for him.

"Yep."

I paid Timothy and cranked the engine. The Metro purred like a young kitten. What did age matter? Anyway, something about the whole brake incident had set my neck hairs aquiver. Why had it happened so quickly? Why were there no brake issues on my way to Creston—only on my way home? I was no mechanic, but it didn't make sense. I didn't care how old the Metro was.

I opened the door to the Windjammer, surprised to find Henry standing in the center of the dining room as if he couldn't believe that the place was still standing. "Hey. You're here early." I was early, and Henry had arrived before me.

"How did yesterday go?" he asked tensely, no doubt waiting for some kind of a kitchen bombshell.

"Remarkably well."

"Really?"

Did Henry seem disappointed? "Wilson was at the top of his game, no spills or accidents, and folks scarfed up the small plates. We sold out."

Henry's jaw dropped an inch. "I suggested a tapas menu last year if you remember," he said darkly, pouting.

Unfortunately, that was the same week Enrico had the flu. We needed a less labor-intensive special. "I know you did," I said soothingly. "Now that we know it's a winner, we could feature a tapas menu more often."

Henry bent down and retrieved a champagne cork. I thought we'd gotten all of them.

"What's this?"

"Looks like a cork to me. I'll have to speak to Gillian about being more thorough when sweeping up," I said with an air of authority.

Henry eyed me with an air of suspicion. "Yeah."

"You haven't told me how your day was. Give me the scoop on the in-laws," I said.

He groaned. "It was like watching paint dry."

"That bad?"

"All they talked about was redecorating their summer home and their trip to Alaska."

"And your future son-in-law?" I asked tentatively.

"The same. Living at home, trying to find a 'better' job...but as long as Leslie is happy."

Henry was a pushover where his daughter was concerned. "You're a good dad," I said and patted him on the back.

"I hope I'm not a regretful dad." He trudged off to the kitchen.

Fathers and daughters. My own dad was a bit of a pushover. He let me choose a college even though he'd have to cough up more tuition, co-signed a loan so I could buy the Metro, kept my past-curfew-nights a secret from Mom. My younger brother Andy always swore that I could do no wrong as far as Dad was concerned. I vehemently denied that I was daddy's little girl. But I was. Reflecting on family jogged my memory. Andy had texted yesterday: *Cape Cod plans for August set - u in?* I had to break the news to him that Bill and I were going to either the Jersey Shore or the wilds of New York State.

Lunch proceeded without a hitch, but it was clear the staff was in higher spirits than usual. Benny was a whirlwind of energy, wiping down the bar and restocking wine, and Gillian actually smiled at customers. Wilson, of course, was his normal, sunny self, and blew kisses to everyone on his way to the kitchen.

Henry was mystified. "I don't get it. Everybody drink happy juice this morning?"

Something like that. Only it was last night, not this morning. "I think it's terrific that everyone is in a good mood."

Benny and Gillian snickered.

When the Banger sisters asked if Henry would be stopping by their table for a chat as Wilson had, I figured our cover might be blown. "Henry's too busy today. Next week," I said quickly.

* * * *

I took my three o'clock break in my back booth. My cell rang just as I'd started to enjoy Henry's crab bisque and a burger.

"Hi Lola," I said between bites.

"Dodie, I'm nervous," she said.

"I know it's drizzling now, but the weather app says tomorrow will be fine. Sunny and dry. Even a bit cooler."

"It's not the weather. It's Dale."

Yikes. "What about him?" I said as innocently as I could.

"Snippets has been buzzing about a rumor that there's an eyewitness to Ruby's murder."

I wanted to correct her: not to the murder, just to a conversation she had with a tall man who had black hair. "You know how people at Snippets get things wrong." I swallowed a mouthful of the bisque.

"I'm not so sure this time. Dale went back to the police station this morning."

"How do you know that?"

"Edna saw him come in. Then he left with the chief for Creston," she said.

For a lineup?

"I tried to reach him on his cell but he wasn't picking up."

I was dying to share what I knew but, one, I had promised Bill I'd keep his confidence, and, two, no sense in creating any more anxiety for Lola than necessary. "There's no point in working yourself into a lather. I'm sure there's a simple explanation."

The line was silent. "You're right. But I wonder if Dale's erratic behavior lately has something to do with Ruby."

"Why do you say that?" I asked.

"Because it all started after her death when he was interviewed by the police. I know the whole cast was called in, but something happened with Dale. I can't quite put my finger on it," she said.

"Why don't you have a cup of chamomile tea to relax and focus on tonight's rehearsal?"

"I suppose you're right. Good thing Walter scheduled the brush-up for indoors, though we'll have minimal set pieces to work with. At least we won't have to deal with the weather." She announced, "This is the last show I'm doing al fresco!"

Benny agreed to close up tonight, so I reassured her that I would pop in, and that Bill would show up during Act Two in time to play a cop. After Lola clicked off, I doodled on a napkin. What exactly had been the connection between Ruby and Dale besides financial adviser and client?

"Hey O'Dell, heard you had a party after closing last night," Penny said, putting an imaginary bottle to her mouth and tipping it upward. She slouched in a theater seat, her legs stretched out in front of her. Very un-Penny-like.

I had yet to understand how word traveled so fast in this town. Like the speed of light. "A staff meeting," I said casually. I sincerely hoped there were no more errant corks hidden in corners.

Penny snorted. "Better get rid of those champagne corks. Could be evidence."

"Penny! Stop!" I yelled. Then more calmly, "Shouldn't you be getting ready for rehearsal?" I peeked at my watch. It was seven thirty.

"Nah. Walter hasn't done the warm-up yet—"

"Penny! Gather the cast!" Walter hollered from the stage.

Penny hauled herself out of the seat. "I'm on it."

I held my ears as her whistle detonated and actors winced, slowly making their way onto the stage to join Walter. Janice and the other young women in the cast yakked and flirted with the guys, who pretended to ignore them while they checked their cell phones. The Creston High athlete was nowhere to be found.

"Hey," I heard behind me. It was Pauli, out of breath.

"Pauli, hi. Did you run all the way here?"

"Like…I thought I might catch Janice before it starts," he said.

We both shifted our attention to the stage where Penny took attendance with her clipboard while Walter prodded actors to hurry up. "You have about a minute. Go for it."

He ran to the stage and grabbed Janice's attention. She focused on him, and I could have sworn Pauli grew an inch or two.

"Hi Dodie." Lola stood in the aisle, as down in person as she was on the phone this afternoon.

"Any word from Dale?"

As though he heard my question, the leading man materialized from the green room behind the stage. He spotted Lola in the house and smiled magnificently. This did not look like a man who had spent his morning in a lineup as a murder suspect.

"Dale?" Lola said, as though she was shocked to see him.

"Let's run through our number," he said.

She flew down the aisle and met him at the piano where Alex was setting up his score.

None of this got by Walter. "Lola, dear, could you help me with the warm-up?" he asked plaintively.

Lola snubbed Walter, and bent her head over Alex's score. Walter, clearly put out, introduced his exercise to the actors who were none-too-enthused about his greet-each-other game. Walter instructed everyone to move around the stage and, as though they were all strangers, introduce themselves to each other, making eye—and physical—contact. He told them to touch, hug, and shake hands to acknowledge one another. Most of the actors went along with Walter and his eccentric pre-rehearsal workouts by now. But not everyone.

"What's the point of this?" Romeo asked, and he sat down on the floor, likely assuming that playing the rock star and parading around in gold lamé gave him some theatrical clout.

The ELT regulars were transfixed. They mocked the warm-ups and fooled around when they were supposed to be focusing, but no one doubted Walter's rationale. "Dear boy, the theatre is a—"

"Family. I know. But if we're a family wouldn't we already know everybody's name? Why do we have to introduce ourselves?" he asked in defiance.

I had to admit that Romeo had a point.

The stage grew quiet, Lola shifted her attention to Walter, whose face turned red. "If you do not wish to participate, please leave the playing area."

Penny gasped. Had Walter ever thrown anyone off the stage before? The cast bobbed their heads like ping pong balls, gazing first at Walter, then Romeo, and then Walter again. Romeo got to his feet and plopped into a seat in the first row of the house. Penny wrote furiously on her clipboard while Lola gestured to Dale and the two of them joined the cast.

As if to make up for Romeo's errant ways, the rest of the cast jumped into greeting each other with a vengeance, running around the stage, calling out their names, fist bumping, slapping hands, and generally creating a commotion. Walter was oblivious, floating through the crowd and greeting folks with gusto. Everyone picked up the pace when Alex played the overture to *Bye, Bye, Birdie*. While the teenagers became hysterical, Edna whirled right then left into Abby and the two of them touched hands awkwardly. Vernon shuffled around the perimeter of the stage, waving away anyone who came too close, until Mildred whacked him on the arm. The Banger sisters hooked arms, twirling together in the center of the activity, tapping everyone who passed by, giggling.

Lola looked into the house, caught my eye and rolled hers. I stifled a laugh.

"What's going on?" Bill stood in the aisle, arms akimbo, staring at the pandemonium in front of him.

"Walter's warm-up. It's about greeting everyone as if you didn't know them. Of course, as Romeo pointed out, if the theater is a family—"

"Dodie!"

"Yeah?"

"I stopped by to let Walter know I wouldn't be able to make it tonight."

I sat up alertly. "Why?"

Bill stooped down beside me. "I can't talk now." He observed the madness on stage. "I see Dale is here."

"Did you think he wouldn't be here?"

"I have to go. Could you tell…" He cocked his head at Penny, who pushed her glasses up her nose and furiously fingered her whistle. With the cast bouncing off each other like bumper cars and the volume level increasing, she was ready to intervene.

"Sure. See you later tonight?" I asked.

"I'll let you know." He patted my shoulder and walked up the aisle to the exit.

I shivered. Something was going on in the Etonville police department.

In the Etonville Little Theatre too. While I talked to Bill, the athlete from Creston sauntered into the theater, surveyed the hullabaloo, and ran onto the stage. He found Janice and, not really understanding the exercise, grabbed her and waltzed her around the space. They collided with several actors, and finally bumped into Pauli who was standing at the outer limits of the mayhem taking rehearsal shots of the cast. Pauli landed on his backside, the Creston kid barely noticing. Pauli had had it. He shoved the athlete, who tripped over his own feet and smacked the floor. The two of them went nose-to-nose, each clutching the front of the other's shirt, both gasping heavily and ready to take a swing.

I rushed to Penny. "Get up there and stop them!"

"O'Dell, it's just some guys messing around—"

One of them could get injured—most likely Pauli. "Penny!" I screamed.

She tooted her whistle, heaved herself onto the stage with me close behind. Actors looked around for direction. Walter broke out of his greeting both Banger sisters at once and said, "Penny!"

I tugged Pauli away from the athlete, who was firmly in Penny's grasp. She was nearly a foot shorter than he was, but her stocky build gave her leverage. "Knock it off you two!"

"Decorum!" Walter cried. "The theater is a sacred space. There can be no conflict here!"

The rest of the cast halted the exercise, panting in place, trying to determine what was happening.

"Why don't you call a timeout?" I asked, my arm around Pauli's shoulder.

"Take ten!" Penny blew another blast.

The onstage assembly dissolved and actors talked among themselves, getting water, resting in a seat, and preparing for the rehearsal. Barely anyone looked over at Pauli and the Creston athlete.

"All good?" I murmured to Pauli.

He stared at Janice who stood apart, stunned. "It's just like in the play," she said. "Hugo punches Conrad Birdie." Her eyes glistened and she turned on her heel running away.

"Janice?" the athlete exclaimed, and then stared daggers at Pauli.

Life imitating art.

* * * *

Dale's positive mood vanished by the end of the break. He had a tense conversation with Alex, which concluded with him storming onto the stage and rebuffing Walter's notes. He also brushed off Lola's request to run their last number. With Pauli and the athlete sulking in opposite corners, Dale stomping off into the green room, and Walter fit to be tied, tension was in the air and flinging a damper on the rehearsal.

Lola, bewildered, sat next to me. "One minute Dale's all charm, and the next he's a monster."

"You should get this rehearsal going before anybody else picks a fight," I said.

"What was that thing with Pauli? I've never seen him like that."

We all have our limits.

Lola urged Walter to get the show on the road. He signaled Penny who corralled the cast while Alex pounded out the overture. Dale made a stiff entrance, and kept to himself. Clearly, the drama had sucked the wind out of the *Bye, Bye, Birdie* sails. The cast was game, and slogged their way through Act One with Dale sleepwalking his part, Lola overacting to keep the energy flowing, and Romeo in a funk. The teen actors were having no fun and simply went through the motions. Only Edna was into the rehearsal, fainting and falling with delight.

What would happen tomorrow night in the park with an audience? I decided to cut out during the intermission break. I gave Pauli—who was hunkered down in the back of the house—words of encouragement ("Janice will get over it and the athlete had it coming") and was about to give Lola a thumbs up when Dale blew out of the green room. He headed straight for Walter. They exchanged words and red splotches formed on Walter's cheeks. Now what? Arms gesticulated, Walter tore at his hair, and Dale huffed off the stage.

"Dale?" Lola said. He kept moving. "Walter?"

"He's sick," said Walter with scorn. "Caught something from an ill acquaintance yesterday. Said he'd be better by tomorrow."

The friend he was supposedly tending to when Lola tried to make contact?

Lola tugged on a strand of blond hair and twisted it feverishly. "We'll have to rehearse Act Two without him."

This change in events spelled trouble.

"Yep, trouble all right," Penny said.

"I don't suppose you have understudies?" I asked.

Penny chortled. "O'Dell this is community theater. We're lucky if we can cast one actor for every role much less have extras sitting around waiting for someone to break a leg."

"Metaphorically speaking," I added.

"Metaphor shmetaphor. Why do you think we say 'break a leg' for good luck?"

I had no idea, but assumed I was about to be schooled.

"The theater is a place of opposites. You say 'break a leg' instead of 'good luck.' Upstage is really downstage and versa vice. And you don't whistle backstage. Singing's okay but *no* whistling."

"Unless it's you," I said without a trace of a smile.

Penny pushed her glasses up the bridge of her nose and clapped her clipboard against one leg. "O'Dell, one of these days you're going to understand how the theater works. It's all for one and one for none. And everything's pretty much ado about nothing."

"Aha." If I hadn't been so distressed about Dale leaving, I might have gotten a kick out of Penny's mishmash of theatrical philosophy and traditions.

"Penny!" Walter searched the house until he spotted her in conversation with me. "Call the cast."

She dutifully blew her whistle; probably better than her singing. I pulled out my cell and tapped Bill's number, texting: *Dale has left rehearsal. Sick??* There wasn't much I could do in the theater now so I hitched my bag over my shoulder. "Night Pauli," I whispered.

He thrust his face in his hands and studied the seat in front of him. I figured two parts embarrassment, one part anger, and one part heartache. I felt truly sorry for the kid, but I supposed his ego would mend in time. I'd been through a ton of teenage angst—

"Dodie."

It was Pauli showing his face.

"Yeah?"

He rifled through his backpack and withdrew a sheet of paper, wrinkled with a brown smudge on it. He smoothed the sheet on his leg. "Sorry about, like, the smear. I was eating chocolate chip cookies."

"No problem."

"I meant to, like, give this to you before but then, you know, Janice… and that kid from Creston…" He dipped his head.

I reached for the paper. It was a list of places and dates. I frowned. "What is it?"

"Like, I put Veronica Passonata into a couple of Internet search engines." A bit of the old confident Pauli began to surface, his eyes perked up, his head bobbed in excitement.

"What did you find?

He pointed to the page. "Boom! There's all this stuff about her piano playing as a kid…"

"The contests and awards. Right."

"I checked the census records and, like, some other databases. Did ya know that she lived in, like, about a thousand places before she came to Creston?" Pauli asked.

A thousand? Pauli was exaggerating, but when I scanned the list he'd jotted down, I realized that Ruby had indeed called many places home. Starting in Indiana, then moving to Ohio, Pennsylvania, and finally New Jersey. Pauli had noted dates and places, but I would need to study these to create her personal timeline. "Pauli, this is fantastic!" I must have gotten too enthusiastic because Penny shot a glance my way, plastered her finger on her lips and shook her head vigorously. My bad.

Alex had finished playing the Entr'acte, and Lola and Janice were well into their duet: "What Did I Ever See in Him?" I could have sworn the two of them were actually consoling each other. Dale? Pauli? The athlete?

16

It was a relief to step into the summer night. The air was fresh and cool. I lifted the hair off my neck to let the breeze waft over me—as I walked two blocks down Main Street to my Metro while contemplating the evening's affairs. I was glad I parked in the opposite direction from the Windjammer—no temptation to drop in and check on things. I wasn't in the mood to listen to Henry kvetch about whatever or share in Wilson's general jubilation over life. I was tired but antsy, and decided that I could confirm tomorrow night's snack box delivery and work schedule from home.

I unlocked the driver's side door. My dome light was on. I remembered needing light to apply lipstick but I thought I had turned it off. Was I that absent-minded? I sighed and inserted the ignition key. One of these days, I'd be able to afford a car that started with the push of a button. I twisted the key and nothing happened. I twisted the key to off, waited a few seconds and tried again. Nothing. The engine was dead. Damn! My little hairs cooled off earlier with the light wind blowing, but now were as active as Mexican jumping beans. What was going on with my trusty Metro? First my brakes, and now the battery? Bill was right. Maybe it was time to consider a newer mode of transportation. Immediately I felt guilty. I couldn't let my Metro get wind of any such plans.

It was almost ten o'clock. I considered my options. Since Bill hadn't answered my text, I assumed he wasn't available; Lola was tied up; Carol would be working late at Snippets and closing up. I could leave a message with Timothy that I needed a tow in the morning, but what was I going to do now?

I went back to the theater and quietly slipped into the house. The show was heading toward the end of Act Two and Vernon and Edna, as Janice's parents, led the company in a reprise of "Kids," bemoaning the state of the younger generation. Of course it was the 1950s, but had anything changed? I sat down next to Pauli who was staring intently into his camera, no doubt anticipating Janice's next entrance so he could snap away.

"Hey," I whispered.

Pauli swiveled in his seat. "Wassup? Thought you left?"

"My car won't start. Could you give me a ride home?"

"Now?" he asked.

"I can wait until the end of the rehearsal."

Pauli considered. "Nah. Like, I'm ready to cut out. I've seen enough tonight."

I'll bet he had. "Thanks."

Pauli drove slowly through the dark streets of Etonville, up Main, over Fairfield and down Ames. He pulled to the curb in front of my house. It felt as though he had something he wanted to say. "Thanks again. I really appreciate you leaving the run-through."

"No problemo." He rubbed the steering wheel of the family SUV. Carol ensured that if Pauli had an accident he'd be protected by lots of car.

"Something on your mind?" I asked gently.

"Like…how do you tell somebody how you feel about 'em?"

I wasn't the best person to ask. Even though Bill and I had taken our relationship to the next level, we hadn't really talked about our feelings. We hadn't discussed my birthday—much less a summer vacation. "It's tough Pauli. The whole feelings thing."

"But how's Janice supposed to know, like, whatever if I don't tell her?" he asked softly.

Good point. I should take Pauli's advice. "Right. But find a good time."

Pauli looked at me. "Not right after I knock another guy to the ground."

"Yeah." We both snickered. Pauli was regaining his sense of humor.

"If Mom hears about this, I might get grounded for fighting."

"I wouldn't worry about that. With all of the madness surrounding the rehearsal tonight…" I was thinking about Dale. "…your minor incident won't be at the top of anybody's chatter list."

"Cool. Gotta bounce."

I opened the door. "If you find any more info on Ruby or Veronica, let me know?"

"Got it. Oh yeah…that other name you gave me? Otto?"

"Heinlein. Otto Heinlein," I said.

"He died like Ruby did." Pauli's voice was hushed.

"I know. Freaky, isn't it?"

"Like, yeah, but why d'ya think he had a restraining order against her?" he asked.

"He what?" I got back into the car.

"I found it in a police file. In 1985."

"Why?"

Pauli shrugged. "The report just said harassment."

* * * *

I said good-bye to Pauli, and watched as he glided down the street. Then I kicked off my shoes, put on a tee shirt and sweat pants, and settled down at my kitchen table with a strong cup of coffee. I needed a jolt of caffeine to keep me focused. I smoothed out Pauli's list of Ruby's whereabouts over the years next to a legal pad. I began to take notes.

Ruby embarked on her concert tour soon after graduating from Maynard Institute. The newspaper clippings in the scrapbook indicated that she was traveling around the world until the late '60s—when the record of her appearances stopped suddenly. Pauli's information from the census bureau database showed that Ruby moved back to Indiana the year after her touring ended. Not to Greenburg but to Indianapolis. Then she showed up in Ohio, and later Pennsylvania. She lived in Pennsylvania until she moved to New Jersey. Gradually, Ruby had been making her way east. Either she was restless or she had no identification with any particular city or state—except for Greenburg, Indiana.

Something was niggling at my memory. I took out a pad I'd scribbled on when I'd spoken with the staff of the *Greenburg Chronicle.* I flipped the pages. There it was: Otto had died in 1986. The same year Ruby left Indiana and moved to Ohio. She lived in Indiana until Otto died. Was it a coincidence? Had she simply wanted to be close to her former boyfriend until his death? He moved on with a wife and a son. Had Ruby? Had there been contact between them? I slapped my forehead, dumbfounded. Of course there was—the restraining order! I scanned Pauli's sheet of notes. The Court handed down a restraining order in 1985, during the time Ruby was in Indiana, and a year before Otto died. What in the world happened between them? Knowing Ruby as an older woman in her seventies made it difficult to envision a younger version who had been guilty of harassment. Or did it?

I shut my eyes and massaged my temples. It was getting late and I had an early day tomorrow…Suddenly my eyes flew open. Had Otto's marriage been the reason Ruby ended her career as a concert pianist so unexpectedly?

Had she moved back to Indiana not to be close to the man she loved but to make him pay for leaving her? Was it a threat Boris overheard that day outside his window? Had Ruby threatened vengeance if Otto left her? I leaned back in my chair. Suppositions filled my timeline, but what if I was correct? I felt a glimmer of triumph for, possibly, having unraveled a piece of Ruby's past. A pang of regret immediately followed that triumph. If Ruby lived for revenge, what did that say about the rest of her life? A sad life. Yet, there were hints about her time in New Jersey that didn't suggest an unhappy, depressed senior citizen. According to Bill, she had money, lots of it. She was independent, involved with the Creston Players. Even the deli kid across the street from her apartment building liked her.

It was more than I could untangle tonight. I switched off the lights and went to sleep.

* * * *

"Talk to me about restraining orders," I said, and flipped fried eggs expertly: one of the only cooking maneuvers I could handle in my sleep, which I was practically doing. I had tossed and turned for hours, mulling over Ruby's life.

Bill buttered a piece of toast. "Why? You locking me out?"

"I see your sense of humor is intact."

He looked as tired as I felt. He had dark circles under his eyes. His brush cut was a jumble of spikes; his tie loosened around his neck, his uniform shirt looked slept in. This was not the fastidiously dressed cop I'd become used to. "It was a long night. Another meeting with the medical examiner, conferencing with the Creston force, unearthing more information on Dale Undershot's financial planning company. It ain't a pretty picture."

I plopped the eggs on a plate and handed it to Bill. "That doesn't sound good."

"It's not. He's had some problematic practices over the years, and complaints from clients. Nothing that led to prosecution, but enough red flags to complicate his relationship with Ruby."

"You think he was guilty of fraud?"

"Could be." Bill dove into the eggs like a starving man.

This was an unusual arrangement. Normally, Bill would be serving me, but he showed up at my place at one a.m. and sacked out on the sofa to avoid disturbing me. It wouldn't have mattered given my on and off insomnia last night.

"But what about the payments to Ruby? If he was writing her checks on a regular basis, how could he have been cheating her?" I asked.

Bill shook his head. "Haven't figured that out yet. Dale is due back in the station this morning."

"Are you going to arrest him?"

"Working on probable cause. We have an eyewitness to a meeting between Ruby and him, and he has no one who can back up his alibi. I'm pressing the county prosecutor for a warrant to check his cell phone record."

Wait until Lola found this out.

Bill wiped his mouth. "So what's this about restraining orders?"

I shared the results of Pauli's digging, without mentioning his name, since I continued to protect the innocent.

"I'm not going to ask where you obtained your intelligence…but at least researching Ruby's life has kept you away from the murder investigation," he said wryly.

"Good point."

"Anyway, it's a court order that protects the victim of domestic abuse or violence in cases of criminal restraint, criminal trespass, stalking, assault—"

"Or harassment. What exactly does the court order do?" I said.

"Keeps the guilty party away from the victim's place of work or home. It prevents contact with the victim in person or on the phone anywhere the victim requests. The order against contact may also protect other people in the family," Bill said.

I wondered if the court order protected Otto's wife and son as well. "What happens if the guilty party violates the court order?"

"It becomes a police issue. If a crime is committed as part of the violation, a criminal complaint is filed."

What kind of harassment had Ruby committed?

"You think Ruby's being served with a restraining order means what?" Bill asked.

"I'm not sure. It speaks to her personality, her need for payback. For example, if Dale was swindling her, she might want to get even."

"You're forgetting she's the one who ended up dead." Bill finished off his coffee. "Thanks for breakfast."

"You're welcome." I stacked the dirty dishes in the sink—time to wash up later—and grabbed my purse. "Ready." Bill had offered to deliver me to Timothy's to pick up my car. Timothy called at seven thirty this morning to say that Timothy Jr. towed the Metro to the service station. He said I could stop by in an hour or so to rescue my chariot. Timothy insisted on a thorough inspection of my Metro to prevent further "accidents."

"By the way, I ordered a rod and reel from a sporting goods outfit in Creston," Bill said. "I'm going to teach you to fish if it kills me."

Or me. "I got a text from my mother yesterday."

Bill blinked. "Yeah?"

"They're thinking of renting a place down the shore for August. Wondering if we want to stop by," I said casually.

"Fine by me. That way I'd get to do some deep sea fishing too."

Too? This vacation thing might require a frontal attack. My cell pinged with a lengthy text from Lola. I could read between the words. She was desperate to reach Dale, who was nowhere to be found.

"What does she mean disappeared?" Bill asked, no-nonsense.

"Lola was frantic, so she drove to his house early this morning and a neighbor said she saw him leave at six a.m." I stopped reading the text and gulped.

"What?" Bill clapped his cap on his head.

"The neighbor said he had a suitcase in his hand."

"Let's go," he said.

"No. You go on. I'll have Lola take me to the shop," I said to his back as he strode out my front door. Things had taken a turn for the worst.

* * * *

"I can imagine how you feel—your boyfriend taking a powder like that," I said to Lola quietly. We sat in a back booth in Coffee Heaven. After we trekked to Timothy's—where I heard that my problem was a dead battery, duh, and received another mini-lecture on the age and generally worn out condition of my Chevy Metro—Lola and I decided to drown our sorrows in sugar. Hot cinnamon buns for both of us.

"It's not that. I'm so over the idea that Dale would have been a permanent part of my life…"

"Still, it's gotta hurt."

"It's the show. How do we go on?" Lola asked—anxiety etched on her face.

"Here you go ladies," Jocelyn said, and placed our rolls on the table. She paused as if expecting a response.

"Thanks. They look especially sweet this morning. Right Lola?"

Lola nodded weakly and reached for a bun.

"You gals don't fool me," said Jocelyn. She stuck a pencil behind one ear. Uh-oh. What had she seen or heard?

"Walter was in here a half hour ago." Jocelyn said, triumphant. "We had a nice conversation. I'll bet he's been talking about me. Like what a nice couple we'd make." She positioned her hands on her hips and waited.

Lola coughed, nearly choking on a piece of cinnamon bun, and I stared blankly at our waitress. "Sure. Walter...mentioned you the other day." Lola gawked at me as if I was crazy. Yes, Walter mentioned Jocelyn. He asked Penny to order his dinner and have Jocelyn add extra gravy to his mashed potatoes.

"Aha!" Jocelyn waltzed away, a happy, delusional woman in love.

"Lola, we need to talk."

We wrapped the remains of our rolls in napkins and darted out of Coffee Heaven, careful to circumvent Jocelyn. I agreed to keep most of the information about Dale and the murder investigation to myself, but with Dale on the run, everything would be out in the open and grist for Etonville's rumor mill within hours. There was, no doubt, an APB on Dale already.

We drove to the Etonville Park and sat in Lola's Lexus. I relayed what I knew about Dale's business dealings with Ruby, the fact that an eyewitness had seen Dale and Ruby in a confrontation the night she died, and that Bill was attempting to search Dale's cell phone.

Lola stared wide-eyed. "Dale could be a killer?"

"Nobody knows anything for sure. That's why Bill wants to check his call record." I held back the report about Dale's previous professional practices—no sense in piling on.

"But I let him into my life, into my home..." Lola cried dramatically.

"Dale was a great guy until ten days ago. Focus on that. Meanwhile, what are you going to do about *Bye, Bye, Birdie*?" I asked.

Lola yanked a fistful of her hair. "I don't know. I don't know. I don't know!"

"You'd better call Walter?"

"Oh Walter! What am I going to say? How is he going to take it?" Lola moaned.

Walter wasn't the only one who could use a chill pill. "I'm sorry to desert you, but I need to get to the Windjammer. I'll call you if I hear anything more. Why don't you go home, put your feet up, have a cup of chamomile tea, and phone Walter?"

Lola, zombie-like, put her car in gear.

* * * *

The dining room was set for lunch, Gillian was texting at a table by the front door, and Benny was deep into a crossword puzzle. It was the calm before the midday storm. In my back booth, I flipped through the pages of the *Etonville Standard* listlessly, scanning the local rag for any articles about the murder investigation. Not one. I paused on page fifteen and read my horoscope. *You will have intense communications today... beware of friends with secrets. Your love life is like a roller coaster, and you are feeling stressed by too much responsibility. Let's face it; a bubble bath would do you a world of good.*

Great.

Benny sidled over. "On my way here, I had to stop in Lacey's market, and I overheard the Banger sisters and the lady in frozen foods chattering away."

"About what?" I asked.

"Our leading man taking off?" Benny asked.

How did they find out so soon? "And we're off to the races. Word leaked faster than usual."

"So it's true?" Benny looked startled.

"Yep."

"Why would he...?" A light bulb went on, his eyes narrowed. "Is Dale running away from the police?"

"I don't know—and neither does anyone in Etonville." I felt exhausted and it was only eleven a.m.

"Okay," Benny said. "But that won't stop them from spreading gossip."

I heaved myself out of the booth. "You got that right."

Henry's homemade chicken noodle soup might have been just what the culinary doctor ordered, or would have been if customers took the time to taste it. Instead, theories about Dale and his vanishing act ricocheted around the room leaving patrons disinterested in Henry's lunch specials. Feeling unusually competitive, he had outdone himself today: fish tacos with cilantro and jalapeno and pounded steak sandwiches with mushrooms and onions. Henry wanted to make up for missing one day this week.

I moved around the dining room, eavesdropping on conversations.

"*Bye, Bye, Birdie* will go bye-bye."

"Good thing we saw it last weekend. Even if it did rain on the last half."

"I heard Dale Undershot was in the Mafia."

"I heard he skipped town to avoid child support."

"That's what the ELT gets for working with outsiders like the Creston Players."

Geez. The town's inner daffy was working overtime. When I couldn't listen any further, I escaped to the kitchen. Henry's silent grouchiness would be a pleasant reprieve.

"*Do-dee!*" Wilson caught me off-guard and delivered a whopping embrace.

"Oops! Hi Wilson!"

He beamed and returned to chopping peppers and spinach for tonight's special—angel hair pasta and chicken—while Henry prepped his chicken breasts and gave me the eyeball. He would never truly understand Wilson, the sweetness, the smiling, cheerful demeanor, the singing of show tunes and tapping his toes while sautéing onions...Wilson drove Henry crazy, but he had to admit that his young sous chef was talented, amiable, and—my mind stuttered. OMG! Wilson was always singing and dancing, Wilson knew the entire score to *Bye, Bye, Birdie*, and Wilson claimed he had memorized the choreography from watching a single performance. What was I thinking? Could this possibly work? I stole a peek at Henry wielding a cleaver as he split the breasts and cut the meat from the bones. How in the world would I convince him of this latest stunt, even if Lola agreed? Wilson, I was certain, would be more than willing. I'd been involved in some fairly outlandish capers during my time in Etonville, but what I was about to suggest might have been one of the wackiest.

"Henry, could I speak with you?" I asked politely.

He looked up, cleaver in mid-swing. "Go ahead."

I inclined my head toward Wilson. "In the pantry?"

Henry frowned. "Now?"

"Uh-huh."

* * * *

"I know it's a bit unconventional..." I said to Lola, whose eyes were bugging out of her head.

"I...I don't know what to say," she stammered.

We sat in her Lexus, which she parked outside the Etonville Little Theatre. "As I see it, you have two choices. You either cancel the show, lose box office, disappoint potential audience members, and alienate actors from both theaters. Or..."

"Replace Dale with the Windjammer's sous chef from Haiti who's never been on a stage but knows the show by heart. Hmm." She leaned back against the headrest. "I'll have to persuade Walter."

"You have five hours til curtain," I said hurriedly.

"I'm amazed Henry was willing to let Wilson go."

"It took some manipulation of his ego…having the restaurant to himself, becoming the town hero when the news breaks…We called Enrico and his cousin. Extra hands. When we get the delivery of snack boxes and drinks to the park, the Windjammer will be off the hook and Henry can concentrate on dinner," I said.

"And Wilson?"

"Thrilled and terrified. You're going to need to run through his scenes and dances and… whatever."

"You're sure he can sing the role?" Lola asked.

"Absolutely." I crossed my fingers. Having Wilson in *Bye, Bye, Birdie* was an act of daring without a safety net: there was no margin for error.

Lola hesitated for a second. "Let's do it! I'll talk with Walter, have Penny contact the cast for an early call, and give Chrystal a heads up. Luckily, Wilson and Dale are about the same size."

True. Both Dale and Wilson shared the same tall, robust physique. We high-fived and I gave Lola a hug for good luck. I smiled my phony grin, the one I reserved for those times when I might be in over my head. This just *had* to work.

Word about tonight's performance went viral as soon as we notified the cast. There was a cyclone of commotion as Wilson and I ran between the Windjammer and the theater. At the theater, Lola and Walter rehearsed the "Albert" scenes and songs before the chef-now-actor transferred to the park. Everyone forgot Dale completely. I tried to maintain some semblance of order, as Enrico and Carmen arrived to help with the dinner rush. I coordinated the shipping of the snack boxes to the park via the Windjammer vehicle and Pauli, who was tickled pink at the prospect of driving a full-sized van.

"Like, I got this," he said, twirling the keys on their chain.

"I trust you Pauli. But take it easy," I requested.

"Piece of cake."

"Some cast members will be at the park, ready to unload."

He smirked and saluted me. "Got it, boss."

I controlled the urge to ruffle his hair, which he would not have appreciated. He climbed aboard and I waved good-bye.

Benny shook his head. "I'd love to catch the scene at the park tonight. Wilson…who woulda' thought?"

"I'll cover for you tomorrow night and you can see for yourself," I said.

"Game on for the ELT."

17

"Step, turn, step, step, slide, step, turn." Walter demonstrated a dance move for Wilson who stood by patiently, and then repeated Walter's instructions perfectly— even better than Walter. When he opened his mouth to sing, Lola's dropped open too.

"I had no idea," Lola whispered as Wilson sang "Put on a Happy Face" with a Haitian accent.

"He's been serenading us at the Windjammer for weeks. Think he'll be okay?" I asked.

"Better than okay." Lola squeezed my shoulders. "Thanks for this."

"What about the lines?" I asked anxiously.

"We read through most of his scenes. He seems to have a good grasp on the story. Anyway, he can improvise or work script in hand," Lola said, ever the theater professional.

"I'm glad the show can go on."

"Lola, love, can you join us?" Walter motioned to Lola, and she dashed to the stage.

Walter had been adamant about not including a non-actor in his musical, insisting he could step in for Dale and play Lola's love interest. As if. Lola put her foot down. Wilson was a natural, she said, and anyway, audiences love to root for the understudy. Walter wasn't entirely convinced, but Lola persuaded him that non-traditional casting would put the ELT on the map.

"Yep. It'll put us on the map, all right." Out of nowhere, Penny was standing beside me.

"Penny! Get out of my mind! I can't take it!"

"O'Dell, you gotta learn to chill," she said and swaggered down the theater aisle.

She was right. I plopped into a theater seat as my cell binged. It was a text from Bill: *will be late to park tonight but will make my entrance.* No mention of any progress in the search for Dale. Never mind, I had enough on my plate to keep my brain occupied. The Windjammer's dinner rush and Ruby's harassment of Otto, and maybe his family, that resulted in a restraining order. What was her *modus operandi*? She may have hassled Otto over a number of years. So…Letters? Phone calls? Stalking? Following him around—

Edna appeared beside me. "That's one heckuva voice." She stood in the aisle watching Wilson sing a duet with Lola. "When I got the call to come in, I thought it was a 10-0." She winked at me. "That's 'Caution!' I figured Walter was taking over Dale's role." She grimaced. "But this… oh my. So much better!"

Abby appeared next to Edna. "What the…? Wilson? He's filling in for Dale? He's supposed to be my son?" she sputtered.

Edna confronted her. "Simmer down Abby. This production was a potential Code 30—"

That was a trauma case.

"—before Wilson got involved."

The Banger sisters waddled down the aisle and stopped when they realized what they were seeing. "Wilson is joining our show? He will be such fun!" said one.

"We love him," said the other.

"Besides, the Etonville Little Theatre needs more diversity in its casting. And Abby, you can pretend that you spent some time in Haiti before you moved to the United States," said the first sister.

"Gimme a break," Abby groused and moved on.

"Come on ladies, let's check in with Penny." Edna grasped each sister by an arm and leaned in to mutter. "Got a 10-36 for you. See me later." Edna escorted the ladies to the green room.

10-36? Was that weather and road advice or a stray animal? I couldn't keep up with Edna's codes.

As the rest of the cast assembled—shocked at Dale's replacement, but equally stunned by Wilson's singing and dancing skills—Penny ran to and fro, Walter flapped his arms dramatically, and Lola wrung her hands. Whew…it was going to be a close call, but it looked as though the co-production of *Bye, Bye, Birdie* would not be a Code 30 after all.

Penny announced that a run-through of Act One would commence in five minutes. That was all the cast and crew had time for if they were going to make it to the park by seven o'clock for the curtain. I supposed that if

Wilson made it through Act One, the audience would be more forgiving if he stumbled some in Act Two.

I located Wilson in the green room, script in hand, repeating lines to himself, his concentration fierce. Was it too much to ask of him? "Break a leg tonight, Wilson. You're going to be great," I said, hoping to encourage him.

I needn't have worried. In the midst of a theatrical crisis, with the whole show riding on his performance, Wilson was his optimistic self. "*Do-dee*, I am so excited. I can do this. And..." he winked, "...I will not break my leg!"

I texted Benny that I would stop by the Windjammer in a second.

"I understand we have you to thank for our new cast member." Alex paused on his way back from a break.

"Wilson does a bit of singing around the restaurant, and he loves musicals. Memorized show tunes as a kid. Serendipity I guess." I smiled at the musical director.

"Serendipity. Yes. Lot of things in life are like that," he said.

"Will you be happy when the show closes?"

"Mixed feelings always. You miss the performing and the camaraderie, but I'm leaving this area next week."

"You are? What will the Players do? Losing Ruby and then you," I asked.

He laughed heartily. "They'll get by. Looks like they will have to do without Dale too."

"So you heard too."

"He always plays fast and loose. I guess it caught up with him," Alex said.

"You know Dale pretty well?" I had no idea.

Alex stuffed his hands in his pockets. "As I told Chief Thompson, I know what I hear through the grapevine. But the word on the street... no pun intended...is that Dale had some...unethical investment issues."

"That would be reason enough to skip town," I said.

"True. If that was the reason. Nice talking to you, but I've got two minutes until Penny discharges her whistle," said Alex.

"Go! You don't want to be late."

The Creston Players were going to miss him whether he thought so or not. Alex was the most levelheaded member of the group as far as I could tell. Penny's blast signaled it was time to get the rehearsal underway. Alex finished the overture, and Lola and Wilson made their first entrance. I held my breath, but even I was pleasantly surprised. Lola, a true pro, took Wilson in hand. She walked him through the scene, improvising when necessary, covering when he missed a line, encouraging him when he hesitated. He wasn't Dale; but he was capable and when he belted his first number, the rest of the cast looked on in amazement. And applauded! I relaxed, but only a bit.

Benny texted that Henry was agitated because he thought the delivery service had screwed up. *Be right there*, I texted in return. I intended to see the Windjammer, and Henry, through the dinner service, and report to the park for Act Two. In exchange for releasing Wilson from the kitchen, I agreed to staff the concession stand with ELT folks which left Gillian and Carmen in the dining room tonight. I hurried quietly out of the theater and ran next door.

I'd barely walked in when Henry burst into the dining room. "I'm missing ten pounds of pasta!"

"Bottom shelf of the pantry. I rearranged things to create more space," I said and trailed him to the storage.

Henry wiped his forehead. "I like the way everything was arranged before. I like knowing where I can find things."

He didn't like change of any kind.

"I know."

"And I'm not running around the dining room to talk to people while they're eating!" he said defiantly, and tromped back into the kitchen.

Oops. Someone had snitched on Wilson.

* * * *

I parked my Metro two blocks away from the park next to an empty lot that had once been home to a two-story apartment building. When the owners put it up for sale, the city fathers purchased the property to build tennis courts on the land. Not everyone in Etonville was delighted about it. Nevertheless, now the lot was home to a backhoe, construction paraphernalia, and the remains of the apartment building. I applied a coat of lipstick, ran a comb through my tangled mane, and double-checked the interior dome light. I had no desire to come back to a dead battery again.

Even a block away, I could hear the combo beating out "Lot of Livin' to Do". As I rounded a corner at the edge of the park, Romeo, Janice, and the teenagers came into view. They bounced and romped around the stage. The audience was sizeable tonight, filling the seats, the grassy slope, and overflowing onto the cement pathways that lined the audience areas. I walked across the soccer field and crept up to the concession stand. Georgette was on duty.

"Good night?" I asked.

"Ran out of everything," she whispered.

The Windjammer was making a nice piece of cash during the run of *Bye, Bye, Birdie*. I took the receipts and relieved Georgette, who scurried to find a seat. I craned my neck to get a better view of the proceedings, and hooted and applauded with the rest of the onlookers when Vernon and Edna sang "Kids," shuffling their way around the stage. Wilson was due on soon.

"Hey." It was Bill, panting and sweating. "Where are we?"

"Midway through the act. You'd better sneak backstage." There was an entrance for the cast behind a maze of curtains opposite from where we were standing. "How is everything?"

"All right." He was cautious, assuming his police chief armor.

"Did you find Dale yet?"

Bill wavered. "Can't talk now. I'd better go."

"See you after. Break a leg." He groaned and dashed off. It was only this morning that I'd whipped up fried eggs for us, but now that seemed like days ago.

Wilson's rich baritone cut a swath through my mental debris. He is on the telephone begging Rosie/Lola to come back to him, but Lola, wanting no part of her former fiancé, is partying with a group of Shriners. Wilson rescues her in the nick of time! It was fun to observe our sous chef "stand up" to Abby, his stage mother, and though the ages and races of Lola, Wilson, and Abby didn't quite compute, the actors took their cue from the patrons, who were having a blast, and enjoyed themselves. Yes! I was feeling vindicated. Now it was time for the Sweet Apple police to make an entrance and wrap up the mayhem. Sure enough there was Bill, looking a bit less awkward in his costume, swinging a billy club, and working to bring things under control. His concentration was impressive given all that must have been on his mind.

By the time Wilson and Lola finished their duet, the audience was on its feet, roaring its approval! The bows were orderly—unlike last weekend—and Lola graciously urged Wilson to step forward and be acknowledged for taking on the role. He shyly did so. It was a wonderful moment and, frankly, I felt like the smartest person in the room though I'd never say that out loud.

Alex and the combo took off and the crew went to work, clearing the scenery and preparing to lock up for the night. The cast was giddy with excitement, running onto the stage, and then off again, yakking with parents, friends, and guests. Chrystal chased them down to seize their costumes. It was typical theater bedlam. Bill, already out of his costume, talked on his cell at the other end of the grassy slope. I grabbed my bag and the cash box and made it halfway to him.

"*Do-dee*!" Wilson picked me up, as usual, and swung me around, but this time I didn't mind. I laughed with him, celebrating his tremendous victory. "It is *ze* best night of my life." He set me down gently and I looked up at him. He'd been crying.

"You were terrific! You might be as good an actor as you are a chef," I said.

"*Impossible*! But for now…" he shrugged.

"Do you want a ride home? We can put your bike in my trunk."

"Thank you *Do-dee*. I will ride home and think about tonight. It is like a dream." He trotted off.

It might be difficult to nail Wilson's feet to the Windjammer floor after this.

"Can you believe it? A star is born!" Edna said. "That kid can sing—and did you see those dance moves? I told Walter we should consider doing *West Side Story* next year. He could play Tony."

Another piece of non-traditional casting? "Well, Wilson might have other plans."

"I think he has a future on the stage. Good night Dodie. Good work saving the show." Edna winked and walked away.

"By the way, what's a 10-36?" I called out.

"Oooh. Forgot!" She came back. "Confidential information."

"That's right. Now I remember. So what's the information?" I asked sotto voce though there was no one near enough to overhear our conversation.

"Dale was spotted at Newark airport this afternoon," Edna said.

Yikes. "Attempting a getaway?"

"Looks like it."

"Was he arrested?" I asked.

"Not when I came to rehearsal. But the chief and Suki were in conference with the Port Authority cops." Edna paused. "I always thought Dale was too handsome for his own good. See you tomorrow. Cheers!"

No wonder Bill was preoccupied. I scanned the area, but he was gone. Oh well…I'll catch up with him later. My cell binged. Bill: *see you at my place?* I texted a confirmation and made a last effort to find Lola. I saw her earlier consulting with Walter and then I lost track of them. The park was almost empty. I headed for my car humming "Put on a Happy Face." This show really was hummable.

The streets surrounding the park were deserted. Trees swayed in the summer breeze—casting oddly shaped shadows on the ground. It was eerie. Houses had dim light seeping out of upstairs windows, but for the most part Etonville had gone to sleep. The only sound was the slap of my sandals against the pavement. I picked up my pace. Normally, I had no fear treading the streets of Etonville alone at night, but tonight the darkness and silence pricked the hairs on the nape of my neck. I could see my Metro fifty yards ahead. I breathed out my angst with relief. Nerves.

I was ten feet away from the rear bumper when I inhaled the odor of gasoline. Oh no. Not another leak. What was happening to my beloved Metro? I instinctively glanced around. The houses on either end of the empty property were dark—one had a "For Sale" sign in the front yard and the other looked as though the occupants were away. I shivered again. A lone streetlight, two doors down, provided limited illumination. The construction equipment loomed larger and creepier. I forced myself to walk swiftly but calmly to the car. Gas had leaked onto the ground and the sweet-smelling stench was so strong it sent a wave of nausea coursing through me. I kept telling myself it was only a gas leak. I might have enough left in the tank to make it to Bill's or I might need to call for a ride. But either way I needed to get in the car and check to see if there was any fuel left.

I yanked the door handle, bounded onto the front seat and inserted the key in the ignition, my hand shaking. I turned it to ACC and sure enough, there was a quarter of a tank. Okay, I told myself, I could make it to Bill's. I turned the key further and the engine leapt to life. As I shifted out of Park and into Drive, I smelled smoke. Bile rose in my throat. What was I thinking—igniting the engine with gas leaking out of the car? I could hear two voices in my head. Bill and Timothy both warning me about the condition of the Metro, that it was time to find another car, and was I crazy turning on the ignition with gas flowing around? Blah, blah, blah. I jammed the car into Park again and shut off the engine. The odor of the gas and wisps of smoke leaked into the interior. I gasped for air, terrified. I had to get out of here! I gripped the door handle. It fell off into my hand. What was going on? My breathing became labored. I grasped the window handle to get some air and it rotated, spinning in place. What the…? I leaned across the seat to check the passenger door handle. It was gone and the window crank was equally useless. I scrambled into the back seat and had no luck with those windows, either.

My hands shook as I punched 911 into my cell. One ring, then two.

"Etonville Police Department." Ralph yawned. I'd woken him up.

"Ralph! I'm stuck inside my car and it's on fire! There's smoke and—"

"Who is this? Where are you?" he asked.

"It's Dodie and I'm on the south side of the park by the empty lot. Get help here now! Before my car explodes!"

"10-4!"

I clicked off. I didn't think I could wait for Ralph to rouse the fire department and send reinforcements. I had to help myself. I found a blanket that I'd thrown in the back seat last winter when the temperature hit record lows and a hammer I kept in the glove compartment…just in case.

Flames licked the edges of the hood. I climbed back into the driver's seat, coughing, and ducked into the blanket to avoid potential flying shards of glass. I attacked the window with the hammer, swinging the thing as if my life depended on it. One, two, three, blows and the safety glass shattered, creating a spider web pattern. One more good thwack and the glass burst out of the car, allowing a gust of fresh air into the Metro. The smoke was thick now, black and oily. The flames sent heat into the interior. I pushed bits of glass out of the way with the blanket and plunged head first through the empty window, landing on the grassy strip next to the curb, banging my shoulder and scraping my head against a tree root. As I crawled away on all fours to a safe distance from my burning car, the alarm of a fire engine cut through the quiet of the evening. Sets of flashing lights meant that Ralph had galvanized all of the emergency vehicles in Etonville. A giant bang overshadowed a series of loud cracks from under the hood as flames completely engulfed the Metro.

* * * *

The street had become a circus. The ambulance arrived with the EMS technicians, who checked me out and provided ice for my aching shoulder, a bandage for a cut on my forehead, and oxygen to clear my lungs. The firefighters cleaned up their equipment after they hosed down the Metro. Timothy was there with his tow truck. He scratched his head as he examined the heap of burnt-out metal and plastic. Once again, Ralph handled crowd control—since the neighborhood that seemed deserted thirty minutes ago was now teeming with life. People gathered in curious knots on the sidewalk and porches. Bill was there, in jeans and a tee shirt. He'd been in the shower—rinsing off the sweat and make-up of his performance—when Ralph reached him.

Bill conferred for a moment with the fire brigade, then shook hands and headed my way. Though the night was still warm in the seventies, I trembled under a mylar blanket that an EMT draped over me. I could not wrap my mind around the fact that my Metro was no more. I was in the first stage of grieving: denial.

"How are you doing?" Bill asked kindly.

"Someone is out to get me," I said, angry. I moved on to the second stage.

"Slow down. What exactly happened?"

"My Metro was destroyed!" I said dramatically, and sipped water to get the taste of burning out of my mouth.

"I know, but I need more information if I'm going to figure this out." Bill was speaking patiently as if I were a kid or an old person.

"I've already figured it out. Gas leaking, a fire under the hood, the door and window handles not working. What does that sound like to you? Duh." I didn't care that I was doing a variation on shooting the messenger. Bill was trying to do his job, but I was right. Someone who knew a lot about cars, my Metro in particular, had targeted me. First, there was the brake fluid, then the battery, and now the leaking fuel from my car with no way out. The thought of my possible demise sent me into a spasm of shivers.

"Do you want to go to the hospital? The EMTs—"

"No!" I said brusquely.

"Let's get you home and cleaned up." He wiped away a smudge of black soot on my cheek.

Bill helped me settle into the front seat of his BMW, and I sank gratefully into the soft leather. Through the windshield, I watched him consult with Timothy, who nodded and gestured to his tow truck driver. It was like being at a funeral, seeing my red Chevy carted off so ingloriously. Spontaneously, tears trickled down my cheeks.

Bill slid into the driver's seat and stared at me. "You've had quite a shock."

I sniffed. "I don't suppose there's any chance my Metro can be repaired?"

Bill's eyes opened as if I was asking to borrow a million dollars. Yep. I was into stage three: bargaining.

* * * *

I stood in Bill's shower. The steaming water nearly scalded the skin of my shoulders and back. I scrubbed at the grime on my face and hands. In addition to my sore joints and scraped forehead, my knees were rubbed raw. I shampooed my hair three times to remove the sooty stink. I scoured myself to a new level of clean.

Bill was waiting with one of his robes outside the shower door. He swaddled me, then held me a moment. "Feeling any better?"

"Yeah. Sorry about jumping on you…" He handed me a face towel, and I wrapped it around my head.

"Not a problem. After the jolt you had."

* * * *

In the living room, Bill laid out wine, glasses, and an array of snacks—cheeses and crackers, some veggies, and ranch dip. It all looked beautiful, but I was too upset and jumpy to eat much. I nibbled on a celery stick and skipped the wine in favor of a glass of water.

"Why would someone want to demolish my Metro?" I asked.

"If that's what happened," he said kindly.

"What's that supposed to mean?"

"Look, Dodie, please don't take this the wrong way, but you've been skating on thin ice with that car since I met you. It has well over a hundred thousand miles."

"But it runs fine." I paused. "Ran fine."

"Until this year. With the brake issue and the battery and now the fuel leak."

"And I still say someone deliberately sabotaged my car," I said.

"I'll have the arson squad give it a onceover, but in its present condition, it might be difficult to find evidence of tampering," he said.

Bill was right, of course. My Metro was a burnt-out shell of its former self. Finding that someone had tampered with the interior handles on the doors and windows was a long shot. "I understand what you're saying, but isn't it strange that Ruby was murdered in a car and I've had a series of 'accidents' in my car?"

Bill placed his wine glass on a coffee table coaster. "So you think the issues with your Metro are related to Ruby's death? How?"

I had no idea. I simply thought it was a coincidence that parallel car events were taking place. "Someone knows I've been looking into Ruby's life while you've been looking into her death."

"Someone? Like Dale?" Bill pinched the bridge of his nose. Tired, frustrated too. "But why would that someone, presumably Dale, want to go after you? Unless something you found would explain her death?" he asked.

"No." I guzzled another eight ounces of water. "How am I going to get around without a car?"

"I have a solution." His quirky grin emerged. "You can use my car until you figure out what you want to do."

I interrupted my hydration to blink and cough. "Your BMW?"

"Why not? It sits in the driveway. I spend most of my life in my cruiser. Unless you have a problem driving a BMW?"

Yowza! I supposed I could get used to it. "Well...if you really think that's the best solution..."

"I do." He put an arm around me. "Let's get some sleep and we can work things out in the morning. This has been a stressful night. The gas leak made you frantic. People in those kinds of situations often lose the ability to accomplish normal tasks."

I eased away from him. "Normal tasks? Like opening a car door or cranking a window?"

"You're taking this the wrong way—"

"If I was so frantic and out of control, how did I manage to have the presence of mind to pound the window to pieces and throw myself out of the car?" I fumed.

"I'm trying to explain that—"

"It's fine. I get it." I stood and tightened Bill's robe around me. "I'm going upstairs," I said politely.

"I have some work to finish. I'll be up later."

I stomped off. Bill had his rational way of justifying events, but my instincts were reliable and my neck hairs were a dependable radar system. Tonight both were off the I-got-a-hunch meter. I had to figure this out by myself.

18

I awoke early…before Bill. He was snoring softly when I crept from bed, pulled on yesterday's clothes, and padded downstairs. The smell of brewing coffee—thanks to Bill's automatic timer—was tempting, but I was a woman with an agenda. I found my bag where I'd dropped it last night and checked messages. It was seven a.m. and already I was bombarded by Etonville's rumor mill. Carol: *Are you alive???* Lola: *OMG!!* Edna: *Heard you had a 10-33 and an 11-85. Glad no 11-80.* Huh? Penny: *O'Dell…you gotta learn to stay out of trouble.*

Empathy was not a tool on her belt.

I stole out the door, shutting it softly behind me, as I rummaged through my purse for my car keys. Then I stood stock-still on Bill's driveway, gobsmacked. I didn't have my Metro to climb into anymore. I felt helpless and overwhelmed.

"Forget these?"

I pivoted and saw Bill, mouth creeping up at one end, tousled hair, in a tee shirt and shorts, the BMW remote key fob dangling from his index finger.

I hesitated, caught between a boulder and the toughest place I'd been in since last night. Of course, I forgot that Bill offered his BMW since I now had no car of my own. My pride suffered and I was looking for a graceful way to accept.

"Ummm…yeah…guess so."

He met me halfway and I reached for the fob. "Thanks. I..."

Bill waited for a second.

"Never mind."

Then he said, "The brakes are a little tight and the gas pedal is very sensitive. Remember it's keyless entry."

"Got it."

"And you might need to fill the tank. Premium." Bill's cell rang. "Hello? What?" He listened. "Be right there."

The tone of his voice and his hasty signoff caused me to pause. "Something wrong?"

Bill looked grim. "They've arrested Dale Undershot. He's being interrogated in Creston."

"That means the murder is solved?"

"Our witness will see him in a lineup later today."

"Things are moving fast."

"If he's identified, he could face arraignment tomorrow."

"I'm glad for your sake. And Ruby's," I said slowly and unlocked the door of the BMW, sliding onto the cool leather. There was something about the smell of a relatively new car.

Bill was at the door before I could shut it. "Look Dodie, about last night, I'm sorry if it seemed like I didn't take your accident seriously."

"I don't think it was an accident." I pushed a button and the powerful engine growled.

"I know you don't and I intend to speak to the county arson guys just as soon as I finish with Dale today."

I nodded. "Let me know what you find out?"

He kissed me on the cheek. "Of course I will."

Bill shut the door and I lowered the window. "Etonville is going to have a field day today between my fire and Dale's arrest."

"Any chance word won't travel from Creston to Etonville?"

"None," I said and backed out of his driveway. Before I could put the car in Drive, Bill was back inside. It was the truth. I was happy for him and the resolution of the murder case, but some things didn't add up for me. There were loose ends that required tying up...such as my car "incidents," the man in Ruby's apartment, for that matter, the man with her in the deli. And the missing Ambien bottle. What about her history of harassing a former love? Had she done something to Dale that set him off? Had there been a ferocious argument resulting in Dale's drugging and murdering her? Had Dale been so upset with me for investigating Ruby's life that he threatened me by way of my Metro? That would mean he was at the park last night and rigged my car. Maybe he hired someone to do it for him... My mind was in a whirl.

I drove carefully through the streets of Etonville. Traffic was sparse at this hour, but still, I was very much aware of driving the luxury automobile. I'd driven it once before when Bill had broken his ankle in New York last

February. I relaxed my death grip on the steering wheel, and enjoyed the experience of a smooth ride, luxurious interior, and incredible pickup.

I eased the BMW to the curb next to the vacant lot where my car had caught fire: the scene of the crime, as far as I was concerned. I got out and checked the street. No one stirred in the nearby houses. I inhaled. The air reeked of burnt oil and twisted metal. Black, grimy patches covered the concrete where the Metro caught on fire. There was nothing to gain by staring at the blackened roadway, so my attention drifted to the vacant lot. Out of curiosity, I picked my way through the dirt and pieces of broken bricks that were scattered around, obviously waiting for the grader to smooth the ground before construction of the tennis courts began. I leaned against an idle backhoe. From this vantage point, my Metro would have been about twenty yards away. I shivered. What if the perpetrator had been on the scene witnessing me struggle to escape the car? The thought made me mad as hell, and sharpened my senses. It couldn't have been Dale, could it? He was at Newark Airport attempting to flee. Maybe an accomplice of his? How would someone know I parked my Metro here? I didn't know I would end up on this street. Unless someone followed me…

The day was getting on. I needed to change, grab some coffee, and head to the Windjammer. I might as well surrender to the fact of the Metro's demise. But something would not let go of my attention. I scanned the area. What was it? The ground was littered with garbage, the residue of workers and kids playing in the dirt—soda cans, Styrofoam food boxes, candy wrappers. Shoe and boot prints crisscrossed the dry mud. Could some of those footprints belong to whomever sabotaged my car?

* * * *

At home, I showered hurriedly—a lick and a promise as my mother would say—since I'd scrubbed thoroughly at Bill's place less than eight hours ago. I pulled on three-quarter pants, as the temperature was supposedly hitting eighty-eight today, and a sleeveless blouse. Might as well be comfortable as I hurtled through the day. I ran a brush through my damp, knotted tresses as my cell buzzed. Again. There were now half a dozen more text messages asking about my welfare. Etonville could be aggravating as hell when one was in need of privacy, but the town could be downright heartwarming when one faced a crisis. The last text was Lola. I tapped on her number.

"Dodie! How are you? Were you in the hospital? Why didn't you—"

"Take it easy Lola. I'm fine. I stayed at Bill's last night," I said.

"Oh. Well. I need details. Everyone is so upset that your Metro was firebombed."

"It wasn't exactly firebombed—"

"Why didn't you open the door and get out?" she asked.

"Good question. Coffee Heaven in fifteen minutes?"

Lola agreed to meet me at the café. I finished dressing, then dashed to my new wheels before my neighbors, who had begun to gather on the sidewalk near my driveway, could comment on Bill's car, my Metro, the fire, or any other aspect of my life. "Good morning!" I exclaimed.

"Dodie? We heard about the fire—"

"All good here!" I left them standing, their mouths agape at the sight of me behind the steering wheel of the gold BMW.

I garnered a few stares as I cruised down Ames and over Fairfield; Bill's distinctive-looking automobile was familiar around town. I found a parking space directly in front of Coffee Heaven. Entering the diner meant risking the full fury of town innuendo, but my need for a comforting caramel macchiato was greater than my need for isolation this morning. The entrance bells had barely jingled when all eyes were on me. I ducked my head as I made my way to a booth. That did not deter the faithful, who, to my surprise, tagged along. Six or seven people formed a knot around me shooting comments so swiftly I couldn't respond.

"Dodie, we're so glad you weren't hurt."

"Your poor Metro…"

"That car was about ready to croak anyway."

"I can get you a good deal on a used Chevy."

"Gas leaks are nothing to fool with."

"All right folks, let's give Dodie some air." Jocelyn shooed everyone back to their respective tables but not before they touched my shoulder or squeezed my hand. Sometimes, you had to love this place.

"Thanks Jocelyn. I'll have my—"

"Regular. Got it right here." She plopped my warm cinnamon bun and caramel macchiato in front of me. "It's on the house today."

"That's sweet. Thanks."

"I heard you were inside when it exploded." She placed her hands on her hips and gazed at me.

"What? No! I was out of the car—"

"When you smell gas, you gotta skedaddle, kiddo," she said.

"Right."

Jocelyn dangled a warning finger in my face. "Cause when things go wrong with a car, odds are its time is up."

I bit into my breakfast. My insides relaxed, and I breathed calmly for the first time this morning.

"You don't look as though you nearly caught fire," Lola said and sat down in the booth facing me.

I lowered my voice. "It was a close call."

Lola frowned. "Dodie?"

I quietly described last night: the gas leak, the broken handles on the doors and windows, knocking the glass out with a hammer, and finally, throwing myself out the window. Lola's expression ran the gamut from horrified to unbelieving to frightened.

"Someone was trying to…?" she said, afraid to finish the sentence.

"Kill me. I think so."

She stared at me in silence. "I don't know what to say. Who would want to do such a thing? What does it all mean?" Lola wailed plaintively. A couple at a table near us looked up, interested.

"Shhh. We'd better get out of here."

"Good idea."

I left a tip for my free breakfast, and Lola and I walked out leisurely, yakking about the weather as heads monitored our progress to the door.

"Coffee Lola?" Jocelyn sang out.

"No thanks. I'll be back later." Lola flipped her hand in a kind of royal gesture and we made our getaway.

We decided that I'd leave the BMW where it was—parked several doors down from the municipal building and the Etonville police department—and climbed into Lola's Lexus. I had about an hour or so before I had to get to work. Etonville was too claustrophobic this morning, so we drove to Creston. I wondered when news would break about Dale and how Lola would take it.

"What did Bill say about the fire?" Lola asked as she maneuvered her car onto State Route 53.

"He thinks it was an accident. That I was so panicked I couldn't get the door and window handles to work," I said.

"He doesn't believe you?"

"Sort of, but he's been telling me for months that I need to ditch the Metro in favor of a newer model—one that doesn't leak brake fluid or gas or have a faulty battery."

"You'll miss the Metro." Lola was all sympathy.

A lump rose in my throat. "Yeah. Like losing an old friend."

Lola turned off the highway and drove down Creston's main street to a familiar café.

"But I could get used to a BMW."

We exchanged smiles. I had a sudden impulse, as long as we were in Creston... "Do you mind if we get coffee somewhere else?"

"Fine by me. What did you have in mind?" she asked.

I explained that I wanted to stop in the deli across the street from Ruby's apartment. I didn't mention a need to confirm that Dale was probably the man with Ruby in the store the day before she died. I simply told Lola that the clerk had met Ruby a number of times, and that I wanted to ask if she ever talked about her past. Now that I knew so much about her. Lola agreed to my proposal, but asked that I talk to the guy by myself. She had to read and respond to texts.

That made things easier.

"Make my coffee a large!" Lola said.

"I'll only be a minute." I hopped out of the Lexus and strode into the deli.

As before, the shelves were half-empty and the overall appearance worn out. Nothing had changed. The same young man was waiting on a customer who had ordered buttered rolls and coffees for four. I checked my phone for new messages—none in the past half hour.

"Can I help you?" Still polite, the clerk acknowledged my presence, and then registered my identity. "Hi again."

"You remember me?"

"Sure. You're Ruby's friend," he said.

"Good memory. I'll have two coffees, one black, and one light cream. Make that second one a large."

"Coming right up."

"Business still slow?" I asked courteously.

"Yeah. If it keeps up like this, we might have to close." He jammed lids on the containers and pushed them toward me.

I handed him a five and three singles. "Keep the change."

The clerk picked up the bills. "You sure?"

"Absolutely. By the way, I'm curious. Did Ruby ever mention her past?"

"Her past?"

"What brought her to New Jersey? I know she was born and raised in Indiana."

"She told me once that her family lived out there, but they all died."

"Nothing else?"

The kid regarded me warily, like last time. I had to finish up and as Jocelyn would say, skedaddle. I pulled up the picture file on my cell. Pauli took photos at rehearsal one night. We used them to promote the concession stand and snack boxes on the Windjammer website. One picture was a performance shot of Dale and Lola onstage. "Do you know this guy? He's with the Creston Players. Was he the man you saw with Ruby that one time?"

He looked from me to the photo and back to me. "Not him. It was somebody else. He was… ordinary. Not like an actor. You sure you're not a…cop…or private eye?"

"Neither. Just a friend." I picked up the coffees. "Thanks."

So, there was *another* man in Ruby's life besides Dale.

Lola was on the phone when I opened the car door. Her voice was high-pitched, almost manic. "He was where? Oh no. What? Yes, of course, if he's guilty…what a nightmare!"

Word was out.

"Carol, I have to go. Talk later."

I handed Lola the coffee as she clicked off. "Dale's been arrested. They found him at Newark airport—trying to get on a flight to Mexico. Fleeing the country. Can you imagine?" Lola absorbed my silence. "You knew?"

"I found out this morning. Bill wanted to keep a lid on things as long as possible. I'm sorry Lola."

"I thought I knew him. We all thought we knew him," she said, clearly disappointed.

"The only one who really knew him was Ruby and it cost her life," I said gently.

Lola shuddered. "What was his motivation? Why would he want her dead?"

"It'll all come out. Meanwhile, there's some things about Ruby that will shock you too." I recounted the story Pauli found on the Internet about the restraining order. "Ruby was no stranger to harassment. Maybe she was going after Dale for some reason."

Lola put her car in gear and we rode back to Etonville, wrestling with the latest news of the case, Dale's possible motives, and the strange life Ruby led. We pulled to the front of Coffee Heaven.

"Hang in there Lola. I'll see you tonight at the cast party." I squeezed her hand and she nodded.

I picked up the BMW and moved it to the front of the Windjammer, where I could keep an eye on Bill's prized auto. Etonville was a safe small town…usually.

I walked in the door and hit a wall of concern. Benny ran around the bar and gripped my arms. "I can't believe your Metro exploded. Good thing you weren't in it at the time, or you wouldn't be here." The thought caused him to turn pale.

"Right. It was something—"

Wilson sprinted out of the kitchen, edged Benny out of the way and, as usual, clutched me in an enthusiastic embrace. "*Do-dee! Mon Dieu!* I am so sorry!"

"It's okay, Wilson," I said, and disengaged myself from his arms.

Even Henry offered sympathy. "That car was a disaster waiting to happen. You have to be more careful in the future."

"Time to look for something newer," I said, attempting a breezy tone.

Benny eyeballed me skeptically. I wasn't fooling him. "You loved that car."

Wilson and Henry returned to the kitchen where the aromas of the lunch specials wafted into the dining room. Lasagna soup in a bowl, without ricotta cheese, and with spiral pasta—filling comfort food—something I could use today.

"Hey, heard about Dale Undershot?" Benny asked, as he unpacked a carton of white wine. "Arrested trying to leave the country. Like something out of a spy novel."

It *was* a pretty dramatic development. "I can't imagine what the gossip mill will do with the story."

"You have an inside track," Benny smirked.

"Very funny." I threw a bar towel in his direction.

"Has the chief said anything about Dale's motive? That's the one thing no one seems to know anything about."

Only the payments to Ruby... "Sorry, no information on that score."

I was correct. By noon, the Windjammer was awash with more rumors than it could properly handle. Folks were giddy, coming up with half-baked theories on everything from why my Metro caught fire to Dale's demise and his unscrupulous association with Ruby. I began the lunch rush roving from table to table to acknowledge customers' sincere distress.

"Dodie, we were so worried about you," said one Banger sister.

"Thanks."

"We keep a fire extinguisher in our car," said the other. "We're prepared in case of an emergency."

I remembered the fire video my parents forced my brother Andy and me to watch when we were teens. I visualized the two sisters yanking the pin, aiming at the fire, squeezing the lever, and sweeping the extinguisher from side to side. *Yikes!*

"We had a fire in my house when I was a kid," said Vernon between spoons full of the lasagna soup.

"You did? You never told me that," said Mildred, huffily. "Husbands are supposed to tell their wives everything."

"If I told you everything, we'd be divorced. Anyway, I had to climb out a second floor window."

"Me too," I said. "Not the second floor. Just the window."

The Banger sisters, Vernon, and Mildred all regarded me, perplexed. "Dodie, we heard they had to use the Jaws of Life to get you out."

"Nope. No jaws. I whacked the window with a hammer."

"You're sure they didn't have to cut you out?" Vernon asked, almost disappointed.

Geez. I excused myself, and moved to the cash register where Edna was taking carryout back to the police station. "That's two lasagna soups, a spinach salad, a special burger, and tuna on rye." I rang up the order. "That's a lot of food."

Edna took some bills out of her wallet. "Some Creston cops are joining the chief at the station."

"Any talk about Dale?" I asked.

"Everything's tight as a tick on that score." She hugged the brown takeout bags and leaned into the cash register. "But I can tell you this. They had Dale in a lineup this morning." She raised an eyebrow.

Did the eyewitness hammer a nail in Dale's coffin? "Doesn't look good for him."

"Copy that." Edna hurried away.

19

The restaurant was full of people who agreed it didn't look good. They had plenty of thoughts on why, which I discovered when I circulated with a coffee pot.

"Dale never should have taken the role in *Bye, Bye, Birdie*. That way he wouldn't have met Ruby."

What?

"I heard he'd known her from the time they were kids."

Was Dale from Indiana?

"They're saying Ruby owed Dale money."

Hardly.

"…or he was getting revenge because she wanted him out of the Creston Players."

That's a motive for murder?

"Ruby knew a secret about Dale," said one patron.

Now that made sense.

My cell buzzed. It was Pauli.

"Uh, like, hi!" he said.

"You're awfully perky. Having fun in the frozen foods?"

"Uh…I'm on my break."

"What's up?" I motioned to Gillian to clean off some tables and headed to my back booth.

"I was doing some lateral thinking again…like you know…coming at Ruby's life from another angle."

"What did you come up with?" I asked.

"I forgot about her and, like, searched stuff on Otto Heinlein, Junior." He paused. "That was the son's name."

"That's a great idea. We know Otto Heinlein Senior died in 1986 and his wife was already dead...but what happened to the son?"

"There's some things on his birth and high school. He graduated in 1987. Then nothing until 1991. He got a speeding ticket in Ohio. Like, he was in college there."

"So he left town too. Guess staying in Greenburg after his father's death was too much for him. Is that all you found?"

"Nope. He moved to Pennsylvania in 1993."

The Windjammer suddenly felt warm.. "Pauli, Ruby lived in Ohio and Pennsylvania too."

"Yeah."

"What are you doing later? Can you come to the Windjammer after work?"

"No problemo. I get off at four," he said.

"We need to do a timeline for Ruby and Otto Junior."

"Awesome. Gotta bounce."

Pauli clicked off. My mind raced. Was it simply a coincidence that both Otto Junior and Ruby moved first to Ohio and then to Pennsylvania during approximately the same years? Was Ruby following Otto's son and harassing him as well? Did he end up in New Jersey too, or had Ruby abandoned her pattern of provocation? If Ruby *had* been stalking Otto Junior, her need for revenge ran deeper than I suspected. I was beginning to see a motive for Dale's actions if he was the object of her persecution.

I was so lost in thought that I missed Bill's entrance until he was leaning against the back of my booth. "Hey, how's the car running?"

I jerked my head up. "*Whoa*! Don't sneak up on me like that!"

"Sneak up on you? In the middle of a busy restaurant?" His mouth ticked up at one end.

"You're in a good mood. You here for lunch? Henry's lasagna soup is almost sold out—"

"I ate. It was excellent. My compliments to Henry." Bill sat down opposite me and withdrew a notepad from his shirt pocket. "Just tying up loose ends, as you would say."

"Meaning?"

He glanced at the pad. "I got a preliminary report on the Metro from the arson squad. Cause of the fire was the gas leak. Could have been the result of a fuel tank rupture. According to them, fuel injectors seldom leak but their rubber components are susceptible to corrosion. They can wear out. Same with fuel lines. Corrosion, road debris...they become more vulnerable as a car ages."

There it was again—road debris. Same excuse given for the leak of my brake fluid. What did these guys think? That I was deliberately running over garbage in the road? "So nothing definitive?"

"The squad is continuing to investigate," Bill said calmly.

"What about the interior? Anything on the door and window handles?"

"They'll take a look but the interior was badly damaged..." He spread his hands as if helpless.

"Right," I said coolly.

"Look Dodie, if there's anything to discover, they'll find it. Meanwhile, you have transport, so let's be glad you weren't badly injured."

I stared at him. "Since when did you become so tranquil? Suki's rubbing off on you." Her middle name was 'om'.

"Things are winding down on the Ruby front," he said confidentially.

Bill described the scene at the lineup, how the witness recognized Dale, how Dale, when confronted with the results of the lineup, broke down and admitted to a fraudulent relationship with Ruby. "She was collecting a thousand dollars a month to keep her mouth shut. It's not an airtight case for murder but the county prosecutor thinks he can make it stick."

I gasped. Dale wasn't paying Ruby the interest on her investments; he was paying her off. "Ruby was blackmailing him?"

"Apparently he's been bilking clients for years. A modified Ponzi scheme—"

"Like Bernie Madoff?" I asked.

"On a more limited scale. But yes, the same principle. Paying off existing clients with new investors' money. All the time Dale is skimming off funds for his personal use."

"He was doing this to Ruby?"

"Apparently with Ruby he was guilty of something called 'churning.' Making unnecessary or weak stock trades to pad his own pocket. Dale was no match for Ruby. She discovered what he was up to and threatened to call the police. When he begged her to reconsider, she offered to keep quiet about his illegal activities in exchange for a monthly payment."

"Wow."

"He's providing a list of other clients who might be victims."

"So when I saw them arguing backstage..."

"Dale had had enough and was pressuring Ruby to let him off the hook. After all, he'd been paying her hush money for a year," Bill said.

"And your eyewitness?"

"She spotted Dale and Ruby on the access road by the highway. He appeared to be physically threatening her."

"And Dale admitted all this?" I asked, surprised.

"He confirmed the fight but denied killing Ruby. He says she was alive when he gave up and left."

"How did he get her out there?"

"He was following her to Creston when she suddenly stopped on the access road. Going in the wrong direction. She'd been driving erratically and Dale thought she might be drunk."

"The Ambien?" I asked.

"Most likely. According to Dale, he pulled over after Ruby did. When he approached the car, he thought she was falling asleep. He tried to talk to her but she pushed him, and continued to drink from the flask. He says he got angry, ripped the flask out of her hands, and threw it away."

"That's why it wasn't in her bag!"

"Supposedly it's somewhere in the grassy area off the access highway. If he's telling the truth we'll find it."

"So he spiked the flask with Ambien?"

"Denies that too," Bill said.

Was it worth mentioning the missing Ambien in Ruby's bathroom? "I hate to bring this up because I know you got your nose bent out of shape when you found out I'd been back to Ruby's apartment but…"

"What?" He became suspicious.

"You know how I like to check out bathrooms? Well, the first time Lola and I went to Ruby's, the Ambien bottle in her medicine cabinet was half full. The lid was off," I said.

Bill tucked his pad into his pants pocket. "And?"

"The second time I was there, the bottle was gone."

"This means what?" he asked, "Besides the fact that you weren't supposed to be snooping around."

"Someone removed it? The man who was measuring the piano?" I added helpfully. "Whoever doctored her flask?"

Unexpectedly Bill chortled. "Dodie, some day that vivid imagination of yours is going to get you into serious hot water. Let's just let the prosecutor take over."

"So your work is done," I said lightly.

"Except for paperwork."

He agreed to meet up after tonight's performance of *Bye, Bye, Birdie*, to make up for last night's unfortunate end to the evening. *Yowza!* My blood pressure shot upward as I envisioned Bill and I lounging in his living room, Norah Jones on the CD player, sipping an expensive bottle of cabernet, nibbling on cheeses while he nibbled on my ear—

My daydream shut down without warning. What was still bothering me about Ruby's death? Was it the loose ends? Dale's firm denial about murdering Ruby, even though he obviously had motive? The other men in her life? I shook the cobwebs out of my brain and went back to work.

* * * *

Pauli showed up at four thirty, backpack with laptop slung over his shoulder, Slurpee in hand. "Hey."

"Hey yourself," I said and delivered a serving of French fries and a slice of Georgette's coconut cream pie to my booth. He'd already begun typing by the time I settled onto the bench opposite him with a cup of coffee. The restaurant was quiet—it was an hour or so before the early birds would arrive for dinner. Enrico was busy in the kitchen assisting Henry 2.0. The new version of my chef, who'd been gracious and cooperative with the ELT and Creston Players, and agreed to release Wilson for *Bye, Bye, Birdie* performances this weekend. "So what do we have?"

Pauli bobbed his head and stuffed fries in his mouth. "I have a spreadsheet on Ruby with years and locations," he said, eyes shining.

Maybe Carol and her husband were wrong to force Pauli into a traditional college program. He was like a kid in a candy store when it came to anything related to digital forensics—online classes, deep searches, unusual databases. He had a career ahead of him, no doubt about it. Now, if only he could straighten out his love life. "Terrific. Let me see."

Pauli whipped the computer around to face me. "Like I started when her touring ended."

I scrutinized the spreadsheet. I knew from her scrapbook that Ruby was born in 1940, and the newspaper clippings stopped abruptly in 1969. Pauli discovered that was the same year Ruby's father died and her mother moved to Iowa where she had family. Ruby returned the same year to Indiana—the year Otto Heinlein married.

"From all the facts I found…like uh census records and whatever, Ruby stayed in Indiana until 1986," Pauli said.

"In Greenburg?"

He sucked on his straw. "Nope. She lived in Indianapolis. It's about an hour from Greenburg."

Close enough. "Any information on what she was doing during that time?"

"Besides harassing Otto Heinlein?" Pauli asked, poker-faced.

"Right."

"So, like, she was teaching music at a high school." Pauli looked up. "You think teaching drove her crazy?" He was dead serious.

"It's always possible." Lola shared horror stories about rowdy students dissecting frogs during her teaching days at Etonville High. She fled education after a decade in the biology classroom. "Anything else?"

"Like Otto junior was born 1969 and Otto Senior's wife died 1985. The obit said 'after a long illness.'" Pauli looked up. "Like cancer or something."

"And Otto's death..."

"Suicide...1986," Pauli added.

"Right. The same year Ruby left Indiana."

Otto's son was about sixteen-seventeen when he lost his parents. About Pauli's age—too young to be left adrift in the world.

We both sat in silence pondering the Ruby/Otto relationship.

"Wanna go on?" Pauli asked.

"Sure."

"Awesome."

"What's next?"

"I tracked her through Ohio and Pennsylvania until 2005. Like still teaching music...a bunch of different schools," Pauli glanced at me knowingly.

Did Ruby switch jobs on her own volition, or did the schools fire her? In the classroom, did Ruby employ the bullying tactics she used on Otto and Dale? "She would have been about sixty-five. Retirement age. Is that when she moved to New Jersey?"

"Guess so 'cause the next thing I located was an address in Clifton, and then the one in Creston," Pauli said.

"This is great detective work. I couldn't have found all of this without you."

He blushed and swiped a hank of brown hair off his forehead. "Like thanks. But there's more," he said eagerly.

"Otto Junior?"

"Remember, he left Indiana after his father died and went to college in Ohio."

"Right. Did he stay there after he graduated?"

Pauli consulted his laptop notes. "For six years. Then he moved."

Benny approached my booth. "Dodie, Cheney Brothers are at the back door."

"Sure. Be right back Pauli."

Pauli nodded and swallowed the last of the cream pie. Benny threw a bar towel over his shoulder. "Where does the kid put it all?" he asked as he went to the basement for a case of red wine.

"Got me." I walked to the rear entrance.

* * * *

It took longer for the delivery guy to haul the meat and vegetables into the refrigerator than I anticipated. By the time I'd signed off on the requisition, popped in the kitchen to check on Henry and Enrico—who were scanning a recipe, snorting at something, and enjoying themselves royally—and returned to the dining room, Pauli was storing his laptop. He stopped to answer a text.

"Sorry it took so long—"

"Gotta bounce. Like...I'm uh...meeting...somebody...sort of like a date." He shrugged.

"Janice?"

He beamed sheepishly. "Grabbing food before the show tonight."

Yahoo! Finally. I was happy for him. "Go and hook up. Uh...you know what I mean," I finished lamely.

Pauli understood.

"Could you text me the end of Otto Junior's dates and locations?"

"No problemo."

"Good luck," I said.

Pauli saluted and loped out the door. Ah, young love...

Gillian set up the dining room and left to manage the concessions at the park while Carmen took over waiting tables. Benny served drinks, and I pitched in where needed. As the dinner hour approached, I was surprised at the lackluster crowd. Patrons wandered in filling half the tables and booths, speaking quietly, fairly subdued. This was Etonville after a series of crises involving murder, fire, financial scams, and an arrest? What was going on? What happened to the mob that blathered during lunch? Could it be the weather? A blanket of clouds slowly covered the sky as the afternoon wore on. Was the resolution of Ruby's murder a sobering experience for the town? That would be a first.

"Table for three," a voice said.

I looked up from the bar napkin that I was doodling on. It was Abby, Penny, and Alex. "Hi. Nice to see you all."

Abby pointed to a table in the corner, and I led the way. "I'm surprised more ELT folks haven't come in for dinner." I handed out menus.

"Everybody's depressed over Dale," Abby said, and plopped into a seat.

"Sure," I said.

"Glad I do my own taxes," Penny cackled. "Who needs a financial advisor in an orange jumpsuit?"

"Isn't that…cruel?" Alex asked.

"Nah. Dale just thought he was too big to fall," Penny said.

"You mean too big to fail," Abby corrected her.

"Whatever. O'Dell, what's on special tonight?" Penny asked.

"Beef Stroganoff and rosemary potatoes."

Alex closed his menu. "I'll have that. And I know I shouldn't before a show…" He peeked at Penny. "…but I'll also have a glass of the house cabernet."

"What the hay. Me too," said Penny.

Abby regarded Alex and Penny. "If both of you are having wine… make that three!"

There would be some happy people doing the show tonight!

My cell pinged. I waved to Carmen to write up their orders, and moved to a barstool. It was Pauli: *Otto Jr. in PA after OH. 1999.* I texted back: *Thnx. Janice?* Pauli: *Burgers now. Real date next weekend.*

Nice.

Otto Junior was in the same states as Ruby. She was following him…did she harass the son as well as the father? Had she been so heartbroken by Otto's betrayal that her life became years of payback? What did Professor Yurkov say about Ruby's confrontation with Otto? *…the rage on her face….* She promised Otto *would be sorry* that day on the Maynard campus. *Hers was a voice full of vengeance.*

I shuddered. Goosebumps rose on my neck and shoulders. "Think laterally," Pauli said, "Turn things around"…What if we had it wrong? Ruby wasn't stalking Otto Junior. He was stalking her for decades because he felt the need to settle a family score! 1969 was the year everything imploded: the end of Ruby's tour, Otto's marriage, the birth of his son. *Yikes!* Was it possible that Otto's wife was pregnant before they married? Did Otto consider himself obligated to marry Junior's mother? If so, a shotgun wedding might have added fuel to Ruby's burning rage. What, as Bill would ask, did any of this have to do with her death?

Alex was returning to his table from the men's room. "You look like you've seen a ghost."

"I'm fine…just some strange news." I waggled my cell phone.

I followed him to the table. "Coffee anyone?"

"And ruin a nice buzz?" Abby giggled.

"O'Dell. You're coming to the cast party after the show tonight? Creston Players are springing for the spread." Penny swallowed the last bit of her dinner.

"I'll be there. How was the Stroganoff?" I asked.

"Best I've ever had," Alex said.

Abby and Penny nodded.

"I'll tell Henry."

Out of curiosity, I texted Pauli to see if he discovered what kinds of jobs Otto Junior had during his time in Ohio and Pennsylvania and if there was any indication he'd ever lived in New Jersey. The remainder of the dinner service was uneventful with few customers, none of whom seemed talkative, many of whom left by seven fifteen to finagle good seats for the show tonight. I was fidgety, organizing the pantry shelves, wiping down the bar, and rearranging the artificial flowers on each table.

"Earth to Dodie. Come on down," Benny said.

"Guess I'm distracted."

"You've been wiping the same spot for the last five minutes."

"Really?"

"Uh-huh." Benny took the sponge out of my hand. "Have you eaten anything today? Take a seat and I'll bring you some Stroganoff."

I plopped onto a barstool. "I'm not really hungry. Maybe a seltzer with lime—"

"Oh no you don't. You're gonna eat. I can't have you calling in sick and leaving me to referee Wilson and Henry." He folded his arms across his chest. "It's been a rough week for you," he said kindly.

I agreed. I jumped up. "I'll get my own dinner, but thanks for the offer." I had no intention of passing out invitations to my personal pity party.

20

By ten o'clock, I figured Bill would be approaching his entrance in Act Two, and Pauli would be mesmerized, once again, by Janice's performance as Sweet Apple, Ohio's heroine. Offstage, it looked like the athlete actor from Creston was out of the picture. My cell binged: *Can't find jobs for Otto Jr. no Jersey connection,* Pauli texted. I was disappointed that he'd found no trace of Junior's work or life in New Jersey.

"So take off already," Benny said.

"Sure you don't mind closing?"

Benny scanned the dining room. "There's nothing happening here. Henry may shut the kitchen early."

"I'll cover for you tomorrow night," I said.

"Thanks. I've wanted to take the princess to that new movie. The one with the talking furniture? She'll get a kick out of it," Benny said.

"Fun. Go make plans."

I stuck my head in the kitchen to let Henry know I was off duty, blew Benny a kiss, and grabbed my bag. I texted Gillian that I was on my way to retrieve the concession cash.

Slipping into Bill's BMW was like sinking into a warm bubble bath—comfort, relaxation, and a sweet aroma. My Metro usually smelled of takeout food. I pushed thoughts of my old companion out of my head, and cruised down Main Street. Etonville was a ghost town tonight. I hoped that meant there was a full house at the show.

As I neared the park, I scoured the adjacent streets for a parking space. No way was I going to end up near a vacant lot or deserted neighborhood this time. I'd find an illegal spot if I had to. After all, it was Bill's car. He wouldn't have himself ticketed, right? As the parking gods were with me, a Jeep was leaving a prime location a block from the stage on the opposite side of the park from the site of my Metro's demise. I checked and double-checked the locks on the BMW and headed toward the raucous sounds of music and audience guffaws. I listened. It was the reprise of the "Kids" number with much of the company on stage. I approached the back side of the portable dressing stalls where a handful of actors were milling around, whispering, or dashing into stalls to repair make-up. I saw Abby, Edna, and a couple of guys from the Creston Players.

"How's it going?" I murmured to Edna.

"It's a 10-2," Edna said.

I assumed that was a positive response.

"Good reception," she said.

"Wilson?" I asked cautiously.

"Like a pro. He hasn't missed a beat," Abby said. High praise coming from someone always fast to criticize and slow to compliment.

One more show after tonight. "Is the chief around?" I scanned the area. He should have been hanging out, waiting for the curtain call unless he intended to get dressed down by Penny.

"Well, we had a situation." Edna and Abby exchanged looks.

Not another crisis! "What happened?"

"There was a pile-up out on the highway—" Abby began.

"Multiple vehicles. A code 10, a code 20 and an 11-79," Edna said firmly. "They asked for backup from Etonville PD."

"What's that mean—?"

Abby harrumphed. "For Pete's sake, Edna. Tell her the—"

"Trauma cases," Edna said and adjusted her costume.

"So Bill never went on tonight?"

"Duty called," Edna said and skittered off. "Got to get back on stage."

"Who's taking his role?" I asked.

"Walter doubled up another cop since he didn't have any lines," said Abby.

Poor Bill. He had to miss his moment in the spotlight. Just when he was beginning to enjoy himself. I gulped and stared over Abby's shoulder. "Is that...?"

She jerked her head around. "Dale."

"What's he doing here?" I croaked.

"Word is he's out on bail. Walter spotted him at intermission. Guess he couldn't stay away. I hear he's been drinking, and is angling to pick a fight tonight," Abby said.

"He's not a flight risk?"

"Not in that condition. Anyway, he must have a good lawyer," Abby murmured.

His bald head was a prominent spot of white. "I think he's missing his—"

"Toupee. Yeah." Abby dashed off.

Whoa. Dale must be really loaded to show up in public without his hairpiece. He was weaving his way through the trees, definitely unsteady on his pins. He stopped and seemed to focus, heading straight for me. Uh-oh. I had two choices: I could beat it out of here and hope that Dale wandered off or stay and waylay any attempt on his part to "pick a fight" by interrupting the performance. Who knew how angry he was? He'd lost his role in the show, his business, his standing in the theatrical community, and maybe his freedom if convicted. I decided to be proactive.

I marched through the stand of trees, and raised a hand to halt his forward progress. "Hey Dale. You can't be back here while the show is going on."

He squinted at me, his face finally registering my identity. "If it isn't Dodie O'Dell. Private eye," he said sarcastically and hiccupped.

"Dale, let's get you some coffee." I had no idea where I was going to find coffee, but it seemed like a good way to keep him occupied until the curtain rang down for the final time.

"You told Lola about me didn't you? About Ruby and me."

Was he confessing to more than the financial fraud? "What do you think I told her?"

"I'm wise to you. All of you." He swung an arm in a wide arc, encompassing the stage, the park, and all of Etonville. He moved forward, now just feet from me.

"Shhh! *Bye, Bye, Birdie's* not over yet." From the corner of my eye, I could see Alex conducting the band as they began the final chorus of "Rosie" with Lola and Wilson in a sweet embrace.

"I should be out there singing." He looked mournful, and for a brief moment, I almost felt sorry for him. "Instead of…who is that anyway?" He peered around me.

"Wilson. From the Windjammer," I said with pride.

"They got a cook to replace me?" He let out a howl that would have carried into the house if the combo hadn't struck their last notes. The audience erupted in cheers.

He stepped to me threateningly, yanking on my arm. "You'll pay for this."

I wrenched myself away from him, falling to the ground in the process, landing on my sore shoulder. "Dale! Stop."

He loomed over me. "Stay away from me. Stay away from Lola."

He was going to jail, and Lola was my best friend. "That's it. I'm calling the police." I whipped my cell out of my purse, but before I could tap on the numbers Dale ran into the trees. I reached Suki on dispatch, and relayed my run-in with the erstwhile actor. She alerted Ralph, who was already on duty at the park. But probably more focused on the musical than on security. I was shaky as I brushed myself off, smoothed my blouse, and cut through the back of the set to the refreshment stand where Gillian was simultaneously watching the curtain call and tapping away on her cell phone. I collected the night's profits and released her.

The audience was on its feet, cheering and applauding. I joined in, smiling at Wilson and Lola as they took their final bow. The curtain fell, lights flicked on, and the crowd morphed into a noisy mass of humanity.

Lola spotted me and waved. I waved back. I sat down on a folding chair to wait for the cast to deposit costumes into Chrystal's ready hands. I texted Bill to see how he was doing. It must have been some kind of catastrophe to call in support from neighboring towns.

One of the Creston Players attached an iPod to speakers, and music poured into the night. More stage lights flashed on, the curtain opened, and the cast, in street clothes, whooped it up, dancing, and generally having a good time. They deserved it after the numerous *Bye, Bye, Birdie* crises! I glanced around—I hoped Dale had removed himself from the scene.

Penny and Edna erected a folding table, and the Creston Players laid out a feast. They'd offered to host the company party tonight, and supplied food and drinks. The Etonville park service, with the encouragement of a donation, agreed to keep their security and maintenance on call for an additional hour and a half after the show closed. Time enough for the cast to party. The Etonville police department's contribution was Ralph, who positioned himself by the food table and munched on fried chicken legs.

Wilson glided past with a plate of pasta salad, and pointed at me. "*Do-dee*, I am coming back to dance with you!"

Before I could respond, he receded into a cluster of actors. I wandered to the concession stand where the Players were dispensing lemonade and sodas.

"Hey, O'Dell."

"Hi Penny. Nice party." I flipped the tab off my drink. The Creston Players had indeed provided quite a spread.

She made a face. "Agreed. The ELT offered to bring stuff, but the Players said they were taking care of everything."

Penny was in my head again…but I didn't mind tonight. I was happy to see everyone celebrating. "Congratulations on finishing another ELT season. Looks like the show was a big success."

"Great box office. It means we don't have to be slaves to the audience. We can do more daring stuff," Penny said triumphantly.

"Like what?" I asked slowly.

"Walter thinks period pieces, classics. He's writing a new show based on the Titanic," Penny announced.

Yikes! Did Lola know about Walter's ideas? "What about a nice romantic comedy? Something that will be an audience pleaser."

Penny chuckled. "O'Dell, you slay me. Don't you know by now that if the theater isn't taking chances it stalemates."

"You mean…stagnates?"

"Whatever." She looked off. "Hey, you guys get down out of those trees." She pushed her glasses. "Rookies." She tromped away.

The music shifted, and Wilson took center stage in the midst of a group of actors. He proceeded to do a solo dance, then dropped to his knees and threw his body back and forth in a Haitian break dance. The cast hooted and cheered. Hello theater, good-bye Windjammer. Maybe Wilson did have a new career as a performer.

"I'm thrilled to see everyone relaxing, but I can't wait until this night is over." Lola collapsed into a folding chair, kicked off her sandals, and kneaded the soles of her feet.

"Been a hectic time," I said.

"I'll say. What with the weather, replacing Dale, and then his arrest…" Lola stopped.

"Did you know he was here tonight?"

Lola froze. "Here? In the park?"

"Angry and tipsy," I said.

"Oh no."

"Yeah. He lawyered up and got released on bail," I said.

"Did you speak with him?" Lola asked.

"Oh yeah. He accused me of ratting him out to you. Then he got feisty so I called the police station. Suki said she'd alert Ralph." We glanced at the food table where Ralph had segued from chicken to finger sandwiches. "No sight of Dale since then."

Lola shook her head and replaced her shoes.

"Listen, I don't think Dale murdered Ruby. And if he's only convicted of charges related to scamming clients, well…that's not so bad."

"I suppose," Lola said.

I quietly presented all of the evidence that Pauli had gathered, along with my instinctive analysis. Ruby's threat to get revenge, the restraining order, her moving around after Otto's death, the simultaneous movement of Otto Junior, and my belief that someone was coming after me via the car incidents. That same someone knew what I had found out. There were simply too many unanswered questions. "Charging Dale completely ignores Ruby's past."

"And what about Otto's son?"

"Pauli hasn't found any evidence of an Otto Heinlein, Junior living in New Jersey," I said.

Lola was silent, staring at the group dancing and eating. "But you think he's involved somehow?"

"I don't know, but I'd sure like to know where he is."

"Have you told all of this to Bill?" Lola asked.

"Most of it. I texted him to see what's happening with the accident on the highway, but haven't heard back."

Walter gestured from the stage, and held up a glass of lemonade. "Lola dear, could you join me in a salute to our theatrical partners?" Now that Dale was out of the picture, Walter was more confident as far as Lola was concerned...too bad for Jocelyn. Her romantic possibilities were diminishing rapidly. And Walter was clueless.

Lola raised her voice. "In a minute." She leaned into me. "Dodie, if what you are saying about the Metro fire is true, you are a sitting duck. You need to get security to stay by your side. Don't walk off alone tonight."

"I'll be careful. You'd better get up there and help Walter 'salute'!"

Lola sighed and trudged to the stage.

"Are you enjoying yourself?"

I looked behind me. It was Alex, snacking on cheese and crackers. "Yes. It's so great to see everyone letting their hair down."

"Especially the newer members of the theater. We veterans take openings and closings in stride." He ate a piece of cheese.

"But it was a pretty extraordinary thing you did, taking Ruby's place like that," I said.

"Me? I'm just an ordinary musician. Ruby was the true star."

"Yes, she was." I lifted my soda can. "Here's to the true star."

Alex lifted his plate. We clinked.

Wilson grabbed my hand. "*Do-dee*! I told you I come back for you!"

I wasn't in the mood to dance, but Wilson was dragging me to the stage where a bunch of actors and crew were twisting and whirling and shaking. As an excellent dancer, Wilson was a smooth partner, twirling me away from him, and then back to his substantial body, dipping me, lifting me in the air. My head was spinning! I landed on my feet and Wilson rotated me away again. I bumped into Pauli and Janice, so lost in each other that neither one was visibly disturbed that I landed between them.

"Hey." Pauli said.

"Oops! Sorry!" I shouted. The music was so loud conversation was nearly impossible. "Hi Janice. Having a good time?" I didn't wait for an answer. Her beaming smile said it all.

"Well…you two have fun." I stepped away—toward Wilson's outstretched hand.

"Wait! Like…I found some things." Pauli leaned into my face.

"Text me."

"Got it," he danced away with Janice.

My neck hairs were jumping, and it wasn't the sassy music. I had to get to Bill and tell him about Otto Junior possibly stalking, and murdering, Ruby. He would resist my theory, but I had to make him listen.

The number ended. "Thanks for the exercise," I said to Wilson.

"*Do-dee*! You are *ze* best partner."

"Thanks, but I know better. *You* could be on *Dancing with the Stars*. The dancing chef!"

Wilson threw back his head and let out a belly laugh.

I moved to the outer edge of the party. If I could locate Ralph, I'd have him walk me to the BMW. My cell rang.

"Bill! I was about to text you again. I heard about the wreck down on the highway and—"

"Where are you? What's all the noise?" He shouted into the phone.

"I'm at the cast party at the park. Where you'd be if you'd gone on tonight," I said.

"I know, but duty called. Listen, can you cut out and get over here?"

It sounded urgent but it was also my opportunity to make a case—

"Dodie? You still there? Because I have something to tell you."

Uh-oh…could that good news or bad news?

"It's about the Metro."

My heart thunked. "My Metro?"

"Yeah."

"I'm on my way."

"Where are you parked? Get someone to walk with you," he urged.

Again I scanned the party. Things were hopping and music was blaring. I couldn't find Ralph.

"Be there soon." I clicked off.

I swung my bag onto my shoulder. I didn't see Lola or Wilson either. They must have melted into the crowd of partiers. I was standing on the upward slope—behind the folding chairs—on the outer rim of the well-lit, portable, seating area. I looked toward the street. The BMW was a block away. I'd promised Lola and Bill that I wouldn't walk alone—but what the heck.

I skirted the festivities, keeping to the edge of the darkness that surrounded the party. I had no intention of being drawn into another dance or conversation.

Twenty yards from the revelry, the music was still hardcore. Good thing the co-production invited people in the neighborhood to join the fun. They'd be included whether they left their house or not! I picked up my pace and jogged to the car. I was only feet away from the back bumper when I heard the clop, clop, clop of other footsteps. I resisted looking behind me. It was probably a cast member walking to one of the other cars on the block. I fumbled for the keys, but then remembered I needed to push a button on the BMW key fob for the doors to open. Unlike my Metro which required traditional unlocking.

"Running away? I thought you'd stay and take a final bow for saving the show," Dale roared.

I recognized the bitter, inebriated voice. I whipped around. "Have you been tailing me?" My voice ran up the scale. Hearing Dale behind me was a scary moment, but I had the advantage. He was bigger, but I was sober. And I had already extricated myself once from his grasp an hour ago. "Go home and sleep it off." Over his shoulder, the lights and music of the party were a world away.

"That was my part. I should have been up there last night and tonight!" He gestured wildly. "And tomorrow night!"

I extended my arm to prevent any advance on his part. "You *should* have been up there, but unfortunately you got yourself arrested for murder—"

"I didn't murder anybody!" Dale cried.

"But you did scam Ruby."

"And she blackmailed me. Call it even."

"Dale, for what it's worth, I believe you about Ruby's murder. I think you're innocent."

"What difference does that make now? The show is over." His shoulders sagged, and he stumbled forward. My outstretched hands landed on his upper chest. He raised his head mournfully. "Lola. She'll never want to see me anymore." There was a rush of movement behind him, the sound of a muffled thud, and Dale crumpled to the ground.

I dropped to my knees. "Dale?"

"I saw him grab you, and I was afraid he'd try something." It was Alex.

I gazed upward. "He wasn't assaulting me. He was going to cry."

"Really? I'm sorry...I didn't trust him in that condition. You left and then Dale left too."

I examined Dale's head. "What did you hit him with? He's out cold."

Alex sheepishly produced a piece of pipe. "I found it backstage, and thought I'd better come prepared."

"I'll call 911," I said.

Alex was already tapping numbers on his cell. "I've got it covered." He spoke into his phone, gave dispatch our location.

My cell phone pinged. It must be Bill wondering where I was. It was Pauli: *Otto Junior rebuilt classic cars. Found name at car show in NJ last year.*

OMG. Otto Junior would know how to rig Ruby's car to kill her, through carbon monoxide poisoning, and manipulate my car's brakes, battery, and fuel line. My pulse began to race.

"Something the matter?" Alex asked softly.

"No. I'm not feeling so hot. I need to get home. Do you mind waiting for the ambulance?" Where was it anyway? We should have heard the siren by now. At a minimum, Suki would have alerted Ralph and he should have appeared on the scene.

"I should drive you home. You seem somewhat shaky to me." Alex took a step closer.

"That's all right. I'll be fine."

"I insist," he said firmly

"But what about Dale?"

"Dale won't suffer any lasting effects. I'm not that strong." Alex smirked. "He'll come around."

My cell binged again. "Thanks anyway." I grabbed the door handle, and then glanced at my phone, which I was still holding. Pauli: *Otto Jr used mother's maiden name Milken...funny... same as music director*! I felt dizzy. I couldn't breathe. Otto A. Heinlein became Alex Milkin. It all fit. An "ordinary guy" with Ruby at the deli...classic cars...and a gut full of vengeance.

"Busy night for you. All those text messages. Why don't you get in?" It wasn't a suggestion.

I shut the door and faced Alex. "The ambulance isn't coming is it?"

21

Alex walked me to the passenger side of the automobile. Then opened the door. "Move," he murmured, and gestured with a gun that he'd kept hidden by his side until this moment.

My hands trembled as I slid awkwardly across the BMW's bench, Alex behind me. "You don't want to do anything stupid. Start the engine," he said.

I tentatively pressed the ignition button. Without the ambulance coming, I had to rely on Bill getting bothered enough that he would contact Lola or someone else at the party. The music was so loud, she might not hear her phone. If she had it on her. I had to face the facts: no one knew I was riding with a murderous psychopath who'd waited nearly thirty years to avenge his father's death. "Alex, I can understand how devastating your father's passing must have been."

The atmosphere subtly shifted.

"Drive," he said.

"Where to?" I asked.

"Across town to the highway."

"Losing your mother so young…" I waited but there was no response. "You were what…sixteen?"

"Stop talking."

I had no intention of shutting up. Talking was the only defense I had—that and driving as slowly as possible to delay the inevitable. I forced myself to breathe through my mouth as I clenched the steering wheel. "I know about Ruby's harassment and the restraining order. How did she stalk your father? Visits? Calls? Letters? It was the 80s so no email obviously—"

Alex shoved the gun into my ribs. "Keep quiet," he hissed—with less conviction, but a tad more hysteria.

"And of course you like cars. Classic cars, right? It makes sense that you would kill Ruby in a car." He was inhaling as heavily as I was. Had I gotten through to him? No time like the present for the knockout punch. "The same way your father died. The Ambien in her flask was a smart way to guarantee Ruby would fall asleep at the wheel. Why did you remove the bottle from her apartment? Evidence?"

Alex jammed his foot on top of mine and the BMW shot forward. "Go straight through the light."

So much for maintaining the speed limit. It was the corner of Main and Anderson. I'd been hoping to ease down Anderson, and somehow cut over a couple of streets and end up at Bill's. Wishful thinking. Alex's knowledge of Etonville's streets was on a par with mine.

"It was just your luck that Dale was scamming Ruby at the same time you were planning on murdering her. Making him a prime suspect," I said with fake bravado.

Alex barked an ugly laugh. "He was a fool to tangle with Ruby Passonata. She was a clever woman. Mean and cruel but clever."

"She must have ruined your father's life—"

"My father, my mother, mine." Sweating profusely, Alex wiped his forehead with the hand holding the gun. "All because he dumped her. The calls, the letters. Stupid love letters I found after my father…" Alex gasped. "It drove my mother insane. Years and years of it. Showing up in our front yard in the middle of the night. Even coming to my baseball games. Screaming stuff from the stands. After my mother died, my father went crazy and had to end it. One of them had to go. He was too much of a coward to kill Ruby so he killed himself."

"That left Ruby for you…"

Alex's face twisted in pain. "You want to know the funniest part of it all? The night before he offed himself, he got drunk. Told me he never got over Ruby. Only married my mother because he got her pregnant. I hated him for that. Almost as much as I hated Ruby."

"I'm sorry Alex. I can imagine—"

"You can't imagine!" he screamed in my ear, pounding his gun on the dashboard. "Nobody can!" He latched onto my right wrist.

I winced. Alex was losing it. "Let go or we're going to crash!" I shouted. Bill's BMW was now a weapon!

"You think I care? Ruby gave my life purpose. She's dead. That's all I ever cared about."

If Alex was on a suicide mission, he was taking me with him. "If that's all you cared about you wouldn't be kidnapping me! Let's go to the police station and you can talk it out—"

"Turn here!" He grabbed the wheel and yanked it.

I fought for control of the car, but Alex had adrenaline on his side. The BMW veered sharply to the right. I kicked his leg and swung wildly at his face. Alex ducked and jerked away.

Suddenly a figure materialized in the road ahead. A man! On a bike! Bigger than life! It was Wilson. I rammed my foot into the brake pedal and wrenched the wheel with all my might, sending the car up a curb, through a line of bushes, and coming to rest on top of a tree stump. Alex boomeranged off the dashboard, his gun flying out of his grasp.

In a flash, Wilson was at the passenger door jerking Alex from the front seat, wrapping his arms around him in a tight clinch. I'd banged my head on the steering wheel and was seeing stars just before I saw red and blue flashing lights, and heard a siren wailing in the dark night. *It's about time.*

* * * *

"Wilson, thank you for following me! But standing in the road like that? I could have killed you." The EMS crew gave me ice for my head, while Ralph attempted to control the neighborhood, and Bill loaded Alex into a squad car.

"*Do-dee*! You would never kill me!"

"Not on purpose," I said, smiling, and gulped from a bottle of water—quenching my parched throat—sore from hollering at Alex.

"I am glad you are okay," he said softly.

"Because of you."

"Those men leave *ze* party after you." He shrugged. "I had to chase them."

"How did you keep up with us on your bike?" I asked.

Wilson broke out in a wide grin. "It has electric motor! Thirty five miles per hour!"

Geez. I never thought to question his insistence on riding his bike to and from work regardless of the hour or the weather.

Bill crossed to us and extended his hand. Wilson shook it. "Thank you. You're a hero."

"Again," I added.

"I am no hero…"

"You saved Dodie," Bill said, all police-chief-like.

"Just like you saved the show," I said.

"My office will contact you in the morning for a statement," Bill added.

Wilson glowed. "I am happy to be here," he said and sauntered off, wheeling his bicycle.

"Me too!" I called after him. I turned to Bill. "What took you so long?"

"I tried to reach someone at the park, but no one answered. Good thing Wilson called 911 and reached Suki." He sat down next to me. "How are you? Scared the daylights out of me."

"Me too."

He examined his gold BMW, now with scrapes along the passenger door and a nice-sized crease in the front end.

"I was steering for my life! I'm lucky I made it out alive."

Bill put his arm around me. "I know. I'm glad you did." His crooked grin emerged.

"Sorry about the damage," I said.

"Did you have to play bumper cars with my BMW? And use a tree stump as a shock absorber?"

"Hey, what happened to your 'glad I'm alive'?" I asked.

Bill sighed. "I guess it comes with the territory."

"What territory is that?"

"You!"

"I left the park to get to your place. What did you want to tell me?" I asked huffily.

Bill cleared his throat. "A detailed report came in from the arson squad. The door handles were rigged."

I was elated that my instincts were correct, then alarmed, again, at Alex's attempt to get me out of the way. "He knew I was onto him."

"Good thing you were." He leaned in.

I put up a hand to stop his progress toward my face. "Here? With everybody looking at us?"

He nodded and kissed me.

Yahoo!

22

Today your passion will rival your common sense. Volatile events are heading your way so be ready for unplanned activities. I shut the horoscope page of the *Etonville Standard*. I could do with the passion, but I'd had enough volatile events for the present. Peace and tranquility, even boredom, were welcome over the week since *Bye, Bye, Birdie* closed. Etonville was deserted as the Creston Players went home, the park closed up shop, and some folks went away for vacations. The Windjammer was especially empty today…for a Friday.

"You look nice. Big night?" Benny smirked.

"Wise guy," I said. It was my birthday. I came in late because I started the day with a lavender bubble bath, splurged on an extra caramel macchiato, and wore my gift to myself: a shimmery royal blue silk blouse and matching leggings. They felt good on my skin. Benny and Gillian ran the dining room for lunch, and I agreed to stay until the supper rush was underway. Then I was off to my own supper event. Bill was cooking at home for us—he'd remembered my day! Steaks on his backyard grill, my favorite beet salad, a fine cabernet. It would be a nice, quiet time. Fine by me.

"Thanks for covering today," I said to Benny.

"Happy birthday. Enjoy your night off."

I waved good-bye and walked out of the restaurant onto the sidewalk. At seven thirty, the sun had just begun to set. It would be another hour before it was gone completely. Lovely…Bill and I could dine al fresco—out in the air like *Bye, Birdie*. Though the show had enriched the theater's coffers, and established détente between the Etonville Little Theatre and the Creston Players for the time being, both Lola and Walter swore it would be a while before they embarked on another musical journey. In fact, it would be several months before they put out a casting call for the fall show. That meant no more theme food for a while.

The muggy day transformed into a pleasant evening, the air was cooler and dryer. I inhaled the soft, inviting smell of a summer night as I unlocked the door of my rental car. Bill's BMW was in the body shop. I would have to decide on a long-term transportation solution soon. Having waded through the first four stages of grief over my Metro—denial, anger, bargaining, and depression—I was approaching the fifth and final stage: acceptance. Yesterday, I stopped by the automobile graveyard in Bernridge where demolished cars sat until they were crushed or chopped up. I wanted to bid my Metro a last good-bye. I was sad, but given the shape she was in, it really was time to move on. She'd been a trusty companion these last hundred and twenty-six thousand miles and she had seen me through some fierce scrapes.

I blamed myself for her torching. If I hadn't been pursuing Ruby's past, my Metro might be with me today. I didn't regret my discoveries about Ruby. Even as Alex broke down and confessed to his life-long mission to punish Ruby, I was astonished at the depth of his and Ruby's fixations. Under skillful police interrogation, it had all come out. Otto's shotgun marriage caused Ruby to quit her stellar career and return to Indiana. Feeling betrayed, she embarked on a different career: years of tormenting the Heinlein family. Otto Junior intended to redress his father's death—triggered by guilt and depression—following Ruby until he figured out a way to get even. He ended up in Creston, and it was fate that the local community theater needed a musical director this past year.

While Alex planned Ruby's death, Ruby blackmailed Dale for his attempt to fleece her. Alex had a prime suspect handed to him on a silver platter. Alex was in Ruby's apartment the day I hid under the bed and Alex accompanied Ruby to the deli on the day she died. He finally confronted her about his father, and she mocked him. She had not an ounce of regret. If Alex had second thoughts about committing murder, his clash with Ruby that day sealed her fate.

My pursuit of Ruby's past created an obstacle he hadn't counted on. His knowledge of car mechanics, and the general gossip about my aging vehicle, set me up for the brake tampering, the dead battery, and the car fire. As Alex said…he worked fast!

A combined Etonville/Creston force scoured the field near the crime scene and, sure enough, found the flask that Dale had thrown away in a fit of anger. The flask was laced with Ambien that Alex swiped from Ruby's medicine cabinet. Though cleared of murder charges, Dale received a fraud indictment and awaited trial. He wouldn't be singing with the Creston Players for a while. Which reminded me…no wonder Alex was so efficient at the technical rehearsal! Bill found the cue sheets in his car.

Ruby…definitely a mystery woman whose life was a complicated maze of extreme habits, events, and emotions.

I cruised through the streets of Etonville, and felt a jumble of emotions myself. I finally admitted my pursuit of Ruby's past had something to do with my great aunt Maureen. Last night, my parents called to say happy birthday. In the course of the conversation, I broached the topic of my aunt.

"Why did Maureen leave banking? I mean she had such a great career going," I asked my parents.

"Life's not only about work," my mother answered wisely.

Was that a reference to my own employment history? "True, but did she ever talk about leaving banking?"

"Once. She said it wasn't fun anymore," my father replied.

Fun. Right. That made sense given my aunt.

"By the way, have you and Bill decided on where to vacation?" my mother asked. "We'd love to see you…"

She let the rest of the thought dangle.

"I'll get back to you."

We chatted a bit longer about their neighbors in Naples, my father's arthritis, and my brother's plans to spend time in Cape Cod this summer. Before I hung up, I had a final question for them.

"You know the picture we found in Aunt Maureen's bureau drawer after she died?"

"The young man in a uniform?" my mother asked.

"Yes. Who was he?"

"That was David."

"A boyfriend?"

"David? Oh no, he was her husband," my mother clarified.

"Great Aunt Maureen was married? Why did I not know about this?" I asked, astonished.

"It was so long ago. They were only married for two years before he died in a car accident. She never wanted to talk about him," my father said.

I wished I had known about this relationship in my great aunt's life, that we had spoken about David.

I turned onto Anderson, and left down Bennington until I reached Bill's place on Gracie Avenue. The weeping willow in his front yard was lush, bending and swaying in the evening breeze. The aroma of his rose beds permeated the air as I walked up the flagstone path to his house. I straightened my silk blouse and tossed my tresses, which were curlier than usual because of the day's humidity, over my shoulder. *It would be a nice night.* I knocked on Bill's locked door.

"Surprise!" screamed a barrage of voices. The groundswell of noise echoed around the foyer and thrust me backwards. My mouth fell open. My pulse pounded. OMG! There was a second of silence as everyone waited expectantly for my response.

"Ahhh…huh…ohh…!" was all I could muster. People broke ranks and descended upon me with congratulations.

"Happy Birthday, Dodie," said Lola with a big hug.

"Th-thanks. I can't believe this!"

"Bet you thought we all forgot!" said Carol with a twinkle in her eye. She paused. "You need a trim," she murmured into my ear.

"See you at Snippets tomorrow," I said.

Mildred and Vernon, Georgette from the bakery, Abby and her husband Jim, Edna and Suki—Ralph was on dispatch—all offered best wishes. I had no idea so many people cared about my big day! It had taken several years but, finally, Etonville felt like my town.

"Hey, O'Dell, pretty good secret, right?"

"Yes, Penny, this was."

"Hard to keep secrets with this crew." She gestured around the room, and then lowered her voice. "By the way, did you hear Walter's ex-wife is taking him back to court? Don't tell anybody." She meandered off.

I laughed.

"We love birthday parties, don't we?" one Banger sister said.

"Especially if they're for us!" said the other.

"Uh-huh," I said.

Bill placed a glass of chardonnay in my hand. "Happy birthday," he said. He kissed my cheek.

"Wow! How did you manage this?" I asked and took a sip of wine.

"It's all in the game plan."

"Spoken like a former running back."

He hurried off. Ever the good host, Bill patiently led the Banger sisters to the dining room where he had a buffet table laden with pasta dishes, cold sandwiches, and salads.

I walked into the living room. Pauli and Janice huddled on the sofa. She was talking non-stop, he was listening, fixated and attentive. Jocelyn attempted to corner Walter, one arm hooked through his, while he looked confused and slightly terrified. Relationships. I guessed Lola missed Dale. She had high hopes for that relationship… Although she'd confided this week that she'd dodged a bullet there. I thought of Great Aunt Maureen and David. Even

Bill and I were navigating our way through this twosome thing. The loss of a relationship had sparked an extreme reaction from Ruby that led to a suicide and a murder. It was true…hell hath no fury like a woman scorned.

The front door opened and Henry, Benny, Enrico, and Carmen came in.

"Who's minding the store?" I asked as the Windjammer staff enveloped me in a group hug.

"Wilson offered to keep it open until ten. He'll be by later," Benny said.

Henry handed me a wrapped package. "Happy birthday. From all of us."

I wiggled it, weighed it, and turned it over and over. "Let's see." I tore off the ribbon and wrapping paper to reveal a high-end first aid kit.

"Just in case," Henry said and we all chuckled.

"Where's the bar?" asked Benny.

* * * *

The sun set. The guests ate. Friends made champagne toasts. We cut the Georgette's Bakery cake. I'd made the rounds, thanking everyone. It wasn't the birthday I'd expected. My horoscope was correct: *be ready for unplanned activities.* Out on the deck, Romeo sang "One Last Kiss" from *Bye, Bye, Birdie* and the rest of the party joined in. Bill motioned to me from across the kitchen and I followed him to the garage.

"What are we doing out here?" I asked, in the midst of his too-neat metal shelving laden with sports equipment, camping gear, and car products.

"Patience!" He smiled sphynx-like and handed me a foam rubber drink holder.

"Thanks. This is nice," I said.

"Yeah. You can take it on vacation," he said.

Right. We had yet to settle that particular issue. "As we sit around the campfire," I joked.

Bill gave me an envelope. "More like the beach."

"What?" I looked inside. It was a computer-made gift certificate for two weeks at the Jersey Shore. Reservation already made and paid for. *Just in time*! "I can't believe it!"

"I know. I like to keep you guessing," Bill murmured.

"Well, guess how much I love this gift."

He held me so close his heart beat against mine. "As much as I love you?"

"Wh-what did you say?" I asked, my pulse shooting from zero to sixty.

"Who? Me?" Bill asked innocently.

OMG!

About the Author

Suzanne Trauth is a novelist, playwright, screenwriter, and a former university theatre professor. She is a member of Mystery Writers of America, Sisters in Crime, and the Dramatists Guild. When she is not writing, Suzanne coaches actors and serves as a celebrant performing wedding ceremonies. She lives in Woodland Park, New Jersey. Readers can visit her website at www.suzannetrauth.com.

Printed in the United States
by Baker & Taylor Publisher Services